W9-DFQ-785

THE
ASTOUNDING
BROCCOLI
BOY

ALSO BY
FRANK COTTRELL BOYCE

Millions
Framed
Cosmic

Frank Cottrell Boyce

THE ASTOUNDING BROCCOLI BOY

WALDEN POND PRESS
An Imprint of HarperCollinsPublishers

■ ■ ■

Walden Pond Press is an imprint of HarperCollins Publishers.
Walden Pond Press and the skipping stone logo are
trademarks and registered trademarks of Walden Media, LLC.

Library of Congress Cataloging-in-Publication Data
Cottrell Boyce, Frank.
The astounding broccoli boy / Frank Cottrell Boyce. — First U.S.
edition.
    pages   cm
Summary: Rory Rooney likes to be prepared for anything, but
when he inexplicably turns green and finds himself in an experimental
hospital ward with his nemesis, school bully Tommy-Lee "Grim"
Komissky, everyone is baffled but Rory believes he and Grim have
become superheroes.
"Originally published in the U.K. by Macmillan Publishers, 2015."
ISBN 978-0-06-240017-8 (hardback)
1. Action and adventure—General—Juvenile fiction. 2.
Humorous stories—Juvenile fiction. 3. Social issues—General—
Juvenile fiction. [1. Bullying—Fiction. 2. Virus diseases—
Fiction. 3. Adventure and adventurers—Fiction. 4. Imagination—
Fiction. 5. Heroes—Fiction. 6. Humorous stories.] I. Title.
PZ7.C82963 Ast   2015   2015005996
[Fic]—dc23   CIP
                                                                        AC

Typography by Carla Weise
15 16 17 18 19   CG/RRDH   10 9 8 7 6 5 4 3 2 1
❖
First U.S. edition, 2015
Originally published in the U.K. by Macmillan Publishers, 2015

■ ■ ■

Ms Annabel Roose—
ever so lovely, whatever the color

THE
ASTOUNDING
BROCCOLI
BOY

WHILE THE CITY SLEEPS, AN UNKNOWN HERO WATCHES OVER IT FROM HIS LONELY OUTPOST ON THE ROOFTOPS

*E*very story has a hero.

All you have to do is make sure it's you.

On my first night in Woolpit Royal Teaching Hospital, I thought my chance had come. The boy in the next bed sleepwalked. Hands straight down by his side, head held high, like a piece of spooky Playmobil he sleepwalked right up to the ward door, which is locked with a security code. I didn't want to bother the night nurse, so I followed him. He typed some numbers into the keypad. The door opened and off he went along the empty hospital corridors, through a staff canteen—where I was distracted by cheese— and out of the fire door.

1

I thought we'd walked onto the street.

I'd forgotten we were twelve floors up.

We were standing in the doorway of a kind of hut thing up on the hospital roof.

Miles below, the city twinkled like a massive Christmas tree. The boy did the Spooky Playmobil right to the edge of the roof. One more step and SPLAT! He would be a splodge of jam on the pavement hundreds of feet below. I thought about shouting his name, but what if he woke up, got scared, and fell?

His name, by the way, was Tommy-Lee Komissky—though everyone called him Grim Komissky. And mine is Rory Rooney. We were in the same class at school. He was the biggest and meanest. I was the smallest and weakest. I could tell you stories about the times he squashed my sandwiches, the times he threw my bag off the back of the bus, the times he threw me off the bus. But I wasn't thinking about that now. I was thinking—this is it, this is 100 percent my chance to be a hero.

All I have to do is save his life.

As long as he doesn't take another step, it'll be easy.

■ ■ ■

There was a flash of lightning.

He flinched.

I blinked.

There was a rumble of thunder.

He took another step.

Then Grim Komissky fell off the roof.

*T*HE NEXT THING
I KNEW . . .

I saw him fall. I was standing in the doorway on the far side of the roof. There was nothing I could do to help him. But the next thing I knew . . .

I was standing next to him.

On the ground.

Between a row of wheelie bins and a Dumpster.

I'd saved him.

I looked up at the roof twelve stories above us. How had we got from there to here?

How?

Well the truth is, I am astounding.

And this is the story of how I became astounding.

■ ■ ■

We had fallen off the top of a twelve-story building. We didn't splatter into pavement jam. We didn't crash through the pavement. We didn't bounce. We weren't even scratched. Our fall had left us completely unharmed, though it had woken Grim up.

He looked around, stretched, and growled, "What's going on? Where are we? Are you trying to dump me in a wheelie bin?!" (This might seem an unusual question, but while we were at school, Grim Komissky had once dumped me in a wheelie bin. He probably thought I was trying to get Revenge.) He shoved me into the corner so I couldn't dodge past him. But I wasn't scared.

Tonight—for the first time since I met him—I was not scared of Grim Komissky.

Tonight I was not scared of anything.

"What are we doing here? How did we get here?"

I looked up at the top of the building—way, way above my head, so high I could hardly see it. "We jumped," I said. "From up there."

He looked up too. "You laughing at me, Rory Rooney?" He pulled back his fist, ready to thump me.

"No."

"We can't have jumped. We'd be dead."

"But we did jump. And we're not dead. And," I said, "the jumping isn't the only inexplicable thing. When we came off the ward, you unlocked the door in your sleep. When we were on the roof, I teleported slightly. What does it mean? Think about it."

Grim Komissky looked as if he'd just swallowed a furious wasp.

I worried he was going to be sick. "What's up? What's happened? Are you okay?"

"I'm thinking."

"Oh. Right."

"No. No good. Nothing's coming."

"Okay, Tommy-Lee, listen." That was the first time ever I called him by his real name, by the way. "They put us in the isolation ward here at Woolpit Royal Teaching Hospital because they think we're sick. What if we're not sick? What if what we are is . . . superheroes?"

*H*OW WE BECAME ASTOUNDING . . .

No one is born Super (except Superman, obviously).

The Incredible Hulk was mild-mannered scientist Bruce Banner until he was blown up by his own Gamma Bomb.

Spider-Man was ninety-pound weakling Peter Parker until he was bitten by a radioactive spider.

Swamp Thing was a botanist. He was trying to find a way to make deserts fertile, but he died and his soul got stuck in a bush.

They didn't choose to be heroes. They didn't even want to be heroes. Something weird happened and they became astounding. Maybe they could have gone to the hospital to have their astoundingness removed. But no. They chose to use it for Good. That's what made them heroes.

That's exactly how it was for us.

When I looked up at the hospital roof, I seemed to see all the weird things that had happened to us, trailing after us like the tail of a comet. My life was flashing past me like the pages of a Spider-Man comic!

And I don't even like comics! (My dad does, but I don't.)

On the front page of this comic was a picture of me and Tommy-Lee and the words *How We Became Astounding . . . Now read on.*

ATTACK OF THE KILLER KITTENS

GOVERNMENT HEALTH WARNING:

Feline-Origin Respiratory Tract Infection—
commonly known as "cat flu"—is a virus spread
by domestic house cats. Although the virus is not
especially serious, it is extremely contagious.
You can avoid infection by keeping your contact
with cats to a minimum. If you have a cat,
please keep it indoors until the epidemic is over.
Thank you.

No one called it cat flu except on the news. Everyone called it "Killer Kittens." Especially my mum.
We didn't have a cat, but we did have a cat flap—the

people who lived in our house before us put it there. Mum nailed up the cat flap and spread anti-cat pellets all over the back garden.

"Don't be scared, love," said Dad. "No one else is scared."

"Just because no one else is scared doesn't mean things are not scary," said Mum.

She was definitely right about this, by the way. No one else was scared the day we started Handsworth Academy. I was scared, and I was 100 percent right to be scared, because on that very first morning Grim Komissky took my bag off me, rooted around inside, took out my sandwiches, and ate them right in my face.

Bonnie Crewe—the Girl with the World's Longest Ponytail—said to him, "Why don't you pick on some-one your own size?"

"There is no one my own size," growled Grim, through a mouthful of my lunch, "and if there was, why would I take that risk? It's much safer for me to pick on someone I know I can squash like a bug."

"That makes sense," said Bonnie, and skipped off with her ponytail swinging from side to side.

Dad explained to Mum that the virus wasn't serious anyway—it caused flu-like symptoms and drowsiness.

Plus, even if you had a cat, you only had a 10 percent chance of catching it.

"If there's a ten percent chance of catching it," said Mum, "that means ten percent of people will catch it."

"No, it doesn't."

"Yes, it does."

"It doesn't."

"It does."

"It doesn't."

"If ten percent of people catch it, that will mean ten percent of people are off work. What if those people are the people who deliver flour to the bakeries or milk from the dairies? What if they're the people who take the food to the supermarkets? Or the people who open the supermarkets in the morning? What then? That'll mean there won't be enough food to go round. And people will be rioting for food. And what if some of the people who are too sick to go to work are policemen? Then there won't be any policemen to stop the rioters rioting, and what then? A total breakdown in law and order, all because of Kittens."

"I think the chances of that are about 0.001 percent," said Dad. "There's nothing to worry about. Or only 0.001 percent."

Mum bought about a million tins of Spam and ten tons of pasta. She didn't buy them in one big lot from one big shop because people might see her, then copy her, and that might trigger a wave of panic buying. She also bought a camping stove with its own gas canister and loads of matches and candles in case the electricity went off, and she made us keep the bath filled up with cold water in case the water went off.

"Now I'm not scared," she said. "Now I'm prepared."

Don't Be Scared, Be Prepared is the name of a book that Dad had bought for her. Under the title it said, *Dangerous situations are not dangerous if you know what to do.*

It tells you:

- What to do about wasp stings
- How to light a fire with no matches
- How to catch, skin, and cook rabbits
- How to stop a nosebleed
- And what to do in the event of a total breakdown of law and order in society, etc.

And . . .

- How to deal with bullies.

Until then everything I'd done to try and stop Grim Komissky picking on me had failed.

There was the night I tried to stop him from throwing my bag off the back of the bus by giving my bag to my big sister Ciara, who went home on the late bus. Instead of throwing the bag off, he threw me off.

There was the time I tried to avoid him by getting the late bus myself. He waited for it with me, complained about the delay to his homeward journey, and threw me off again.

Every day he'd take my sandwiches out of my bag and lift off the top layer to check on the filling. If it was something he liked—say, ham—he would eat the whole sandwich. If it was something he didn't like—say, cheese—he'd roll the whole sandwich into a ball between his chopping-board hands, drop it on the floor, and stamp on it. SQUELCH!

In the comic-book version of my life story, there was a drawing of me hiding in the geography storage cupboard, which was surprisingly comfortable. The caption said: AT LAST RORY ROONEY FINDS PEACE IN HIS FORTRESS OF SOLITUDE.

The Fortress of Solitude is a vast complex hidden away under the polar ice, where Superman goes to do his thinking. Except Superman has droids to serve him food, whereas I had a big papier-mâché model of the West Midlands in the Ice Age, which I used as a table to put my sandwiches on while I was listening for Trouble.

And the next picture was Grim Komissky bursting into the geography storage cupboard with his almost-as-big-as-him mates (Kian Power and Jordan Swash) shouting, "Surprise!!!"

In the drawing you can tell from the expression on my face that it's no surprise to me.

The next picture after that would be just the store-room door with *POW! CRASH! THUNK!* written across it and the word "Ow!" sneaking through the gap under the door.

In *Don't Be Scared, Be Prepared* it says that if you're being bullied, the first thing you should do is inform a responsible adult—for instance, a parent.

"Mum," I said, "bad things are happening at school."

"Have you disinfected your hands?" She'd put a squeezy bottle of disinfectant gel by the front door.

"Yes."

"Then don't worry. We're not going to catch the virus, and even if there's a total breakdown in law and order, we've got pasta. We've got candles. We've got water. We could last out for weeks. We're not scared. We're prepared."

"Great."

I also mentioned it to my dad.

"When I had trouble at school," he said, "you know what I did? I sneaked into our yard when everyone else was asleep and tried to summon Batman. I got a big rubber bat from a joke shop and shone a flashlight at it onto the side of our house—to make the Bat-Signal." Dad has always been unusually serious about comics.

"Did it work?"

"No. You know why?"

"Because Batman's not a real person?"

"Exactly. If you need a hero, you have to be one. Sometimes—for instance, if you are the youngest and the littlest in your year—you might think, How can I be the hero? I'm the littlest in my year. But there's more than one kind of hero. There are heroes with shocking great muscles who can stop a speeding train with their bare hands, thus saving the passengers from Certain Death. But there are also skinny little heroes who destroy big bullies using only their superior intelligence and cunning."

"But I don't have superior intelligence or cunning."

"But I do." And to prove it, he showed me his anti-gravity trick. In the Rory Rooney comic, there was a diagram to show you how to do this trick.

HUMILIATE BULLIES WITH THIS
SIMPLE ANTIGRAVITY TRICK

1. Ask the bully to pick you up, and then they pick you up.
2. Ask them to put you down and try again.
3. While they're getting ready to lift you, allow your own body to go limp. Concentrate on a spot on the floor, between their legs.
4. Put your arms out, forcing the bully to pick you up by your forearms. When they pick you up, gently press on the inside of their elbow joint with your thumbs. Continue to concentrate on the spot on the ground and to keep your body limp.
5. They will not be able to lift you up. Works every time.

"Are you sure it works every time?"
"Absolutely."

■ ■ ■

So I tried that.

After Grim picked me up the first time, I was about to say, "Now . . . put me down and try to pick me up again." This is when you do the part with the thumbs and staring at the floor, etc. In fact, when I said, "Now put me down," Grim did put me down—facedown—DUNK!—in the wheelie bin.

In every story there are Heroes and Villains, winners and losers. If you don't decide which you are, someone else will decide for you. Someone like Grim Komissky.

THE WAGON WHEEL
OF DOOM . . .

Every superhero has a nemesis. Batman has the Joker. Spider-Man has the Green Goblin. Superman has Lex Luthor.

My nemesis was Grim Komissky.

If I was a superhero, how would I fight my nemesis?

"If you were a superhero," said my sister Ciara, "what would you be called?"

"I don't need a secret identity. I need Grim Komissky to stop hurting me."

We were flicking through *Don't Be Scared, Be Prepared* together, looking for nemesis-crushing notions. "Look at this," said Ciara. "It says here that

18

hippopotamuses kill more people than lions do. How depressing is that? I thought hippos were nice, but, no, violence is everywhere."

"I'm not being bullied by a hippopotamus. I'm being bullied by a bully."

"Anti-Bullying Suggestion Number Two—try to make friends with the bully. For instance, find out if he's got a hobby or something and start a conversation."

I said, "He has got a hobby. His hobby is picking on me. We have lots of conversations about it. They go like this:

"Me: 'Please don't rip up my homework/eat my lunch/snap my ruler/throw me off the bus.'

"Him: 'Try and stop me.'"

"There's got to be more to his life than that." She asked around at school and discovered that Grim did have a hobby.

Kickboxing.

"Advanced kickboxing, apparently. He's really good at it. He's the Under-Sixteen British Champion. Could you have a conversation about kickboxing?"

I tried that.

Me: "Please don't kickbox me with your killer feet."

Him: "Why not? Kick."

Ciara had one of her brain waves. "Let's be logical about this—Grim steals your food. What does that tell you about him?"

"That he can do what he likes, due to his highly trained feet."

"What else?"

"That I'm always hungry. That I'm going to be the smallest in my class forever because of malnutrition."

"No, no. *He's* hungry. Otherwise why steal food? He's hungry. All you have to do is offer him some food before he asks for it. Hungry people will do anything for food." She makes some sandwiches.

In the comic-book version of my life, there was a picture of her making sandwiches with a slightly-too-pleased-with-herself expression. I didn't notice this expression at the time.

"If he's going to eat your sandwiches, don't let him take them. Go and give them to him. Show some style."

That lunchtime I walked right up to the Table of Fear—the table where Grim eats with his two nearly-as-big mates. I opened my lunch box and said, "Mind if I join you?"

Tucked in next to the sandwiches is a Wagon Wheel. A nice little touch from Ciara. I love Wagon

Wheels. I said a little prayer that Grim would hate that combination of light milk chocolate, crunchy biscuit, and squashy marshmallow.

Grim: "Wagon Wheel . . . I love that combination of light milk chocolate, crunchy biscuit, and squashy marshmallow . . ."

Curses.

"But I don't do sweet before savory. Let's see the sandwiches first. . . ." Maybe he'd be so full after the sandwiches he wouldn't want the Wagon Wheel. He opened the top sandwich like he was defusing a bomb. Top layer of bread—thrown away. Crunchy fresh lettuce, in the mouth. Under the lettuce—ham spread with a thick layer of . . . what was that? A knife of cold fear stabbed my heart. I knew what that was. It was Dad's Rocket Chili Sauce. My gran sends a bottle over from Guyana every Christmas. It's called Rocket Chili because one tiny teaspoonful is enough to send you into orbit. One tiny teaspoonful is enough to spice up a big pan of curry. Ciara had spread it on the ham like jam. Ciara had made a lethal Ham and Chili Rocket Volcano Nuclear Meltdown Sandwich.

Me: "No . . . don't eat that."

Grim: "I eat what I like."

Grim rolled the ham up, brought it to his mouth,

chili sauce leaking out of the sides like chemical waste. I could feel the heat of it, singeing my nasal hairs.

"But . . ."

Grim posted the chili-smothered ham into his mouth.

He chewed.

His eyes narrowed.

He stopped chewing.

His eyes closed.

Then they opened again.

The pupils were tiny black dots.

Then they were big black pools.

His nostrils flared.

Then he did the last thing I was expecting.

He swallowed.

He licked his lips.

He took another bite.

Eyes closed. Eyes opened. Pupils tiny. Pupils huge. Nostrils flared.

Then . . . the rest of the ham vanished into the mouth.

He opened his mouth, wafted a bit of air into it with his hand. "Nice." He nodded. "Do me another one like that tomorrow."

Grim Komissky has asbestos taste buds. Astounding.

What can a big sister, or a dad, or a mum, really

do against someone who can't feel pain even with his tongue?

"Now," he said, "for the light milk chocolate, crunchy biscuit, and squashy marshmallow of the Wagon Wheel."

Jodi Swash said, "Tommy-Lee! No!!! You said lunch was Cheestrings and apple. You can't eat the Wagon Wheel."

"'S a present," said Grim Komissky, "so it doesn't count." He Frisbee'd the entire biscuit into his mouth.

"Don't swallow," said Jodi.

"I," said Grim, shrapneling crumbs and chocolate flakes, "swallow what I like."

SLURP.

He swallowed the Wagon Wheel.

YUM.

In my comic-book life story, the next picture was an ambulance screaming onto the playground. WAH WAH WAH WAH WAH WAH. Worried faces were looking out of the school windows. People were standing on benches to get a better view of Grim Komissky being carried out of the building on a stretcher, with an oxygen mask over his face. Within minutes of eating my Wagon Wheel he had turned bright blue, because he couldn't breathe. It turns out that Grim Komissky has a serious nut allergy.

Ciara came and stood next to me as the ambulance drove away. "Wow," she said, "you really crushed your nemesis."

"I didn't do it on purpose. I didn't know he had a nut allergy."

"The chances of you accidentally giving traces of nuts to someone with a nut allergy must be less than one percent. You hit the bull's-eye. You should be proud. What are you going to do now?"

"About what?"

"Like all archvillains, Grim Komissky has henchmen. As you've hurt their leader, I'd say that there's a solid ninety-eight percent chance that Kian and Jordan will come after you for . . .

"REVENGE!"

Oh.
Great.

REVENGE OF THE HENCHMEN

*D*ad keeps all his *Amazing Spider-Man* comics in a box under his bed—each one in its own little plastic folder. In *The Amazing Spider-Man* #8, Peter Parker is still at school and a football player called Flash Thompson keeps picking on him and calling him "Puny Parker." They end up having a boxing match, and Flash Thompson is completely confused because he can't land a punch on Peter Parker due to Peter Parker's Amazing Spider Speed. Then—WALLOP!— Peter hits Flash with his Amazing Spider Punch and sends him flying out of the ring. Peter Parker is the new hero of Midtown High School. All the kids give him a rousing cheer as he walks to his locker.

■ ■ ■

Is this what happened to me when I defeated my nemesis? Did I get a rousing cheer as I walked to my locker?

No.

Everyone thought I was a poisonous little snake who had tried to kill poor Grim Komissky with a biscuit.

In fact, no one called him Grim Komissky anymore. From then on everyone in school called him "poor Tommy-Lee."

"You tried to kill poor Tommy-Lee with a biscuit," said Kian Power, blocking the entrance to the boys' toilets. "He has a chronic nut allergy."

"I was trying to be friendly. I didn't know he had a chronic nut allergy. I didn't even know that Wagon Wheels had nuts in."

"Traces of nuts," said Kian. "That's all it takes. Just traces of nuts. We have lunch with him every day to make sure he doesn't eat a nut by accident. We all eat the same lunch so he doesn't feel left out."

"We haven't eaten a nut, or a trace of a nut, all year," said Jodi.

I said, "He never told me he had a nut allergy."

"So you're trying to blame *him* now!? You're saying

it's his fault he's sick? Are you saying we should go and beat him up just because he's got an allergy?"

"No."

"Who do you want us to beat up then?"

"I don't think you should beat anyone up."

"He's our mate. We have to beat someone up."

"And that someone is you," said Kian. "We're not going to do it yet, though. We're going to make you wait in fear. You won't know the time or the place."

"And then," said Jodi, "we'll get you the Monday after next in Colomendy."

The Colomendy "It's Great Outdoors" Center was where we were going for our Year Seven trip. When our geography teacher, Ms. Stressley, gave us the final details about the trip, she said, "Sadly, poor Tommy-Lee won't be joining us for this trip. Thanks to the aftereffects of the recent attempt on his life, he has now been transferred to a special hospital." She gave me a dark look and asked that everyone remember Tommy-Lee in their prayers.

I did pray that he wouldn't die. But even in my prayers I couldn't call him Poor Tommy-Lee. He was still Grim to me.

Monday morning . . .

I t's a bright autumn morning. A group of innocent schoolchildren is crowding excitedly onto a bus bound for the countryside. One boy stands a little apart, less excited than his classmates. . . .

I stayed at the back of the queue. Everyone had to wipe their feet on a disinfectant mat—to help defeat Killer Kittens—before getting on the bus to Colomendy. When the last person had done that, the driver asked me to help him get the mat onto the bus.

"Thanks, son," he said as I shoved it on board. Then he closed the door in my face and drove off without me.

I was saved!

Until Ms. Stressley pulled up in her little Fiat and accused me of trying to dodge the trip. I told her the driver didn't see me.

"You should make yourself more obvious. Get in."

She was following the bus in her car so we would have a vehicle for emergencies when we got there.

We did have an emergency in the end.

But it was too big for a Fiat.

I opened my sandwiches so I could eat them before Kian and Jodi could take them. "Those look nice, Rory," said Ms. Stressley.

"Thank you, miss. Made them myself. Cheese and ham and tomato."

"My favorite." She kept looking at them instead of looking at the road. In the end I decided to give her one in order to prevent a fatal car crash. She shoved it into her mouth more or less whole and put her hand out for another one.

"When we get there," she said, spitting bits of tomato everywhere, "you'll be split into groups. Each group will be named after their dormitory. There's Badger Dormitory, Fox Dormitory, Falcon Dormitory. You'll be in Bat Dormitory. That's way up in the roof, up a rickety old staircase, on the far side of the house. Nice and quiet. That's why it's called Bat Dormitory. You'll be in there with Kian Power and Jodi Swash."

"What?! No! Please, miss! No! Why?"

It turns out that we were all supposed to write down the names of anyone we'd like to share with and no one had written me down, except Jodi and Kian. She said, "They might be very hurt if you said you didn't want to share with them."

I said, "Someone will be hurt, miss, but I don't think it will be them."

"This is your chance," she said, "to show some remorse for trying to kill Tommy-Lee Komissky."

No, I thought, this is his henchmen's big chance to get revenge.

■ ■ ■

When we arrived, a man in a pom-pom hat gave us a talk about making sure we washed our hands in disinfectant after any contact with the animals, and about avoiding any contact with cats or catlike creatures due to Killer Kittens.

Bonnie Crewe said, "Apart from cats, what creatures are catlike?"

"Lions, leopards, lynxes, pumas, tigers, cougars . . ."

"Do they have lions in Wales?" asked Kian.

"Not as a rule, but you can't be too careful."

"What about tigers?"

"No. As I say, big cats are not indigenous."

"Leopards?"

"That's right. No big cats. Usually."

Then he explained the emergency procedures—what to do if someone broke a leg or similar.

Kian whispered in my ear, "You should listen to this. You're probably going to need emergency procedures."

The first activity at the "It's Great Outdoors" center was kayaking. The man in the pom-pom hat led us on a walk up the river to where the boats were kept. On the way he pointed out various geographical features. "Here is where the river meanders," he said. "Come back in a couple of hundred years and you'll probably find these meanders have turned into an oxbow lake. Course, you'll probably be dead by then."

"Or before then," said Kian, digging me in the ribs.

The kayaks were about a mile upriver, where the water—said Pom-Pom Hat—was "a bit more exciting but not too exciting." Kian and Jodi stayed one on each side of me, walking more and more slowly and closer and closer to the bank as we got farther up the hill. Soon we were way behind the others and right on the edge of the water.

"Ready for your bath?" asked Kian. So they were going to dump me in the river. Fine. I wasn't scared of getting wet. I could swim. I could just swim away from them. I could swim upriver to where the kayaks were, and when they asked me what I was doing, just say I preferred swimming to walking—especially in exciting water. It would actually be cool. I might even look like some sort of hero.

"What are you doing?" said Kian. Jodi was looking around all over the place. He seemed to have lost interest in hurting me.

"I'm keeping an eye open," he said. "For lions."

"That gnome man just told you," said Kian. "There are no lions in Wales."

"He said you can't be too careful."

"Don't worry about lions and leopards," I said. "All you've got to do is make yourself look as big as you can. Stand on tiptoe, stretch your coat out. Spread your legs. Anything. Lions hate to waste energy. If you look like you might be hard to kill, they'll leave you alone. Besides, if I'm with you, the lion would go for me and leave you alone, because I'm the littlest." They looked at me. I shrugged. "I read it in a book."

"Great. I feel a lot better now, thanks," said Jodi. "What are we going to do? Drown him?"

"Yeah. Come on. Let's do it."

"Lions aren't a problem anyway," I said. "Hippos kill a lot more people than lions do."

"Hippos are vegetarian," said Kian, grabbing me. "Come on—get his other arm, Jodi."

"Being vegetarian doesn't make you gentle," I said. "If you scare a hippo, it will trample you and possibly bite you in two. You don't even have to scare it on purpose. If you stand between a hippo and the water, that is an emergency situation as far as a hippo is concerned. And in an emergency situation, a hippo does not roll up in a cute little ball, or change color. It bites you in half. There's no point trying to reason with a hippo, because the hippo is three meters long and weighs as much as fifty men." This was all in *Don't Be Scared, Be Prepared*. By now Jodi was anxiously scanning the horizon for signs of hippo activity. He was worried, and as long as he was worried, he wasn't dumping me in the river. All I had to do was keep him worried.

Kian wasn't worried, though. "There are no hippos in Wales," he said. "Someone would have mentioned it."

I pointed out that there were six hippos in Conwy

Zoo. "I know," I said. "I checked."

"Exactly. In the zoo. Behind bars."

"Yeah, but how did they get there? They weren't born there. They didn't swim to Wales from Africa. Someone brought them. In a lorry, probably. For all you know, the roads of Wales are stuffed with lorries taking hippos up and down the country. And lorries can crash and hippos can escape. There could be hippos in this very river."

"Yeah? What's the chance of that?"

"Small. Maybe ten percent. You could risk it. I'm just saying, that means there's a ten percent chance of us ending up with a lot of empty kayaks and loads of bitten-in-half kids, going, 'That hippo attack was ninety percent unlikely.'"

Jodi scanned the water anxiously. "I just wish poor Tommy-Lee was here," he sighed. "I never worried about hippos when Tommy-Lee was here."

"But he's not here, is he?" snapped Kian. "And why is that? Because *he* put him in the hospital, that's why." He poked me in the chest as he said this, then poked again, and each poke shoved me a little bit nearer to the edge. "Are you trying to scare us? Are you? You don't scare us! We scare you! Understand? Do. You. Under. Stand?" One last poke and I was in the water.

■ ■ ■

My nostrils filled up with water. It was so cold inside my nose, I couldn't think of anything else. I tried to stand up. But I was the wrong way up. I banged my head on a rock. The water gurgled around me. It was like being swallowed by a polar bear. I rolled over. At last I could hear something other than water. Laughter. Kian and Jodi laughing their heads off as they ran off up the hill.

I managed to get up on my knees. I breathed in.

The next page of my comic-book life story was a half-page picture of me on my knees in the middle of the river. There was no way I could swim up to where the kayaks were. The water was too shallow, too fast, too cold, and too full of rocks. There was no way I could actually look quite cool, because I was dripping wet and muddy and shivery.

But I wasn't drowned.

No one was trying to kill me. The bite of the cold water was a good feeling once you got used to it. I liked the sound of it churning in and out of the glacial meander. I even liked the sound of the shouting that came from my year group up the hill. Kian and Jodi had reached them now—they were pointing down the river and waving their hands. They were probably telling everyone that I'd just fallen in, making out that they had been trying to save me. There were shadows of clouds chasing over the hill. The birds were twittering overhead in the blue, blue sky.

I remember all this because it's the last time in my life that everything seemed sort of normal.

Everyone in the year group came running down the hill toward me. It was like the bit in *The Lion King* where the stampeding wildebeests come over the edge of the cliff and trample Simba's dad. Parkas and Puffa jackets flashed in the sun. The man with the pom-pom hat shouted to everyone to slow down, they might get hurt.

I got to my feet. I was planning to walk out of the water, a smile on my face, and shrug it all off. I might say, "Come on in—the water's lovely."

They were all lined up on the bank. Laughing, pointing, jeering. Ms. Stressley had her arms folded. "I. Might. Have. Known," she sneered. "If anyone was going to fall in the river accidentally on purpose, it would be you."

There's no way you can look good trudging out

of a river after you've been pushed in. If you smile, it looks fake—and you look like a loser. If you look sad, you look like a loser. If you look angry, you look like a loser.

Also, the bank was slippery, so I got even more muddy climbing out. Pom-Pom Hat offered me his hand to help me up. I was about to take it when he snatched it away and stepped back.

I looked up.

I noticed that everyone had gone quiet.

Everyone was staring at me.

Some of them covered their mouths with their hands.

Bonnie Crewe burst into tears.

Some of the boys laughed.

Some of them came toward me, staring, but the Pom-Pom Hat turned to them, airplaned his arms, and shouted, "Back! Back! Right back! He may be contagious." I looked around, trying to see who he was talking about. I thought he might be talking about a Killer Kitten, but he turned to face me and shouted, "You follow me. Let's get you out of here." Then he asked Ms. Stressley to take everyone else up to the kayaks.

"I wouldn't worry," she said. "This is probably his idea of a joke. Rory thrives on negative attention, don't you, Rory? He tried to kill one of his classmates with a biscuit."

"Maybe he's contagious. Maybe he's just a show-off. Either way he's a health and safety risk," said Pom-Pom Hat. "Come with me, Rory."

I followed him through the middle of the crowd. As I came forward, everyone stepped back. They drifted into two lines, one on either side of me. They were all silent now. None of them could take their eyes off me. Except Bonnie Crewe, who gave a little sob and turned away. I felt like a bride walking up to the altar. Which was weird.

Pom-Pom Hat took me all the way back to the center. He asked me if anything like this had ever happened to me before.

"Well, it's the first time I've been pushed in a river, but they did push me into the pool in the Perry Barr leisure center once. They also pushed me into the Curly-Wurly Canal, which really hurt because I actually landed on a shopping trolley. Mum said I was lucky I didn't cut myself because—"

He gave me a harsh look. "This isn't some kind of stunt, is it? You haven't just painted it on?"

"Painted what on?"

He showed me into a tiny room with a single bed in

it. He brought me my bag and a cup of cocoa. "Change into some dry clothes," he said. "Get yourself warmed up. I'll make a few calls." But as he was leaving, he seemed to change his mind. He looked back into the room and said, "Wash your face. Let me see you do it."

There was a sink in the corner. I scrubbed my face with soap and then turned to face him.

"Good grief"—he whistled when I'd finished—"that looks worse." Then he left and—unbelievable this—he locked me in! As though I was the bad guy!

There was a hand towel on a hook by the sink. I picked it up to dry myself off. That's when I saw my face in the mirror.

That's when I saw why everyone was scared of me.

My face had changed color.

My face had gone green.

*T*HE WEIRD MUTATION OF RORY ROONEY

When I say green, I don't mean greenish. I don't mean looking-a-bit-pale-maybe-about-to-throw-up green. I don't mean flesh-with-a-hint-of-green green. I mean a bright, lettucey green.

I took off my wet shirt. The green wasn't all over. It was just my face at first, and my neck. The rest of me was all right. I thought, Don't panic. Read a book. Ciara had put *Don't Be Scared, Be Prepared* in my bag in case of emergencies. As soon as I picked it up, I noticed that my hands had gone green too. And when I put on a dry T-shirt, my arms were going green. Green color moving up toward my elbows. That was almost the scariest thing about it.

Scary but kind of cool too. When I was little, running around in my Spider-Man pajamas, I liked to pretend that a radioactive spider had bitten me and that I could feel my muscles swelling up. Okay, my muscles weren't swelling now, but something was happening. Something weird. Inexplicable. Just like in a comic. As the green rose up my arms, I could feel my skin tingling. Maybe it was excitement. Maybe it was a symptom.

I looked in the mirror and my face was still green. No. *More* green. Before I had been lettuce-colored. Now I was verging on broccoli.

A key turned in the lock. Ms. Stressley brought a man with funny little egg-shaped specs into the room. He took one look at me and more or less ran out again, shutting the door behind him. I could hear him arguing with Ms. Stressley on the other side of the door. She was saying, "It's your job. You're a doctor."

"What if it's catchy? Health and safety, isn't it?"

"Of course it's health and safety; that's why I called a doctor. So he could be healthy and we could be safe."

Ms. Stressley shouted through the keyhole that I should stand as far away from the door as possible. The door opened and the doctor edged in with a handkerchief over his face and nose. He seemed to be asking questions, but I couldn't hear what he was saying, just hanky-chewing noises.

"He's asking what color you are normally," said Ms. Stressley. Then she answered his question for me. "He's normal color. Dark normal. His father's from Guyana. His mother is Irish."

"I know this may seem a strange question," said the doctor, "but have you been drinking at all?"

"I just had some cocoa."

"He means alcohol," snapped Ms. Stressley. "Have you been drinking alcohol?" She made it sound like I was forever chugging vodka in class.

"No, miss. Course not! Where would I get alcohol?"

"It does seem unlikely," said the doctor.

"So does turning green," said Ms. Stressley.

"Was anything unusual going on when this happened?" asked the doctor.

"He was in the river. Showing off."

"I wasn't showing off. They pushed me in."

"He has a bit of a history," said Ms. Stressley, as though that explained everything. "He tried to kill another child with a biscuit."

"Are you saying you think this is something he caught from the river?"

"I don't know. You're the doctor."

"The river feeds one of the main reservoirs for Birmingham," said the doctor. "If the infection is caused by the water, we could be looking at a catastrophe on a massive scale." He made it sound as though it was my idea to poison Birmingham. "Our resources are already stretched. So many of my staff are off work with this Killer Kittens virus. This could be very difficult." He seemed to think I should be locked up.

Then they left, locking me up.

A few minutes later someone opened the door very slightly. I said, "Hello?"

A girl's voice whispered, "Can you get far away from the door so we can look at you?"

"I'm over by the window."

Around the edge of the door came the face of Bonnie Crewe. Bonnie Crewe—the girl with the longest, shiniest hair in the school. In eight years of school she has barely ever spoken to me. Now she looked at me and burst into tears. "The key was in the other side of the door, so we thought we'd take a peek at you," said one of her friends. There were four of them, crowding into the doorway behind her.

"Poor, poor Rory," sobbed Bonnie. "I wish I could give you a hug." I thought this sounded like a good idea. I moved toward her, but she jumped back. "Not literally," she said. "Not while you're gravely ill."

"I actually feel okay."

"So brave." She sighed. The others agreed that I was brave. "It's so unfair for this to happen to you. You're only little."

"That's true."

"Though you did try to kill poor Tommy-Lee with a biscuit, so maybe this is some kind of cosmic karma."

"Cosmic what?"

She stepped into the room and dropped a huge greeting card on the floor. "We made you this," she said. It had a picture of the Colomendy activity center surrounded by flowers glued to the front, with a photo of my face glued to the flowers. The photo of me was from the chart in the foyer, where there were ID photos of all of us so that the people at the center knew who we were. Underneath in glittery writing they had written:

We will always remember you.

:-(

I said, "Oh, a get-well card. Thanks."

"It's not really a get-well card," said Bonnie. "It's more of a farewell card."

"Farewell?"

"Everyone says you're . . ." She choked a bit, trying to get the word out, then wailed, "Incurable!"

For days and nights I'd been worried about what Kian and Jodi might do to me. I thought I'd planned for every possibility. The one thing I never expected to happen to me on a school trip was that I would mutate. *Don't Be Scared, Be Prepared* tells you how to cope with spiders, kidnappers, forest fires, hurricanes, problems with your plumbing. It has nothing at all to say about what to do if you change color.

Maybe you would expect me to be upset to see my incurably green self. But I looked at the photo of myself that Bonnie had stuck to the good-bye card. Then I looked at myself in the mirror. The me in the photo was usual me. Puny me. Hiding-in-the-geography-storage-cupboard, no-sandwiches, pushed-in-the-river me. The me in the mirror was . . . different. I didn't yet know just how different. But just then any kind of different was good.

Unless of course they'd decided I was too green to ever be seen again and were planning to keep me in a maximum-security bedroom forever.

■ ■ ■

There was a sound like a cyclone somewhere outside, and shouts and doors banging and windows opening. Outside the window, the trees were thrashing about. Ms. Stressley opened the door and told me to follow her, "But not too close."

She led me out onto the lawn in front of the activity center. All the upstairs windows were full of staring faces. Bonnie Crewe blew me a kiss! I was going to blow one back, but as we turned around the corner of the building, the wind attacked us like a giant leaf blower. It swirled around us, making me screw up my eyes, or turn my back to it. Ms. Stressley yelled into my ear. "Go on! Hurry up!"

I turned round and saw . . . not a giant leaf blower but a neat blue helicopter, dangling over the back field like a mad Christmas decoration.

"Hurry up!" yelled Ms. Stressley. "This is messing up my hair!"

"Me?! In there?!"

"Yes, please, on the double. Some of us have abseiling to do."

DESTINATION-SECRET

I wasn't surprised that someone had sent a helicopter. Once one weird and terrible thing has happened to you, you sort of expect more unusual stuff—for instance, someone sending you a helicopter, probably to take you to a secret government installation where they give you special training and gadgets. And for instance, the pilot to be wearing a massive crash helmet with a black visor and also black gloves so that you can't see his face or his hands and you think he might possibly be a robot.

"Hi!" I said.

"You are a category-ten risk. Please confine yourself to the yellow area," he said in a voice that definitely sounded a bit electricky. Part of the floor and one of the seats in the back of the helicopter had been painted yellow. I clipped myself in and gave the pilot a thumbs-up to show that we were ready. I sort of thought helicopters just went straight up into the air. But they don't. The tail shot up and the nose pointed down, like something on a thrill ride. Then it powered over the grass, nose still down, until it came to the edge of the hill, where it dropped like a stone. I pushed myself back into my seat, screwing my eyes up, thinking, This has all gone wrong, we are going to die. Maybe they were right to give me a farewell card.

But we didn't hit the ground. I opened my eyes. We were whirling up into the air. The center was already far below us, falling away like a dropped toy. The roads and the hills spread out all around the building like a giant painted fan opening. The river meanders were a glitter-pen scribble.

Mountains crowded up around the rim of the fields. There was snow on top of one, and I swear I saw the sea. Then a city that I knew must be Birmingham. Houses, chimneys, factories, gasometers. I saw the Bull Ring, the station, the Lickey Hills. All these places that I knew really well—places I've been to on different days at different times—but now I was seeing them all at once. I felt like I was traveling in time instead of space. And my whole life had shrunk down to a minute. "This is amazing," I called to the pilot. The electric voice said, "Please do not engage the pilot in conversation."

There were some more hills. Another city came marching over them toward us in ranks of towers and steeples and skyscrapers. For a little while we followed a river like a winding, shining road. Then we dropped onto the roof of this tall gray building. A man in earmuffs and a high-vis jacket came to help us out of the helicopter. I strode across the roof next to him toward a door marked ACCESS LIMITED, feeling exactly like a proper hero. I thought that probably the prime minister or some kind of secret super-genius would come out of the door and shake my hand and say, "Ah, Mr. Rooney, we've been expecting you."

But it wasn't the prime minister. It was three men in high-visibility jackets and big orange plastic earmuffs. One of them had a walkie-talkie. It took me a minute, but I recognized the middle one.

"Dad!" I said.

"What?" said Dad. I pointed to his big orange

earmuffs. He said, "Oh," and lifted them off. "This is him," he said to the others.

"I can see that," said the one with the walkie-talkie. "Please don't make any physical contact. Follow me." He led us inside, talking into his walkie-talkie "Yes, he's here. We'll take him straight down to A and E to be processed. We'll use the emergency stairs to avoid unnecessary human contact."

The one with no walkie-talkie kept looking back at me as we clattered down the stairs. "No offense," he said to Dad, "but your kid is really very green."

"Well, yes, he is. He is indeed," said Dad, then added, "I think kids are like gummi bears. The green ones are the best."

Mum and Ciara were waiting for us at the bottom of the stairs. When they saw me, their mouths opened. No sounds came out, but they wouldn't close again. They looked like shocked fish.

Dad said, "So our Rory's traveling by helicopter now! Not like us normal people. We had to deal with a contraflow on the A38. Then we took the M6 toll. Once we got on the M1, we had a good run—with a loo stop and a sandwich at Newport Pagnell. Then the A5, which becomes the Edgware Road . . ."

Whenever Dad's feeling emotional, he gets all geographical.

Mum doesn't worry about the geography. She focuses more on the question of who is to blame. "Rory Rooney," she said when she finally got her mouth working, "what have you done to yourself?!"

"If you'll follow us to Accident and Emergency," said the man with the walkie-talkie, "they'll do your paperwork."

"We can't let people see him like that," said Ciara. "Can't we put a bag over his head or something? Everyone's going to be staring at him."

"Don't you think," said Mum, "people will stare just as much if he's got a bag over his head? He's my son," she said, "no matter what he's done."

"I haven't done anything. This just happened."

"Whatever. We'll stand by you. That's the point."

Diagnosis: super

Me walking into Accident and Emergency was a double-page spread in the comic book of my life. Everything else was in black and white, but I was really, really, bright, bright green. There were people there whose heads were dripping with blood, whose children were weeping in pain. There was a little girl with a potty stuck on her head. There was a television showing a report about how the prime minister had decided that Figaro—the Downing Street cat—would have to be put down due to concerns about Killer Kittens. No one was looking at the television. No one was looking at any of these things.

Everyone was looking at me.

Everyone except the reception nurse, who was too busy typing my details into her computer. She asked for our address, so Dad went geographical again. "Handsworth Wood. Not far from Perry Barr. If you're coming north on the M6, you merge with the A38 at—"

"Thank you. We don't need directions. Just a postcode. And door number."

"One sixty-three."

"Thank you. Name?"

"I'm Len and this is my wife, Siobhan, and—"

"Patient's name."

"Oh. Rory. Rory Rooney."

"Thank you. So, has Rory had any recent contact with cats or catlike creatures?"

"No."

"Do you own a pet cat or catlike creature?"

"No."

"Thank you. And what seems to be wrong with Rory?" She hadn't looked up yet.

"Well," said Mum, "he's gone green."

"And is that not something he's done before?"

"Love, it's something that no one has ever done before in the whole of history."

"Presenting a new symptom: green discoloration. Is that in the eyes, the extremities . . . ? Where is it?"

She was still head down, typing.

"It's all over. It's absolutely all over. Just look at him."

"And how green exactly is he, would you say?"

"We don't have a color chart with us. But I'd say a light broccoli."

Now the nurse put on her glasses and looked up from her keyboard. She managed an "Oh," and then she had to take a breath. "And is"—she took a sneaky peek at her monitor—"Rory . . . is Rory not normally that color?"

"As I already explained, no one is normally that color, love. That is not a normal color."

"What is his normal color?"

"Well, he's normally a mixture of me and his dad," said Mum.

Mum is sort of pale and freckly, and Dad is sort of dark.

"My mother is from Guyana," explained Dad. "It's on the north coast of South America, at the southern tip of the Gulf of Mexico, just next door to—"

"Ciara, come here," snapped Mum.

Ciara stood next to me.

"That's his sister. That's his normal color," said Mum.

The nurse's eyes didn't leave my face, but her

hands were rooting around in her drawer. She pulled out a white face mask and came scurrying out from behind her desk, pulling on some rubber gloves. "I'll get the mmmmmm weeehhhh," she said, and tied the mask on.

"Thank you," said Mum, taking a step toward the seats. Everyone on the seats leaned away, scared that we might sit too close to them.

The nurse said, "Not there. Come with me."

She showed us to a kind of alcove with plastic curtains across it. "You should be comfortable back here." She twitched the curtain open for us, and we crowded in.

"She thinks you're contagious," said Mum. "I'm sure you're not, though."

She said it as if, if I was contagious, that would be letting her down.

"Nice curtains," said Dad. They were covered in pictures of fun things to do on the beach—donkey rides, sand castles, beach huts. "Probably meant to be Norfolk, what with the beach huts. Could be Cromer or Wells. What do you think?"

We could hear the nurse coming back, explaining to someone that she'd put us behind the curtain because she was worried that I might be infectious.

"Oh, don't worry about that," said a big, cheery

voice. "Some of my best friends are infectious." The curtains were pulled back, and there was a tiny woman with short blond hair and a diamondy stud in her nose. She looked like I imagined a top secret government scientist would look. "All right, nurse," she said. "You get on with your accidents. And your emergencies. This one is mine."

*R*ORY ROONEY, WE'VE BEEN EXPECTING YOU. . . .

*S*he said a few polite things to me, such as "How did you like the helicopter?"

"Great. Thanks."

But she didn't really want to talk. She wanted to look. Her eyes flickered all over the place, like swivelly scanners, checking my fingers, my eyes, my ears. She looked at me as though I was her best-ever Christmas present. "Brightside, by the way." She shook hands with Mum and Dad. "Bernadette Brightside. I'm a specialist in this field."

"There's a field?" said Mum. "People turning green is a field?"

"Not yet. But it's getting that way. Oh, I've got so

many questions for you, Rory Rooney. First the obvious, boring ones. Do you have a temperature?"

"Errrm . . . I don't think so."

Mum went to feel my forehead, but then pulled her hand away at the last minute and asked me if I felt hot.

"Eaten anything unusual? Could this be a reaction?"

"Not unless cheese and tomato is unusual. And I haven't drunk any alcohol."

"I should think not."

"What made you say that?" asked Mum. "Have you been drinking alcohol?"

"No."

"Why are you talking about alcohol?"

"The doctor at the center asked me about it. I thought it might be medically relevant."

"Follow me," said Dr. Brightside, "to HQ."

HQ!!

She pushed the curtains aside so hard and fast that the curtain rings tinkled like bells. Everyone in A & E looked at us.

"Ladies and gentlemen"—the doctor smiled—"I'd like to assure you that there is no need to panic. . . ."

The moment she said that, everyone panicked. People shuffled, limped, and sidled toward the exit. Chairs were knocked over. The kid with the potty on her head kept asking, "What's happening? What's happening?" We were emitting some kind of Fear Force Field.

"Whenever I say don't panic," the doctor whispered in my ear, "people panic. I love that."

Dr. Brightside took us up to the twelfth floor in a lift and then along a corridor with about a million doors, all locked with codes that she had to punch into their keypads.

"Makes you wonder . . . ," whispered Ciara.

"Wonder what?"

"If you have to lock something up behind a million electronically coded doors, it must be something dangerous. There's got to be at least Dementors in here."

The doctor asked if any other family members had ever turned green. Mum said no, right away. But Dad said, "Actually, sweetheart, you went a bit green on the ferry once."

"Interesting," said the doctor. She muttered a voice memo into her phone. "Possible genetic component. Mother has experienced similar—"

"What are you talking about?" wailed Mum.

"You were seasick and you turned green. You even said, 'I've gone green.'"

"I was a bit off-color on the Dublin boat. I did not suddenly turn into the Incredible Hulk's little brother."

"In fact," said Dr. Brightside, "Rory has not turned into either the Incredible Hulk or his little brother. I can be certain of that."

By now we were in front of a blue door with a singing duck painted on it. The duck was wearing galoshes and carrying a sign that said JUNIOR ISOLATION—ABSOLUTELY NO ADMITTANCE.

"Except for very special people." The doctor smiled. "If you all wait here, Rory and I will go through and do some tests. Wipe your feet, Rory."

There was one of those disinfectant mats in front of the door. Also an antiseptic gel dispenser with FIGHT THE KITTENS! written on it.

There were some chairs and a drinks machine in the corridor outside. Mum, Dad, and Ciara settled down and I went with the doctor.

I heard the Singing Duck door click shut behind me.

I looked back.

I could see the door with its two portholes—Mum looking through one, Dad looking through the other. They weren't smiling.

But maybe they couldn't see me because of the reflection. Maybe it was one-way glass and they couldn't see at all.

Junior Isolation was a big white room with a desk in the middle and four or five doors leading off into mini rooms. Each door had a window next to it. Each room had a couple of beds, a sink, some cupboards, and a telly. No windows to the outside. The only way you'd know if it was day or night would be by looking at what was on telly.

That day, the rooms were mostly empty except one where the duvet was piled up in the corner of the bed as though someone was hiding, like in an aquarium when you tap on the glass to try and get the fish to move about. I almost tapped on the glass to wake the sleeping kid, but Dr. Brightside saw me and stopped me.

"What's wrong with him?"

"We're . . . not sure yet. But we will be soon." The doctor smiled reassuringly. "In fact, I'm going to look at his lab results right now. Nurse will look after you."

I turned round and almost jumped out of my skin. Standing right behind me was the tallest nurse in the history of the world. At first I thought she was a statue or some kind of landmark. But then she looked down at me. You could tell that it was hurting her neck just to get me in focus.

"I'm Nurse Rock," she said in a voice like gravestones falling over. She pointed to the lab door.

The lab was full of test tubes and charts and a big white machine with flashing lights.

I looked back toward the Singing Duck door. Mum's face was still there. It looked so far away, though.

"Don't worry, I'm not going to dissect you."

I hadn't thought about being dissected until she mentioned it.

She measured my height and my weight. She made me breathe in, breathe out, reach up, reach down, blow into a metal tube. The thing with the flashing lights turned out to be a running machine. She fitted electrodes to my chest and made me run on it.

Dr. B swept in, waving a clipboard, and started taking notes. She was really impressed by everything I did. Everything I did was either great or brilliant. Normally when older people talk to me they're saying stuff like "Now look what you've done," or "Just try," but she was all like "Your blood pressure is perfect," and "Wow, great lungs!" and "Brilliant stretching." She asked me to go to the toilet and wee in a bottle, which was a bit embarrassing, especially when she was so enthusiastic about it. "Your wee is green!" she whooped. "Want to look at it under a microscope?"

"I'm not even that keen on looking at it normal size, so I definitely don't want to see it magnified ten thousand times."

"Very funny. You should look at it, though. Honestly, this wee is outstanding." Then, "This won't hurt," she said, grabbing my thumb and jabbing it with a needle. She squeezed blood out into a test tube. It really, really hurt. "I lie"—she smiled—"a lot. But always for your own good. Here." She gave me a certificate that said "I've Been Brave."

I have outstanding wee.

I am officially Brave.

I felt that Spider-Man would be impressed.

After the tests, she took me to the room with the piled-up duvet. The duvet grunted and then curled itself into an even tighter ball. "Maybe you can cheer him up," said Dr. Brightside. "I'll go and let your mum and dad onto the ward." She left, closing the fish-tank door behind her. Then she opened the Singing Duck door. Mum and Dad came to the fish-tank window and peered in at me, waving. Ciara had a packet of crisps.

Dad had a canned drink. They each gave me a thumbs-up. I really was in the aquarium now.

Dr. Brightside was saying, ". . . all normal—hemoglobin, proteins, physical tests. Not even normal, they're great. I mean, they're terrific. He is really very well indeed. You are obviously doing everything right."

"We do our best," said Mum. She was trying to sound proud, but it came out annoyed. "We have always tried to do our best. And then he goes and turns himself green." She was still convinced I'd done it on purpose.

I said, "I didn't turn myself green!" None of them even looked at me. They couldn't hear me. Their voices weren't coming through the glass but from behind me, from a little blue intercom on the wall. I thought I might be able to use it to make them hear me, but it didn't seem to have any buttons.

". . . whatever is wrong seems to be asymptomatic," said the doctor's voice.

"Is that really bad?" asked Dad. Ciara explained that "asymptomatic" meant that I didn't have any symptoms.

"That's right. He's completely normal."

"But green."

"Yes."

"Broccoli green."

"I don't mean to be picky," said Dad, "but isn't being broccoli green a symptom?"

"Strictly speaking, yes, it is," agreed Dr. Brightside. "But you wouldn't say he was suffering from it. In fact, it looks quite groovy, don't you think? Sort of like Mystique in the X-Men, but green instead of blue. And male instead of female."

Dad pointed out that the X-Men are mutants.

"I believe in being honest," said Dr. Brightside. "And the truth is, I have never examined an X-Man."

"We thought you were going to fix him. We thought we'd bring him in here, you'd fix him, and we'd take him home." That was Dad.

"It's not as simple as that, I'm afraid."

"You mean he might be green forever?" That was Ciara. She did not sound strictly unhappy about this possibility.

"Has he gone a bit greener, d'you think?" asked Mum. "Is he going a bit spinachy?"

"No, it's definitely broccoli," said the doctor. "I was thinking of calling it broccolitis, in fact. As it's a totally new medical condition, I get to name it. How exciting is that?! Broccoli syndrome or broccolitis—which do you think?"

"Emerald," said Ciara suddenly. "What about emeralditis?"

"Oh, now I do like that," said the doctor. "Lovely."

Emerald—I liked that too. You could imagine an X-Man called Emerald. Then Ciara said, "But if you think he's contagious and he might be green forever . . . will he have to stay in that fish tank forever?"

It gave me a funny feeling that Ciara had decided to call it a fish tank too, without even talking to me. Like we both saw everything the same. I shouted, "I can hear you! I can hear what you're saying!"

"And how do you know," went on Ciara, "that it's not going to get worse? What if he gets greener? Or starts to grow gills or webbed feet like a giant frog?"

"I think gills are unlikely. But I believe in being honest. . . ." Dr. Brightside glanced at me through the glass. "So, I'll say yes to your first point. Yes, Rory could be green forever."

"Couldn't we take him home and keep him in isolation there? He's got his own room, and we could take precautions," said Mum.

Dad explained that Mum was worried about the possibility of a total breakdown of law and order. Dr. Brightside looked a bit confused.

"Killer Kittens," said Mum. "At home we're

completely prepared for any crisis, but here we've got nothing except a few sandwiches."

"All the same," said the doctor, "I can't let him out until we know more."

"I CAN HEAR YOU. . . ."

Nothing.

"I CAN HEAR YOU!!!!"

"Aahh, look at him," sighed Mum. "It's like he's trying to tell us something."

"I think he is trying to tell us something," said the doctor. She flicked a button, and I could hear my own voice coming back at me, yelling, "I can hear you."

They were all quiet for a bit.

"How long have you been listening?"

"The whole time."

"It's good that you can hear us," said the doctor. "It's right that you're part of the conversation. Say hi to Rory, everyone."

Everyone said hi and waved at me. It made me feel weird. I said, "Don't do that. It makes me feel weird."

"You do look weird," said Ciara.

"I've changed color, not species. I'm not a leprechaun."

The moment I said leprechaun, the hunched-up duvet began to rumble like an unextinct volcano.

Dad said, "The doctor says you're going to be all right. Isn't that right, doctor?"

"I'm a great believer in honesty, so I'm going to be honest with you . . ."

No, don't, I thought.

". . . so I'll say . . . I have no idea. Rory is a medical mystery. No one knows what's causing this or how dangerous it is. But I'm determined to find out what it is."

"Is he going to die?" asked Ciara, sounding more interested than worried.

"No. I don't think so. Well, yes he is. We all are. But he's not going to die from this. He's really healthy. His scores are terrific. He's a very, very well young man. Amazingly well. Though his wee is bright green."

"Oh, please," said Ciara. "Too much information."

"If you'll come with me, there are some forms you need to fill in."

They moved away from the window.

There was a soft click, and Dad's face was peeping in at me around the fish-tank door. "Son," he whispered, "I'm not sure I'm supposed to be in here."

"I think you're probably not."

He looked at the rumbling duvet on the other bed. "Is he okay?"

"I don't know."

"Rory, I don't know why this has happened to you, but I know this: everyone is good for something. Really tall people make great basketball players. Unusually small people make good jockeys. Really, really fat people can be sumo wrestlers—"

"Only if they're Japanese."

"Everyone is good for something, Rory. Everyone has their purpose. If you're green for life, then I'm sure it must be good for something. All you have to do is find out what."

"Okay."

"And you know I've been thinking? When you look at all the people in history who have turned green—"

"Other people have turned green?"

He listed them. "The Incredible Hulk, Swamp Thing, the Green Hornet, the Green Goblin . . . what do they all have in common?"

"They're all not real people?"

"They're all superheroes. All green and all superheroes. It seems to me that if you turn green, there's only one possible diagnosis. Namely—Super."

When he turned to go, the big tall nurse was standing in the doorway, giving him the bad look. "Sorry," said

Dad, and dodged past her. But just as he was leaving, he said, "Scampi. He really likes scampi. I know you probably don't have any control over the menu, but if you can manage it every now and then, he really likes scampi." And he went.

That was the last time I saw my dad, by the way.

ENTER THE BOGEYMAN . . .

Icontemplated my fate in the mirror, partly because I couldn't take my eyes off myself. My face was so familiar and so strange at the same time. I thought about what Dad had said about superheroes. In a mad way it made a lot of sense. The things that had happened to me in the last twenty-four hours were more like things out of a comic than things in real life. Being pushed into a mountain stream and coming out a different color. Being taken away by a possibly robot pilot to a high-security installation. Having scientifically outstanding wee.

Most of all I felt safe. All right, I was locked up in an isolation ward miles from home and family. At least that meant no one was going to beat me up and eat my sandwiches. For the first time in ages I wasn't worried or scared. If anything, people would be scared of me. The once-weedy, misunderstood and undersized Rory Rooney was now . . . what? Who was I? Captain Emerald, maybe. Dr. Emerald, perhaps, this being a hospital. Or just the Emerald. The Astounding Emerald. Or what about the Bogeyman—because I'm green like a bogey. No, that's horrible. The Leprechaun? Was that too kiddy? Or too creepy? I sprawled on my bed, making myself at home, and said it aloud, trying it out. "The Leprechaun."

"I hate leprechauns." It was the voice of the duvet.

I didn't turn round.

I stood very still.

Because I knew that voice.

"Don't ever call me a leprechaun again."

I still didn't look round, but I knew what was happening to the duvet. Thick, sausagey fingers would be pushing it down. Massive, muscular arms would appear from underneath. A huge head would push itself out, like a baby dinosaur head butting out of its egg. The head would turn toward me, its eyes focusing on me like gunsights.

"Oi. I'm talking to you."

I turned round.

The face of the boy in the duvet was bright green.

It was also instantly recognizable.

It was the face of Grim Komissky.

REVENGE OF THE NEMESIS!!

My first feeling was . . . WHATAMIGONNADO? I'm locked in a tiny cell with my own lethal kickboxing nemesis!!! I thought I was safe, when what I really am is Dead-in-Two-Minutes.

My second feeling was Unexpected Disappointment. I'd been enjoying the idea that I was the only green person in the world, so I felt a bit like Santa Claus coming down the chimney and finding another bloke dressed in red with a big white beard putting presents under the tree.

I could practically hear Grim's brain beeping as he tried to figure out what I was doing there. "Is that . . .

no, it can't be . . . so who . . . permanent fatal error, please quit your brain and restart."

"You're bright green," he said.

I was too scared to say, "So are you."

In the end he figured it out. I could tell from the way he hurled himself across the room toward me.

I dived under the bed.

He grabbed the bed and pulled it toward him so that I couldn't hide underneath it.

But . . .

I had somehow already had the brilliant idea of grabbing the bedsprings and clinging on underneath.

So when Grim looked at the space where the bed had been, there was no me. It looked as if I'd vanished. Ninety percent of Grim's brain was so confused it shut down.

The other 10 percent of Grim's brain was pure fury. That carried on working fine. When pulling the bed didn't work, he shoved, dragged, spun, and banged it all around the room. Maybe he thought it was all the bed's fault.

All the time I clung on underneath, the wires digging into my fingers and grating against my toes. The bed screeched and skidded over the polished floors. It was like surfing but upside down.

While I was upside-down surfing, I had time to think. . . .

And this is what I thought. . . .

Yes.

Just like the Hulk and Swamp Thing, I have undergone a strange mutation.

Unlike them, I have no superpowers.

I'm as small and weak as ever, but now I look weird too.

*T*EAM GREEN

Hospital beds have loads of wires connected to them. These all got wrenched out of the wall once Grim got going. Quite a few chunks came out of the actual wall too, when Grim rammed it with the bed. Alarms were bleeping and howling all over the place.

The voices of Dr. Brightside and Nurse Rock came over the intercom.

"What's going on in there?"

"Seems like poor Tommy-Lee is having one of his panic attacks. Best wait for him to calm down."

"No!" I yelled. "DON'T WAIT!"

"That other boy was in there with him. Can you see him?"

They hadn't heard me. The intercom was only working one way again.

"Rory seems to have vanished. Maybe he's in the toilet."

"No! NO! I'M NOT IN THE TOILET! I'M IN INCREDIBLE DANGER! HELP ME!"

"He seems to be doing a lot of damage. Maybe we should intervene?"

"YES! YES! YES, PLEASE. INTERVENE! HELP ME!!!"

Dr. Brightside couldn't hear me.

But Grim could.

He growled.

Then everything went quiet for a bit. I stayed still, expecting his head to peep under the bed.

But no. Grim didn't peep under the bed. He turned the bed completely over.

Now he could see me. I was spread out on the springs like a burger on a barbecue.

But before he had the time to take a bite out of me, the door opened and Dr. Brightside stepped in.

"Tommy-Lee Komissky," she snapped, "what's going on?"

"He made me eat a Wagon Wheel and that's what turned me green—"

"Where? What Wagon Wheel?"

"At school."

"What school? What are you talking about?"

"Handsworth."

"Wait. Wait a minute. Are you saying . . . are you trying to tell me . . . that you two went"—she had that look of exploding happiness on her face that you only normally see on people who've just won *The X Factor*—"to the same school?"

"We're in the same class."

Dr. Brightside clapped her hands. "Oh, oh, oh. This is so the best!"

Seeing a grown-up so excited about what school we went to was so strange that Grim briefly stopped trying to kill me and I even more briefly stopped being scared.

"Don't you see?" Dr. Brightside clapped her hands again. "This opens up so many avenues. You were in contact. I'm guessing you must have been in physical contact. Maybe one of you caught it from the other."

Grim rumbled, "Yeah, he tried to kill me with a biscuit, and he made me go green."

"Oh. Poor Tommy-Lee," said Dr. Brightside. Then she thought for a moment. She did not seem to appreciate that for that moment my life was in her hands. "No," she said finally. "You went green first. So if anything, it seems more likely that you made Rory go green."

"Good," grunted Grim. "I hope I did."

"Or perhaps you were both in touch with some third party. Or some foodstuff or chemical or . . . anything. The point is, you are medical mysteries.

"Normally when you get a medical mystery, it's like Killer Kittens. You get hundreds or thousands of patients coughing or scratching or sweating. Then doctors test all those patients—look at their symptoms, their blood, their wee—and compare the results. That's how we work out what's wrong and how to fix it. But when Tommy-Lee turned up here, he was the only person in the world who was green. But now you're here, Rory. Everything is twice as easy. We're twice as close to solving the mystery. If we work together . . . if you do what I ask and we work as a team, we can beat this. What do you say? Do we want to beat this?"

Neither of us said anything, though I think Grim may have made a weird noise in his throat.

She stuck her hands out and smiled. She was wearing rubber gloves. I wasn't sure what she wanted us to do. Then she grabbed my hand with her left hand and Grim's with her right and said, "Let's say it. We are a team and we want to beat this."

"I hate leprechauns," said Grim, ignoring her and addressing me. "You are a leprechaun. You're little and green. I am not little. I'm big."

"But you are green," said the doctor. "So you could be the Jolly Green Giant."

"If anyone ever calls me a leprechaun, I'm going to forget all the anger-management techniques they taught me in the special place."

"It's absolutely fine for you to raise that objection," said Dr. Brightside. "Now, are we a team and do we want to beat this? Yes, we do! Go, Team Green!"

Finally we all shook hands. She was still wearing her rubber gloves.

*I*NSIDE THE FISH TANK

We had to move to a new fish tank because of the damage that Tommy-Lee had done to the plasterwork. He put a framed photograph of a woman in kickboxing gear on top of the cabinet next to his new bed. The woman was looking at us over her shoulder, with her back to the camera. On the back of her jacket were the words ALL-ENGLAND FEMALE KICKBOXING CHAMPION, written out in metal studs. I asked him who it was. "That," said Tommy-Lee, "is my mum." He seemed really proud of her. There are no pictures of my mum looking like this. He also had twenty-one "I've Been Brave" certificates Blu-Tacked to the wall above his bed, three rows of seven.

"You've been brave a lot," I said. "What have you been doing? Bullfighting?"

"You'll find out," said Grim.

After we'd finished moving our stuff, it was time for more blood tests. I gave Dr. Brightside my thumb. She took another blood sample. Gave me another I've Been Brave certificate and trilled that it was Tommy-Lee's turn now.

"Don't want to," grunted Tommy-Lee.

"Don't be silly. I need to test your blood."

"Don't stick things in my thumb."

"It doesn't have to be your thumb." Dr. Brightside smiled. "I'm quite happy to stick it in your bum. And if you're uncooperative, I'm quite happy to call for a general anesthetic."

Very slowly Grim put out his thumb. He looked away while she got the needle ready. When she tried to stick it in him, he yanked his thumb away so quickly she ended up sticking the needle in the back of her own hand.

"Ow!"

"See? It hurts, doesn't it?"

"Yes, it does." She put a bit of cotton wool over it. "Can you hold that in place, Tommy-Lee? While I get a plaster."

He put his thumb on her cotton wool, but instead of getting a plaster she whipped out another needle and jabbed it into his thumb.

"Ow! Ow! Ow! That's cheating."

"It would be if this was a game. But it's not. It's me trying to cure you."

"If going green hadn't destroyed all my confidence, I'd've thrown you out of the window for stabbing me."

"Then it sounds as if you're a much better person without your confidence." Dr. Brightside smiled again. Then—of all the unbelievable things—she gave him an I've Been Brave certificate.

"What!?" I said. "He's getting a certificate for that?!" I was completely scandalized. How could she give him a bravery certificate when he was crying like a baby? "He's not been even a bit brave!"

I'd somehow forgotten who I was talking about. When Grim swung his head around and gave me his Bad Look, though, I remembered. I stopped talking, but the thought didn't go away: Grim Komissky is big, but he's not brave. And if someone's not brave—how can they be scary?

"You weren't brave yourself," said Grim, as if he could read my thoughts, "when I chucked you off buses. You screamed and moaned and cried. Want me to do it again?"

"Now, now," said Dr. Brightside. "We are here to fight the problem. Not each other. Tommy-Lee, you have to understand—your best hope of getting better is Rory. And Rory, your best hope of getting better is Tommy-Lee. You need each other."

"He tried to kill me with a biscuit," grumbled Grim.

I thought about Grim's gallery of I've Been Brave certificates—twenty-one of them, pinned to the wall—and realized they were meaningless. Grim Komissky had never been brave. He had only had some blood tests. Twenty-one blood tests. Did that mean we were going to have twenty-one blood tests per day? "How long exactly," I asked, "have you been here?"

"Two weeks, two days, and thirteen hours."

"Two weeks? And you're still not better?"

I'd been thinking that we would be going home tomorrow.

"Two weeks and two days and thirteen hours," said Grim.

The biscuit thing reminded Dr. Brightside about allergies. "Do you have any allergies, Rory?"

"No."

"I want you both to think about food and tell me what your most favorite and least favorite foods are. Talk about it together. Let's see if we can find a pattern."

I told her that Grim really liked ham-and-tomato sandwiches, but not cheese and tomato.

"How do you know?" asked Grim.

"When I have ham-and-tomato sandwiches, you always take them off me and eat them, whereas when I have anything involving cheese, you take them off me and stamp on them."

"Cheese has traces of nuts, that's why."

I pointed out that if he didn't want the cheese ones, he could have just let me eat them.

"How about . . ." said the doctor, ". . . I leave you two with this big piece of paper and a pen and you make a list of your favorite foods?"

"Do you have to leave us alone?" I asked.

"I've got blood to test." She waggled the test tubes of our own blood at us.

At school, whenever one of the teachers asked if we had any questions, Grim would always put his hand up and say, "Who would win in a fight between a badger and a rattlesnake?" or "a vampire and a zombie." It turned out he was the same about food. In Grim's head all the different foods in the world were at war and you had to choose sides. "What about prawn crackers?" I said.

Prawn crackers versus Snack-a-Jacks rice crisps

took hours and involved him punching the wall and kicking the air.

The Snack-a-Jacks versus prawn crackers show-down was nothing compared to the battle of the breads—naan versus pita.

Chicken tikka versus scampi wings was more or less the Third World War.

Custard versus ice cream was nuclear meltdown.

Anyway, here's the final list . . .

- Thin-and-crispy pizza with pepperoni
- Chicken tikka (I couldn't believe that scampi lost!)
- Fish fingers
- Special nut-free supplements that help kickboxers get bigger muscles
- Snack-a-Jacks (Salt & Vinegar only)

I'm not saying it took a long time to agree on this menu, but it might have been quicker to grow up, go to catering college, then go to sea in a trawler and catch some fish and sail back home and cook them.

Dr. Brightside read the list, nodding her head. "This," she said, "has given me the idea for an experiment." The word "experiment" made me think of Magneto firing bullets at various X-Men to see if they were really, really indestructible. Dr. Brightside's experiment was different.

Ages and ages after we gave Dr. Brightside the list, Nurse Rock came in with a food trolley, parked it in the middle of the room, and said, "Enjoy."

The plates had metal covers on. I couldn't wait. I pulled the cover off mine and underneath was . . . not a pizza. It was something—but it didn't look like food. Someone must have thought it was food, because it had a knife and fork next to it, but it very much did not look like food. In fact it very much looked like frog spawn. Frog spawn with dead beetles on top.

I tried speaking into the intercom.

"Yes?" said Nurse Rock.

She could hear me! "I think there's been a bit of a mix-up."

"Yes?"

"I ordered pepperoni pizza, thin and crispy."

"This is a hospital, not Pizza Hut. You don't order food. Food comes and you eat it."

"Dr. Brightside told us to make a list of our favorite foods. Thin and crispy with pepperoni came out on top."

There was a sound like bits of paper being rubbed

together. I realized after a while it was the sound of Nurse Rock laughing.

Dr. Brightside explained the food situation.

"What if you've got an allergy?" she said. "What if that's what's making you green? The best way to find out is to put you on a very simple diet, of food you wouldn't normally eat. That way the reaction might fade away quite quickly."

So that was her experiment—a diet. Not Magneto firing bullets.

"Wait," said Grim. "You mean if we eat this, we might get better?"

"It's a possibility."

Without even tasting it first, Grim shoveled the frog spawn into his mouth. After the first three mouthfuls he paused and glared at me. "Eat your food," he growled.

"It looks vile."

"It tastes vile," agreed Grim. "Now eat it. Do what the doctor says."

At school I always did as I was told. Grim Komissky never did anything unless he wanted to do it. His motto was: "No one tells me what to do." But here he was, doing everything the doctor told him—even eating frog spawn and cockroaches without asking what they were.

"There is every possibility," said Dr. Brightside,

"that your greenness is diet related. Green turtles are green because all their food is green. The chlorophyll dyes their body fat."

I said, "Can I just point out that scientifically speaking I've been eating pepperoni pizza for years and never once turned green?"

"Hmmm," said Dr. Brightside. "Good observation. Maybe you've eaten so much pizza over the years it's turned you green incrementally. We have to look into every possibility."

By the time she'd answered my question, my plate was empty. Grim was licking his lips.

Our skin color had changed but nothing else had changed. He was still bigger than me. He was still eating all my food.

The frog spawn, by the way, is called quinoa. It's pronounced "keenwa." They spell it differently from the way they say it in a pathetic attempt to disguise it.

The cockroaches turned out to be roasted peppers that had been roasted too much.

*T*HE NIGHT WALKER

Nurse Rock gave me a new set of pajamas. I asked her what they were supposed to be.

"Pajamas."

"Yeah, but they're so bright blue. Are they supposed to be Smurfs or something?"

"Pajamas."

I'd never had a pair of pajamas before that weren't also some kind of dressing-up. When I was little, Dad once got me a pair of Spider-Man pajamas that were actually padded out with foam to make it look like I had massive Spider-Man-type muscles. I used to love turning the biceps inside out and waiting for them to pop back into place.

"These pajamas are hypoallergenic," said Nurse Rock.

They were also very scratchy. They crackled with static electricity when you put them on. If you stroked one sleeve over the other sleeve, the two sleeves clung to each other, and then when you pulled them apart, sparks flew everywhere.

"I think these might be a fire risk!"

"There is a fully tested sprinkler system installed in your ward. So no need to worry about fire."

"Thanks."

"The doctor asked me to say, 'Sleep well.' So. Sleep well. That's an order."

"Okay," said Grim. "If that's what the doctor says." He got into bed, closed his eyes, and started snoring right away.

Could anyone really get to sleep that quickly? I whispered, "Grim . . ."

No answer.

I went to turn the light off.

His massive security-light eyes flashed open.

"Where are you going? Doctor said go to sleep. Go to sleep."

"I was going to turn the light off."

"The light switch is in my territory."

"Your territory?"

"Yeah. See that line there? That's the border. This side is my territory. That side is yours. You can't come into my territory, so you can't turn the light off."

"What line? I can't see any line."

"I drew a line. In my imagination."

"If it's in your imagination, how can I see it?"

"If you can't see it, you'll just have to be extra careful, won't you? I can see it. That's what matters."

"So you're telling me not to cross a completely invisible line and you're not going to tell me where it is?"

"I'm telling you to be very, very careful."

"But the light switch—"

"Is in my territory."

"Right." I headed back to bed.

"What did you call me?"

"What?"

"Just before. You called me something not my name."

"Did I?" I remembered now I'd called him Grim. "I don't think so."

"You didn't call me leprechaun, did you?"

"No! Why would I do that?"

"You would do that if you wanted your life to end soon and painfully."

"Right. Well, I don't. So I didn't."

"Good. Go to sleep."

I climbed back into bed. My fire-lighter pajamas made the sheets crackle like firewood. I actually moved the fire extinguisher a bit closer just in case.

I had mutated into a green thing, been locked up in a high-security secret laboratory, forced to share a bedroom with my nemesis, and on top of all that I had to sleep with the light on! Why did he want to sleep with the light on? *Because he was scared of the dark.* It seemed that Grim Komissky was scared of all kinds of things. I almost thought about saying something about this. But I was every bit as scared of Grim as Grim was of the dark. I gave up on trying to find some darkness under the duvet. I thought I'd try reading myself to sleep, but when I pulled the duvet down, I nearly jumped out of my skin. When I pulled the duvet down, Grim Komissky was standing right in front of me. Breathing on my face. He wasn't looking at me. He didn't seem to know I was there. He just walked past me, straight to the door—a slow, dreamy walk, with his hands hanging down at his sides, like spooky Playmobil.

Sleepwalking.

And then, just like that, he sleepwalked right out of the fish tank.

I'd never seen anyone sleepwalk before. I followed him just to see what would happen. It was interesting the way he never bumped into anything even though he was asleep.

I'd thought the fish-tank door was locked with some kind of special high-tech lock. I'd never even tried to open it. Now Grim Komissky pushed it open with one hand. It wasn't locked at all.

Nurse Rock was at her desk, staring at her phone—maybe she was playing a game or checking Facebook. Unbelievably she was eating chocolate. There was something in her hand that was blatantly a Toblerone.

More injustice!

There was a tapping noise.

The Singing Duck door was locked with a security code. Grim was typing numbers into the keypad.

Obviously they couldn't be the right numbers.

THUNK!

The door opened.

He had unlocked the door in his sleep.

■ ■ ■

He did the Spooky Playmobil out into the corridor.

I followed him down the million-door corridor. But he didn't go back the way I came in. He turned right. There were no doors, no exit signs, no lifts, just a long, long corridor with no windows and a massive silver pipe running down the middle of the ceiling like an armor-plated draft excluder. Finally we came to a door.

I was expecting a room full of screens and monitors and phones and buttons—the technological nerve center of the building.

It was the staff-only café.

A deserted café in the middle of the night is a creepy thing. The chairs were all at funny angles to the tables, as though invisible people were sitting in them. The vending machines hummed like ghosts. Where the food should have been, there were empty tin trays. There were big, soggy footprints in the anti-Kittens disinfectant mats in the doorway. The only thing that moved was Grim—floating past the empty tables, like a waiter that no one was waiting for.

Grim kept moving. I kept following. It made no difference to him whether it was dark or light. He was asleep anyway. I brushed against something. A door handle. Maybe it would lead to a room with a light in it. I yanked the handle. Light and cold and mist burst out. It was a massive freezer—a house with walls of ice, just like the Iceberg Lounge—secret lair of Batman's archenemy, the Penguin. The light from the freezer lit up the whole room. Now I could see that we were in a kitchen. I don't mean a sitting-on-the-table-eating-cake-mix-off-a-spoon-while-your-mum-is-baking type of kitchen. I mean a kitchen the size of a railway station. Everything in it was made of steel—steel knives, steel shelves, steel floor even, and rows and rows of steel pots and pans hanging off steel pegs like bits of armor. If medieval knights ever went to a swimming pool, this was what the changing rooms would have looked like. The stove was the length of a bowling alley. It gonged when Grim sleepwalked into it.

He didn't wake, but he stopped. Maybe he was trying to sniff out where he was. All around him there were shelves and shelves of food. Boxes of cereals and rice, baskets of fruit, rows of fresh loaves, towers of biscuits. This was a warehouse of snacks! I was starving due to Grim having eaten all my "food." Now I could eat what I liked as long as he was in the kitchen.

There was a wardrobe-sized fridge packed with hunks of cheese, fat red tomatoes, buckets of milk and yogurt and juice, a tower of thinly sliced bacon, and even a pie. I didn't take the pie because it had a card

propped up against it with MAUREEN'S—DO NOT TOUCH!!!
written on it. There was something about those excla-
mation marks that said that if I did touch that pie,
Maureen would hunt me down like a dog. So I broke
off a chunk of cheese and grabbed a packet of crackers from a shelf. Then went to look in the freezer on
the off chance that there'd be ice cream.

I stepped inside it.

RORY ROONEY–PRISONER OF THE ICE!!!

As well as being inside the Rory Rooney comic book, this was also the front cover. There was me, looking around inside the freezer, trying to decide between a gigantic tub of Raspberry Ripple and a bucket of Honeycomb Smash, while Grim sleepwalks by. You can tell what's going to happen. Grim sleepwalks past the freezer door, nudges it with his shoulder.

CLUNK.

It shuts.

I'm locked inside.

And it's very dark.

I dive for the door.

Too late.

I look for the handle. There is no handle. I try to force the door open with my shoulder.

Nothing.

Push.

Nothing.

Push harder—HRRRRRRRRRR GRRRRRR . . .

Still nothing.

It gets colder and colder.

I'm only wearing pajamas. I try to call Grim, but my teeth are chattering too much to speak. They shiver the words to pieces.

I think to myself: What would Batman do?

Obviously Batman would have a special gadget on his belt for blowing doors off inadvertently locked freezers. In this picture my thought bubble says, "Maybe I can dig my way out with an ice-cream scoop." Then there's a close-up of me noticing a button that glows with a dim red light. I go closer. It has EMERGENCY written on it. EMERGENCY and SUPER FREEZE. I press it. It glows a bit brighter. There's a hissing sound and the icy mist begins to swirl and thicken around me like accelerated fog. It's getting colder. I still have cheese in my hand. I can feel it turning hard and brittle. I try screaming for help, but the speech bubble is empty with icicles hanging off it—my voice freezes in front of me. Words clunk to the floor like ice cubes. I try screaming again. Desperately I shoulder-charge the door.

It opens, and I almost fall out.

Warm air pours in.

I can breathe.

I stroll out into the kitchen and close the door on my potential icy grave.

Looking back at this picture now, it's obvious what happened. When I first went in, the temperature in the freezer rose a bit because I'd left the door open and let the warm air in. The door sealed itself automatically to allow things to get back to the right temperature. Then when I pressed Emergency Super Freeze, things got cold enough almost immediately, and that meant the automatic seal on the door was released. So I could open it again.

The next picture in the comic is me with my eyes popping as I realize with horror that there's no sign of Grim.

There was a sound like a boiler starting up. A sudden square of light. It was a small access door. He must have gone through it. I followed him. There was a ladder on the other side. At the top everything was dark, but there were little flecks of light high up. One massive yellow light over to the left. Something quick and quiet flittered past my face. Then there was a crack of brilliant light. So bright I had to blink.

Lightning.

■ ■ ■

We were outside.

We were on the roof.

Grim was standing right at the edge of the roof. A few big drops of rain fell. The storm was starting.

There's a picture of Grim, his Playmobil arms straight down at his sides, x-rayed by lightning. And . . . well, you already know what happens next.

Tommy-Lee fell off the roof.

THREE . . .

I don't remember anything about that first second after the fall. One moment I was standing in the doorway, looking at the space on the edge of the roof where Grim had been standing. The next I was standing in that space myself. I'd gone from there to here, but I didn't remember moving. It seemed like I'd teleported.

TWO . . .

I remember everything that happened then—as though someone had got hold of Time and stretched it like a rubber band. I remember thinking, Don't look down! Then thinking, Well, if you don't look down, how are you going to save him!? I looked down. It was amazing—miles below, the blue light of a tiny ambulance was flickering as it pulled out of the hospital. A pigeon flew by just below Grim's falling feet. I felt like I was just arriving on planet Earth from some distant galaxy. Everything looked new. I was noticing every detail. I wondered why my brain hadn't always noticed everything. What had it been doing with itself all these years? Didn't matter. Now, finally, it had switched on. It saw everything. Knew everything.

My brain had been upgraded.

There was thunder. The storm was unexpectedly close. My hand swept through the air and grabbed Grim's wrist and . . . yes! I saved his life!

Then my brain said . . . very slowly . . . Oh . . .

no . . .

you . . .

for . . .

got:

he weighs more than you do . . .

much . . .

much . . .

more . . . so this won't work . . . isn't working . . . you're falling . . . let go . . . let go . . . go . . . go . . .

no . . .

oh . . .

too

late . . .

oh.

Big Grim Komissky pulled me right off the roof.

ONE . . .

I thought the elastic band of Time would have been pulled to its limit. But now it just kept on stretching.

And stretching.

And stretching.

I was falling like a stone, but I felt as if I was drifting like a leaf. I was moving like a bullet, but my brain was moving superfast.

The billion pixels of the city below twisted and tangled. On either side of me were big bright billboards. When I looked, though, the billboards weren't showing adverts.

They were showing bits of my life. Scenes and memories of stuff that had happened to me. These weren't photographs, like memories usually are. They were drawings, like the drawings in a comic. They had captions, speech balloons, thought bubbles, and words like:

CRASH!

THUD!

KERPOW!!

splashed across them.

There was a picture of Grim x-rayed by lightning as he fell off the roof.

One of my hand grabbing his wrist just in time.

One of my face staring into his blank eyes while two thought balloons bubble out of the back of my head. One says, "Saved him!" The other, "But how did I get from there to here so quickly!? I must have teleported!!"

How 100 percent annoying is that—discovering that you can slightly teleport and then immediately using that ability to teleport yourself to certain death?

The last picture shows the two of us falling off the top of the twelve-story hospital. The word:

AIIIEEEEEEEEE!!

is splattered across our tumbling bodies.

It was just me screaming, not Grim. He was still fast asleep. Snoring and falling.

A NEW AGE OF SUPERHEROES BEGINS. . . .

*T*HUNK!

There were black walls around me. A gap above me. I was in some kind of box, open at the top. The opening was full of stars. I was 93 percent sure that I was lying in the bottom of the hole I'd made in the pavement when I'd smacked into it at a million miles an hour.

But the other 7 percent of me was still wondering . . . maybe I was in heaven.

There was metal under my hands. Also there were thick oily cables shuddering in the air above my head. It didn't seem heavenly, but then who knows?

At the edge of the box of stars I could see the slope

of the hospital roof. It wasn't in the distance.

It was three, maybe six meters away.

I lifted my head a little.

Grim was standing next to me. Staring into the night. Not looking at me.

Where was I?

If Grim could stand up, so could I.

Very slowly, I tucked my knees in, put my hands on the floor, pushed myself up. I was inside some kind of metal Dumpster. The oily cables were holding it to the side of the building. There was a thick plastic water tank strapped to the inside.

We had landed in the window cleaners' cradle.

We had fallen just a few meters.

The whole plunging-to-our-doom, life-flashing-before-my-eyes thing had only taken one millisecond.

I was alive.

And so was Grim.

He was holding on to the side of the cradle, staring into space. He wasn't screaming or panicking. He was staring straight ahead. He was still asleep! He had fallen off the side of a twelve-story building and not even woken up!

His fingers fumbled along the metal sides of the cradle, searching for something. They found it. A catch. A bolt. They grabbed it. They rattled it. The whole front of the cradle was a sort of gate—so that the window cleaner could step out of it when he reached the ground. Grim was trying to open the gate. But we weren't on the ground. We were twelve stories up.

It seemed that he just loved to sleepwalk off great heights. Quietly I slid myself between him and the lock. He reached around behind me. One of us must have knocked a switch. There was an electric groan. The cradle swayed. Then it started to sink, very slowly, down the side of the building, heading for the ground. As soon as we started to move, Grim stood still. In his sleep he probably thought he was in a lift.

The air was freezing. It was like breathing lolly ices. There was a tower block to the left, a multistory car park off to the right. We were alone in the air, in the middle of the night. We weren't dead. We weren't even in danger really. The lights of a hundred thousand streets glittered like hot confetti. We could see a million houses, but no one could see us. This must be what it's like for Spider-Man. When you see him swinging from skyscraper to skyscraper, you think it's just his spidery way of avoiding traffic. But when you are actually dangling off the side of a skyscraper, like we were, it's not like that. It's windy, strange, lonely, and amazing. The thing that's most amazing isn't the height or the cold, it's you. You're up there. No one else is. You're looking down at everything and everyone. No one can even see you! No one even knows you're there. You feel . . . Super.

You notice that the wind has different smells in it—frost, car exhaust, the oil from the cradle cable, the toasted dust from the top of its electric motor. You notice all the sounds of the air—the way it creaks through the cables, snuggles in the cradle, fidgets in your hair. You feel that the night belongs to you. You know without looking everything that's in the cradle—the motor, the rivets that hold it all together, the pair of dropped cigarette ends in the corner, the oily hinges of the gate.

You notice everything.

Now my brain is finally switched on. It sees everything. Knows everything. Probably I could open that gate, step into the air, and glide down to the ground.

Actually, probably best not to try that.

And then the cradle hit the ground, just next to the wheelie bins. And that's when Grim woke up. I explained about how he had opened locked doors in his sleep, and how I had teleported, and how we had jumped off the roof of a twelve-story building and survived. He looked up at the faraway roof of the hospital. "We jumped off there—" He looked at his feet, safely on the ground. "You laughing at me, Rory Rooney?" He pulled back his fist, ready to thump me.

"No."

"We can't have jumped. We'd be dead."

"But we did jump. And we're not dead." I realize now that I'd left out a few details—such as that we hadn't actually jumped seventy meters, more like one really. And that we had not swung down like Spider-Man, more like a window cleaner. But those things didn't feel important just then. I FELT super. I was tingling with Superness. That's when I told him my theory. "They put us in the isolation ward here at Woolpit Royal Teaching Hospital because they think we're sick. What if we're not sick? What if what we are is . . . superheroes?"

Without saying anything, he kicked his right foot up into my face, stopping just short so that his toe was almost touching my nose. He held the pose for a while, then snapped his foot back to the ground. "You know what, Rory Rooney?" he said, "I believe my confidence is coming back." He proved this by kicking his foot right into my face again. Then he jumped back, spun around, and did the same thing backward. "I've still got my moves."

"Yeah, you have. Just wondering if you could make them somewhere else."

He looked up at the roof again. "So how do we get back up there?" he said.

The moment he asked me, I knew we weren't going back up there. Not yet. We couldn't just press the up button and go back to bed and quinoa in the fish tank. Dad was right. We had turned green for a reason. Up there they wanted to know what had turned us green. I wanted to know *why*. Surely the answer lay out there, in the city.

"We are not," I said, "going back up there. We are going out into the city!" I pointed to the underpass, which you could just see between the wheelie bins.

It was as though he had been awaiting my order. "Yeah!" he whooped, and did a kind of flying kick right out of the cradle, yelled, "The Green Goblin!" and off he ran.

The wheelie bins clattered into one another like bowling pins, and I thought . . .

The Green Goblin is not a superhero.

The Green Goblin—aka the billionaire director of Oscorp, Norman Osborn, nemesis of Spider-Man—is not a superhero. He's a supervillain.

He's not a good guy.

He's a bad guy. A very bad guy.

A LONE FIGURE PACES THROUGH THE CITY ALLEYS AND UNDERPASSES

When I caught up with him, Grim did his kickboxing stance and a long, loud evil laugh. "Fools!" he chuckled. "Little do they suspect . . ."

I tried to figure out what he was so pleased about. There was a queue of mostly women in sparkly dresses with bare legs and tottery heels. Plus also a gang of lads with their arms around each other, shouting at the girls and bursting into song. I don't think I'd ever walked around a city at night before. It was much noisier, busier, and more exciting than I expected. But I wasn't scared. I was ready and hoping. Hoping that something crazy and dangerous would happen so that we could sort it out—a runaway train we could stop or a bank robbery we could foil.

"Ha! Perfect!" laughed Grim.

"What's perfect?"

He pointed to the head of the sparkly dresses queue. Two massive men were standing, with their arms folded, outside a big, chunky building with no windows. Across the backs of their silky black jackets was the word SECURITY in fluorescent letters. Over the door of the big, chunky building it said THE BANK in curly flashing lights.

"A bank," said Grim. "Let's rob it."

"Rob a . . . what? What are you talking about?"

"There's a bank. Let's rob it."

"What?! *Why?!*"

"For money. Why else would you rob a bank? If the Green Goblin saw a bank, he'd rob it, wouldn't he?"

"Yes, he would, because the Green Goblin is not a superhero, he's a supervillain. Think about the Green Hornet. Think about heroes. Being good. Foiling bank robberies, not doing bank robberies."

"But I'm not good. I'm bad. Surely you know that. Don't you remember when I used to throw your bag off the bus?"

"Yes, I do remember."

"Doing good, it's just not my thing. I'd probably get

it all wrong. Stick to what you're good at, that's what my mum says. I'm good at being bad."

"You were certainly good at being bad to me."

"I've been stuck in that ward for weeks. This is the first chance I've had in ages to really go and frighten someone. Come on."

"There's a queue."

"Evil doesn't queue." So he strode right to the front of the queue. I went after him. I felt as if I could stop a runaway train in its tracks, but stopping Grim Komissky was a different thing.

When I fell off the roof, my brain seemed to notice everything that was happening everywhere—the sound of a bird's wings, the lights of the city, even how I was falling. It was like I'd had a brain upgrade. Like now my brain was working at 200 percent normal capacity.

Anyway, now my 200 percent brain was noticing stuff and asking questions. For instance . . .

—Do banks usually have flashing neon signs over the door? (No.)

—Do they usually have loud music pumping out of them like this one does? (NO.)

—Aren't banks usually called something a bit more

specific than "the Bank"—such as "Bank of Ireland" or "the Co-Op Bank," not "the Bank"?

—And do banks usually stay open in the middle of the night?

I said, "Do banks usually stay open in the middle of the night?"

"Haven't you ever heard of twenty-four-hour banking?"

I had heard of twenty-four-hour banking—I just never expected it to look so exciting. A lot of the people going in and out were singing and dancing.

"Fools," snorted Grim. "Soon their laughter will end."

I was so surprised to hear how good he was at sounding like a supervillain that I forgot to be surprised that he was robbing a bank. He even had a proper plan. "Okay," he said. "You can teleport. Teleport us to the vault."

"I can't *teleport* teleport, not like that. I just . . . When you fell, it was just . . ."

"Don't say stuff like that. Say, 'Yes, Master,' or something."

"Okay."

"And don't say, 'Okay.' Say, 'Copy' or 'Understood.'"

"Sorry, Tommy-Lee."

"And don't call me Tommy-Lee. Telling everyone my name when I'm robbing a bank, idiot. We need supervillain names if we're going to rob banks. What about the Green Robbers?"

"If you're going to take robbing seriously, you probably don't want to tell people in advance that you're a robber. Better to keep it as a surprise."

"Oh yeah. What then? Green Kickboxers? Or the something gang."

"The Grim Gang?"

"Why Grim?"

"Your nickname. In school. Remember?" As soon as I said this, I realized that probably no one had ever called him that to his face. He looked as if he might cry.

"That's not very nice," he said.

I tried to change the subject. "What about the Broccoli Boys? We could be the Broccoli Boys?"

"Why Grim?"

"What?"

"Why did they call me Grim? Who called me Grim?"

He looked so sad, I said, "No one. It was just me. Because you threw me off the bus. Which was grim." He looked less frightening when he was sad, which was how I felt brave enough to say, "I'm not going to help you rob this bank. Robbing banks is wrong."

Suddenly his supervillain confidence came back. "Resistance," he roared, "is useless."

"No, it's not. Resistance is actually really useful. Look, there's you telling me to rob a bank. And here's me resisting. And are we robbing a bank? No."

"That's just where you're wrong." He grabbed me by the arm and marched toward the entrance. The two massive security guys stepped sideways, into our path. One of them put his hand more or less right in my face. "No kids. Over-twenty-ones only."

But the other one stared at us. "These kids are green," he said.

"Excellent," said the first one, bending down to get a better look at me. "How did you do that? They look like . . . What are they called?"

I was thinking, Please don't say leprechauns.

"Munchkins," said the second one. "They look like Munchkins."

The other one disagreed. "Munchkins are yellow," he said. "You mean Oompa Loompas."

"Oompa Loompas are orange," says the first one. "It was the Yellow Brick Road that was yellow. The Munchkins were green."

"It's definitely not Munchkins."

My upgraded brain warned me that they might be about to say the word "leprechaun."

"Santa's helpers," I said. "We're the elves that help Santa."

One of them growled, "Are you trying to be funny?"

But the other one asked, "Is it for charity?"

"Yes! Yes!" I said. "This is for charity. And it's Christmas!"

"Why didn't you say? Go on in. Don't forget to wipe your feet on the mat." We crossed the big, squidgy disinfectant mats and entered the Bank.

I'd never been in a bank before. I'm not sure what I was expecting, but I know it wasn't loud music and flashing lights. Or people jumping up and down and waving their arms in the air. Putting money in and out of your bank account seemed to be a lot more fun than I would have thought. The women seemed to be mostly in dressing-up clothes. One of them had a long pointy tail, and red horns growing out of her head. She was carrying a big pitchfork and wearing a T-shirt that said LITTLE DEVIL, even though she was absolutely huge. Another was dressed as Santa Claus—if Santa Claus was a woman who wore a really short red skirt and massive boots. Quite a few were dressed as cats, with CAUTION: THIS KITTEN'S A KILLER written across their T-shirts. I'd had no idea that when Mum or Dad had to go down to the bank they were having such a great time.

"My mum," said Grim, "used to guard a bank. She never said anything about people dressed up as chickens."

A little flock of chicken women were dancing around a man with very, very blond hair and a sparkly jacket, who was holding a microphone.

The music stopped. The man with the very, very blond hair got up and said into a microphone that his name was DJ Iceberg and that this was a very big night for someone called Wendy, who turned out to be one of the chickens. Wendy had a poster on her back that said I AM A HEN AND THIS IS MY NIGHT, and she was going to sing for us. DJ Iceberg gave Wendy the microphone and asked everyone to clap before she started, "Because you might not feel like it afterward." But before Wendy the Hen could cluck one note, Grim had grabbed the microphone.

"Obey," he said, "and you will not get hurt. Know that we are . . ." He paused. He still hadn't thought of a name. "Know that we are . . . here to rob the Bank."

Everything went quiet.

No music.

No talking.

My 200 percent brain was still taking in lots of details, such as the fact that we were a very long way from the exit, that there were hundreds of people in the room, all of them bigger than me, that we didn't have any of the advantages of normal bank robbers—for instance, guns.

"Now hand over your money to my henchman," said Grim.

I did try to explain that I wasn't his henchman, but the microphone didn't pick it up.

I tried again to convince Grim to stop, but he only said, "Henchmen don't argue."

A woman with a tinsel halo and feathery wings stepped out of the crowd. Her wings were too small. She looked as if she had been in a nativity play when she was a little girl and never took off the costume. She yelled, "Me first!" and pushed a ten-pound note into my hand. "After all, it's for charity." We never said we were collecting for charity. She just assumed we were. She put her arms around Tommy-Lee and asked someone to take her picture.

"No pictures!" said Grim.

But no one took any notice. Dozens of phones

flashed as all her friends took pictures of her with her arms around Grim.

The women dressed as Killer Kittens pushed forward, gave me another tenner each, and stood one on each side of Grim, making Killer Kitten faces.

Wendy the Hen shouted, "I want one!" and ran over to me, her wings flapping. "My purse has got snagged under my beak, look. Can you take some money out for me?" she clucked. I took a fiver out. She snuggled in between me and Grim and had her photograph taken. We were surrounded by strangely dressed women, hugging us, patting us, and most of all, giving us money. Lots of money.

"This is the easiest bank robbery I was ever in," said Grim. Everyone laughed.

It wasn't that easy, in fact, because we had no pockets in our pajamas. Also we hadn't brought a bag, because we hadn't known we were going to do a bank.

A very loud nun in a very short nun-skirt asked if we were collecting for charity.

"No, it's all for us."

She laughed, and when she laughed, all the others joined in.

"Don't laugh," I pleaded. But somehow this only made them laugh more.

My upgraded brain could hear bad thoughts and crackling noises going on inside Grim's head. It also noticed something else—the security guy pushing through the crowd toward us with a big smile on his face. It knew right away what was causing the smile. He had remembered the word he had been trying to think of. He pointed to us, looked at the women, and said the word. "Leprechauns!" he said. "They're leprechauns!"

Grim's two worst things were happening at the same time: People were laughing. And someone had said the Leprechaun word. His brain was no longer crackling. It was ticking, like a bomb about to go off.

He suddenly leaned back and kicked the air somewhere just above his head. No wonder he was British kickboxing champion. As he kicked, he shouted, "Pow!" I swear the air went "OW!!"

Everything went quiet. Everyone jumped back.

Grim turned on his heel and did the kick again, backward this time, like a donkey—a green donkey in Ninja pajamas. "Kerpow!" he cried this time.

He whirled around to kick again. This time when he kicked, though, all the chickens kicked too. And they all shouted "Kerpow!" When he stood with his fists raised, they raised their wings. When he turned round to do another backward kick, everyone—chickens, nuns, Santa Claus, and Killer Kittens—they all turned round too. They all tried to kick backward. They all shouted, "Pow!" They were rubbish at it, but they were having a good time. They were trying to copy every move he made. They thought he was teaching them some kind of dance. He shook his fist, they shook their fists back. He threatened them, but they couldn't hear him because DJ Iceberg had started playing a record over him. It was called "Kung Fu Fighting."

I turned round. A Killer Kitten jumped back. She had been looking really hard at the back of my neck. Now she was right in my face. She squashed her head next to mine and took a selfie of the two of us. "How did you do it?" she shouted right in my ear.

"What?"

"The color?"

"Oh. It's just a spray. We sprayed it on."

"That's never a spray. It's too smooth. . . ."

She was looking into my eyes now and at my fingernails. "I'm a nurse," she said. "We're nearly all nurses."

I said, "We're not sick."

"No. But you are . . . green. . . . You're really green, aren't you?"

There was trouble coming. I could feel it. I had

already noticed the door behind DJ Iceberg. It had a bar across it that said EMERGENCIES ONLY. It wasn't my 200 percent brain that noticed this, by the way; it was me—if you're used to being hunted down by bullies at school, the first thing you look for when you walk into any room is the way out. But it was my 200 percent brain that figured out our escape plan.

"This isn't makeup!" yelled the Killer Kitten. "I'm a nurse. I'm telling you, these kids are actually green, possibly contagious. . . ."

People frowned. The Hen Whose Night It Was screamed and cried and said was it catchy? Was she going to be green on her wedding day? "Oh my days, get me out of here! Get them out of here!"

The Sparkly Nun stared me in the eye. "You made Wendy cry on her Big Night," she growled.

Wendy the Hen punched numbers on her mobile, her little wings flapping like angry fingers. I knew she was ringing the police.

"We've got to get out of here," I yelled.

"I'm not scared. I can fight all of them."

"You're doing a robbery. What do robbers do at the end of a robbery? They get away."

"Oh yeah."

Vampires, nuns, and nurses closed in on us like

wolves. I grabbed the money out of Grim's hand—
there was a lot, notes and coins—and threw most of it
up into the air.

Nurses, angels, hens, and Killer Kittens saw the
cash confetti falling and dived on it.

For a few seconds they forgot we were there.

I grabbed Grim and dragged him to the Emergencies
Only door, and we were out on the street.

"That was fun," he said.

*H*OLY TELEPORTATION, RORY. YOU'VE TAKEN US TO CHINA!

We were in a street, but there were no cars. There were lots of people standing around talking and smiling and waving to each other. The street was mostly cafés with red paper lanterns hanging over their doorways. Some of them had little stalls with boxes of fruit and vegetables outside. There was a big statue of a dragon with a long, sloping back. Some kids were using it as a kind of slide. Everyone looked Chinese. The writing on the street signs looked Chinese. The posters on the wall, the signs above the shops— all Chinese. Even the phone box behind the stone dragon had a pointy, curly roof like a pagoda's, with four little stone dragons, one guarding each corner.

"Excellent work, my trusty minion," said Grim, patting me on the shoulder. He really was good at this supervillain thing. It's a shame it was evil, really.

I tried to make it look as though I was used to teleporting to China. I should have been worrying about how to get back to the hospital, but I hadn't eaten all day and the air was spiced with all kinds of cooking smells. The cafés' windows were decorated with roasted ducks and chickens, sparkling with crisp skin. Outside one shop were piled the brightest, weirdest fruits I'd ever seen—tiny round ones colored like Smarties, something that looked like a purple hand grenade, things a bit like apples but shaped like rugby balls, a box of papery lantern things with berries inside. MOONLIGHT DELIGHT it said in silvery writing across the shop window. "I'll say one thing for China," said Grim. "It smells good. I bet it tastes good too."

He reached for a papery fruit. I said, "Hey. They're not ours."

"I'm evil. I take what I want, remember? I've just robbed a bank. I'm not going to worry about stealing a weird tomatoey thing." He did his evil laugh. But stopped when someone else joined in. It was a little girl with bunches in her hair, standing in the doorway of the shop. She said, in English, "Are you two goblins?"

"Oh. No. Not goblins, no. Definitely not. Nothing like that." I didn't want to say we were Superbeings, because it sounded a bit showy-offy. At the same time I wanted to make sure she didn't mention leprechauns.

She shouted something in Chinese. From somewhere inside the shop an old lady appeared and put her hand on the little girl's shoulder, chatted to her for a bit in Chinese.

"She's not going to laugh, is she?" asked Grim.

"They won't laugh at you."

"Or mention leprechauns?"

"Or mention those small people."

The old lady went back inside and came back with little bamboo boxes with wisps of steam coming out of their lids and big, pale, hot meat dumplings inside. They were soft and melty. Grim went to take one, but I grabbed his hand just in time. "Traces of nuts," I said.

"Oh," he said, "yeah."

I sat down on the step to eat.

"Tell me what they taste like."

"Won't that make it worse?"

"No. I like it when people describe. My mum always eats whatever she likes and then describes the taste of big bowls of steaming pastas swimming in thick, creamy tomato sauces to me. She says—let's share. You have the smell and I'll have the taste."

So I tried describing the dumplings for him—how the meat was a bit chewy and how you could feel the steam on the roof of your mouth. I was going on to tell him about the honey aftertaste when the old lady came back with two old-lady mates, and all three of them started patting us on the head.

"Whoa! What's going on?!" whined Tommy-Lee.

"They think you look like lucky goblins," said the little girl. "They're patting you for luck."

Apparently the harder they patted us, the more luck we would bring them. Tommy-Lee was getting twitchy.

"They want to know where you're from," said the girl.

I told her we were from Birmingham.

The girl said something in Chinese and then explained, "I told them you were from Greenland."

Now the ladies were laughing.

"Are you real?" asked the little girl. "Or are you an advert? Like for frozen peas or something."

"We're real. Of course we're real."

She said something else to the old ladies. They laughed even louder. Grim jumped up.

"Rory Rooney," growled Grim, "old ladies are laughing at me."

"They like us!"

These people were giving me food instead of grabbing it off me. They were patting me on the head instead of throwing me off the bus. I was having the best time ever.

"They love us."

"Old ladies are laughing at me, Rory."

"You said that before."

"It was happening before. And it's still happening now. Make it stop. My anger-management issues are coming back."

"What anger-management issues?"

"Kicking people. I have an issue that makes me kick people when I get angry."

"I know. I was one of those people."

"I had to go and see a special doctor about it."

"And?"

"He gave me special anger-management techniques."

"Great. Why don't you use them?"

"I always forget."

"But you could use them now."

"Great idea."

He put his head down and walked off up the road. It turned out his number one anger-management technique was walking away.

MOCKED BY MERE MORTALS,
THE GREEN SUPERVILLAIN
SWORE THAT HE WOULD
AVENGE HIMSELF ON ALL
NORMAL-COLORED PEOPLE!!!

"**T**hat was my worst night ever. I'm never going outside again. Not until I'm well."

I said, "I don't know what you're so upset about.
People gave us food. They gave us money! We were in
China—sort of."

"Big women dressed as chickens attacked me. I
want to go home."

It's always easy to find your way back to a hospital. All
you have to do is follow the ambulances. I took Grim
around the back to the window cleaners' cradle.

"What is it?"

"This is our shortcut back to base."

He didn't like the cradle either. By the time we were just a little bit above the wheelie bins, he was already complaining that we were too high. "Get used to it," I said. "We've got eleven stories left to go."

By the time we were level with the roof of the multistory car park, he had his back to the city and was holding the side of the cradle so hard his knuckles bulged. I said, "Turn around—you're going to miss the view."

"I can see the view. It's reflected in the windows."

"It's better if you look round. Honestly, don't be scared."

"Stop telling me I'm scared when I'm not scared. You're the one who should be scared."

"Why should I be scared?"

"I could throw you out of here if I felt like it. You'd be jam on the pavement."

Maybe it was because he was threatening to turn me into pavement jam after I had just saved him from being turned into pavement jam.

Maybe it was because I was still feeling indestructible after falling off a high building without a scratch.

Whatever the reason, that's when I knew one thing: I wasn't scared of Grim anymore. Not even a bit.

It felt as if I'd been cured of a long illness.

I pulled the oily handle. The motor ground to a

halt. The cradle rocked in the air, just a little bit.

"We've stopped? Why have we stopped? Why have we stopped?!" Tommy-Lee was having a panic. A proper eye-popping, hands waggling panic. "We've stopped. What are we going to do?"

"I'm just appreciating that river. And the big wheel thing . . ."

"Make it go again. We can't stay here. We're in the middle of the air."

"In a bit."

"Make it go . . . ," he yelled. He swung around to face me, but when he was facing me, he also had to face the view. His eyes bulged in fright. "What is it?"

"That? It's a city."

"Why's it so small?"

"It's not so small. We're so high up."

"Get us out of here! PLEASE, get us out of here."

Komissky said "please" to me! I said, "Sure." There was always the possibility that he might get angry and throw me out of the cradle. "No bother." I cranked the handle. We wobbled up the side of the building. I watched the city get smaller and smaller. At the top I undid the catch and led Tommy-Lee onto the roof, through the little access door, and down the ladder onto the corridor.

He followed me all the way to the first locked door.

Then I thought, Oh, we're in trouble now—how are we going to get through? But he just slid past me and typed a code into the keypad, and the door opened. I didn't say anything in case it ruined his concentration or something, but I did wonder if being able to open locks was like being able to slightly teleport—something that only green people could do.

When he opened the Singing Duck door, we both froze. Nurse Rock was at her desk, staring right at the door, her hands on the table in front of her.

The door clicked shut behind us.

Even the 200 percent brain couldn't think of anything to say. We walked toward her with our heads down. She never said a word. She never moved a muscle. Even when I said, "Sorry." Even when Tommy-Lee said, "It was him, not me. He made me do it."

I went a bit closer.

"Is she dead?"

She gave a loud, horrible, gluey snore. She was asleep! She slept sitting up with her eyes wide open.

We ran back to the fish tank and hid under our duvets.

■ ■ ■

In the course of one evening I had saved Tommy-Lee's life at least twice—once from falling off a building, once from a mob of potentially furious chickens. More if you counted the traces of nuts. I'd also foiled a bank robbery. Even though the Bank hadn't been an actual bank—and even though it was a bank robbery in which I had been one of the bank robbers—that was still a good night's superhero work.

I was just about to fall asleep properly when a voice from the other bed said, "Grim, though? That's so harsh."

"I'm sorry," I said. "I won't do it again, okay?" Then I added, "Tommy-Lee."

"Okay then."

And I really did never call him Grim again.

BRITAIN'S TOP-TOP-SECRET-
SECRET SCIENTISTS ARE
SUMMONED TO THE TOP
SECRET GOVERNMENT
INSTALLATION WHERE THE
ASTOUNDING BROCCOLI BOYS
ARE BEING HELD . . .

When I opened my eyes next morning, Nurse Rock and Dr. Brightside were staring in at me through the fish-tank window. Behind them were about a million other grown-ups in white overalls, all talking and making notes.

"Tommy-Lee . . . ," I hissed.

"He's awake! Rory's just opened one eye!" shrieked Dr. Brightside.

"I told you they weren't in a coma," sniffed Nurse Rock. "They are practically teenagers. Teenagers sleep until lunchtime. Even the ones that are washed and dressed and sitting in school are mentally asleep until lunchtime." She probably didn't know that the intercom was on.

"Tommy-Lee . . . ," I hissed again.

"No one is looking at me," he growled. "Not while I'm green." He wrapped his duvet tight around him. He looked like a massive floral caterpillar.

Dr. Brightside tapped at the window with her pen and pointed to the intercom, which was in Tommy-Lee territory.

"No, you don't . . . ," rumbled the floral caterpillar when I tried to cross his invisible line.

"They want to talk to us."

"I don't want to talk to them."

Now that I'd opened both eyes and counted, I could see there weren't a full million people. It was closer to seven people. They were all making notes, though.

One of them—a massive bloke with a massive beard—leaned into the intercom and boomed, "Is your friend the same shade of green?"

"Yes, he is," said Dr. Brightside. "Exactly the same, even though they were different colors to start with."

Massive Beard wanted to see.

"Of course. Rory, tell Tommy-Lee to get out of bed."

"Not getting out of bed," grunted Tommy-Lee.

Other questions were flying out of the intercom and squawking around the room: Could I lift my top up so that they could see my chest? Was I in pain? Had I experienced any strange hallucinations? If Tommy-Lee wasn't getting out of bed, then he couldn't stop me from talking to them, could he? I padded across the room. The caterpillar duvet froze.

I spoke right into the intercom. "We don't feel ill. We feel great. The truth is, we're not sick. We're just . . . different." When I looked back at them, they were mostly holding their ears. Apparently if you speak right into the intercom, it makes a weird wailing sound.

I stepped away from the intercom and said it again. "We're not sick. We're just different."

They all looked at Dr. Brightside. She smiled. "While it's true that their health indicators are generally very good, I think we'd all agree that if we were to let them go into the outside world looking like that, people would stare and call them names. They'd suffer enormous psychological damage. We need to protect them."

"Good point," said Massive Beard. "Also, in the current medical climate—with the whole country in a State of Emergency about cat flu—the prospect of an epidemic of green children could trigger a highly

138

volatile situation. We need to protect these boys."

"We don't need protecting," I said. "We feel Super."

"Such a positive outlook," said Dr. Brightside. "It's heartbreaking."

"Dr. Brightside is looking after you very well," said Massive Beard.

"No. I don't mean super as in good. I mean super as in Super. Like *Superheroes*. We feel different."

The caterpillar duvet shuffled.

The doctors stopped making notes.

They stared at me through the window. It made the fish tank feel less like a fish tank and more like a television set. And I was the program.

"Think about it—who else in history has ever turned green?" They all looked blank. I listed the only other green people in history as told to me by my dad. "The Incredible Hulk, Swamp Thing, the Green Hornet, and the Green Goblin. What did all these people have in common?"

"They're all fictitious?" said Dr. Brightside.

"But besides that?"

They still looked blank.

"They're all Super. With superpowers."

"Actually," interrupted Dr. Brightside, "the Green Goblin is a supervillain, not a superhero."

"But he's got superpowers. That's my point."

"I believe I'm right in saying," said Massive Beard, "that he was originally a billionaire chemist who created a serum to turn himself into an evil genius."

Why were they talking about the Green Goblin?! I was talking about US!! They were missing the whole point. "The whole point," I said, "is he was green. He was green and he had superpowers. Okay? If you turn green, there's only one possible diagnosis—and that's Super."

It went very quiet inside the fish tank all of a sudden. Dr. Brightside had muted the intercom. I could see her discussing what I'd said with all the other doctors. I couldn't hear their voices. But I could see that Massive Beard was saying, ". . . for all we know, these delusions of grandeur could be a symptom."

"No, Dr. Big Beard, we don't have any delusions of grandeur. We ARE grand!"

"How does he know I said that?" said Massive Beard. "Can he hear through walls?!"

"That's exactly my point. My brain has had an upgrade. I notice all kinds of things I never noticed before. I can hear things, smell things. I could tell what you were saying just by looking at your face."

"Lipreading is not a superpower," growled Nurse Rock.

"It is if you don't actually know how to lip-read," I said. "Also, I slightly teleported."

"You slightly teleported?" asked Dr. Brightside.

"I don't want to go into details"—I didn't want to tell them about walking around London at night in pajamas in case they decided it was bad for us and tried to stop us—"but I definitely teleported a short distance."

"Interesting," said Massive Beard. "Is there anything we can do to help you in your work?"

I thought about asking for gadgets, or for some sort of training, or maybe a proper outfit.

"How are you for capes and masks?" said one of the doctors at the back. "Have you got a name or a logo?"

Then they all started suggesting names.

"What about Broccoli Boy?"

"The Broccoli Kid?"

"The Mean Green Team?"

"Lettuce Man?"

"The Chameleons. Because you changed color."

"Captain Chronic, because it's a chronic condition."

"Bogeyboy . . . because you're the same color as bogeys."

"The Bogeyman. The Bogeyman is good."

"Then you can say you've been picked for your mission!"

Everyone laughed. While they were laughing, Tommy-Lee rolled off his bed and gave the intercom one of his bad looks. "They're laughing at us," he growled. "I hate that." Through the window, grown-up faces in white coats were talking, shouting, nudging one another, and most of all laughing. The laughing seemed louder now that you couldn't hear it. "Right," he growled. "You'll pay for this." He thumped the intercom. "You're all laughing," he roared, "but it's really true. Rory CAN teleport. Look. He does it like this." The doctors looked round.

Tommy-Lee picked me up and flung me across the room.

"See?"

I smacked into the wall.

"Interesting," said one of the voices. "Do you think the green pigmentation has in some way made this boy more aggressive?"

"No!" I yelled. "He was always like this! This is exactly my point!" Tommy-Lee hoisted me back into the air. "He's behaving exactly the same as he did before he went green. Going green hasn't affected his health at all." He proved my point by throwing me clear across the room onto my bed.

"He's strong!" I bawled. "Would he be this strong if we were sick?"

When Nurse Rock burst in, I was lying on the bed, noticing the fact that I didn't hurt. Once you've jumped off a twelve-story building, being shoved around a bedroom doesn't bother you. I, I thought to myself, am possibly invincible. Or indestructible. But definitely quite comfortable.

"*I***F I'D KNOWN THERE WERE GOING TO BE FISTFIGHTS, I WOULD HAVE SOLD TICKETS."**

That's what Dr. Brightside said as she looked down at the two of us sprawled on our beds. "Please don't kill each other. You're my favorite specimens."

"Yes, miss," said Tommy-Lee.

"Your fates are intertwined. Your best hope of a cure, Tommy-Lee, is Rory—and Rory, your best hope is Tommy-Lee. You're blood brothers. Well, skin-pigmentation brothers."

She pinned a big color chart on the wall. "It's got every shade of green known to man," she said, "from Light Pampas to Vivid Vomit. Come and stand with your backs to it." She pulled a big chunky camera out of her shoulder bag and pointed it at us. "Give me your biggest superhero smiles, please." I am actually smiling in that photo, even though Tommy-Lee was crushing my little toe with his big, kickboxing heel at the time. "You two get more interesting by the minute. We are on the brink of something really special here. Can you feel it?" All I could feel was Tommy-Lee's heel grinding into my toe.

"I'm going to take a photograph like this every day so that I can monitor any fluctuations in your pigmentation."

There never were any fluctuations, by the way. We went green and we stayed green.

After the photo it was all the usual stuff. Blood test. Wee in a bottle. Blowing in a tube. Quinoa.

Tommy-Lee reached over to take my quinoa. I tried to grab it back. He hissed. "You're not hungry. You ate loads last night. I wasn't allowed to eat then. You're not allowed to eat now."

I glanced at the intercom, then the window. "Someone might be listening," I hissed back.

"From now on, you do everything I tell you, or I'll tell her what you did."

"What did I do?"

"You went outside."

"No. You went outside. I followed you. I saved your life!"

"When I tell her, then you'll suffer. She's a doctor.

This is a hospital. That means she can do what she likes. She can stick needles in you. She can put you in a ward on your own with no telly. She can keep you locked up forever."

"She's a doctor, not a Dalek. She's trying to make us better."

"They do terrible things to you in the hospital if you don't do what they say. So we are going to do everything she says, including not jumping off buildings or robbing banks."

"Robbing banks was your idea."

"You led me astray. People are always leading me astray. From now on, whatever she tells you to do, you do."

And what she told us to do that day was drawings. Dr. Brightside gave us a box of felt pens and some big sheets of paper. She said drawing would keep our minds active and also give her a window into our minds. Which might be useful if going green is psychosomatic.

"You're saying we made ourselves green with our brains?"

"I'm not discounting anything at this point."

She asked us to draw something to do with Undersea Exploration. "Imagine going down into the darkest depths. What will you find?"

I drew a giant squid attacking a submarine. One of the squid's slimy tentacles was stuck in the propeller, and another one was reaching inside the submarine through the periscope. It was a masterpiece. I'd never drawn a masterpiece before.

"Hurry up," snapped Tommy-Lee. "The doctor said to draw a picture, so draw a picture."

"I've drawn a picture," I said, and turned it around for all the world to see.

"I've drawn one too."

Tommy-Lee had drawn a completely square house with a completely square lawn. At each corner of the completely square lawn he'd drawn a big lollipop-shaped flower. Bright yellow curtains on each of the four square windows. "What do you think?" he said.

I said, "It's a house."

"Yeah."

"What's it got to do with undersea exploration?"

"It's the house," he said, "of an undersea explorer."

When she came back, Dr. Brightside said Tommy's drawing was "very good" and she gave him a little gold star to stick on the corner of it. I thought, If she thinks that's worth a gold star, wait until she sees mine! She'll probably call the National Gallery and tell them to get over here quick. In fact, all she said about mine was "very good" too and gave me a gold star. Our Fate was in the hands of someone who thought Giant Squid Swallows Entire Submarine is about the same level of artistic as "Square House with Lollipop Flowers." It was the I've Been Brave certificates all over again, only without the blood.

There is no justice in the world.

Which is why we need superheroes.

She asked us to do another drawing. This time the subject was "My Favorite View."

I sucked my felt pen. "Get drawing," growled Tommy-Lee. He was already scribbling away. Apparently his favorite view was another square house with lollipop flowers.

"I'm thinking," I said. (I was actually thinking, Is this worth the effort?)

"The doctor didn't ask you to think, she asked you to draw."

"Yes, but she doesn't want you to draw another square house with lollipop trees outside."

Tommy-Lee couldn't have looked more surprised if I'd told him I'd been asked to join the Power Rangers. "What do you mean?"

"She doesn't want you to hand in some neat little box. She wants you to look into your imagination and see what you can find."

"Like what?"

"That's exactly what I'm trying to think about."

In the end, I drew "The West Midlands in the Ice Age," which was slightly cheating, but it gave me a cozy feeling to think about the papier-mâché model in the geography storage cupboard, which also helped me remember various sandwiches I had eaten safely there. Then I thought maybe I would sketch some sandwiches. If I never got to eat food, at least I could draw some. I was just deciding on the fillings when Tommy-Lee said, "Get me some more paper."

He'd already covered one sheet in furious scribbles. I couldn't see what it was supposed to be, so I said, "What's it supposed to be?"

"It's supposed to be my favorite view. It's too big for one piece of paper."

He wasn't drawing his usual square house.

He was drawing a whole city.

A sunburst of roads, streets, avenues and lanes and bypasses and dual carriageways spread out from the middle of the page. It was the view from the window cleaners' cradle. It was already spilling off the edges of the page. I helped him sticky-tape some more sheets together so he could spread out.

"Color the houses in," he said, without looking up. Now that I looked more closely, I saw that it wasn't just roads—it was houses, pubs, churches, schools, supermarkets, car parks, crammed into every bit of space. I colored in their fronts and doorways, roofs and road signs. Tommy-Lee drew in the river, with the big Ferris wheel on its bank. The rockety tower with its huge yellow clock. There was the dome—a big, blank bubble blowing out of it all. Once he made me stop what I was doing and rubbed out a great big patch of the drawing.

"What are you doing?"

Where the streets and a chunk of river had been, he drew a pigeon flying over the city like a big, raggy jumbo jet. It really made you feel like you were looking down from the cradle. I said, "Tommy-Lee, that was a brilliant idea."

"It wasn't an idea. It's real."

That's when I realized he wasn't looking into his imagination at all. He was looking into his memory. Tommy-Lee remembered everything. Every corner. Every doorway. Every passing car. This wasn't a picture. This was a map.

■ ■ ■

"It'll look better," I said, "if we stand on the bed." It really did. Looking at it from up there, it felt as if we were really flying over a real city. We stayed up there for ages.

"Any good?" asked Tommy-Lee when Dr. Bright-side came in.

"You did this together?"

"No," said Tommy-Lee. "I did it. He just sharpened the pencils."

"And did the coloring in," I added.

"You both cooperated—that's my point. Also you spent some time on it. . . ."

She was right. We didn't realize until we looked at the clock, but we'd been doing this for HOURS.

"Well, this picture shows a marked improvement in your powers of concentration and cooperation."

"So we're getting better? If we keep drawing, will I stop being green?"

"Tommy-Lee, when you first came in here, you were so miserable I wasn't sure there was any point trying to cure you. I thought, this boy is getting so little out of life, he might as well spend the rest of it in isolation. Now that you're starting to wake up, I'll try a bit harder."

Then she gave us a "Very Good" sticker to stick on the bottom of the painting.

We put the picture up on the wall when she'd gone. Nurse Rock looked at it with her head on one side.

"What's it supposed to be?"

"My favorite view. It's what she told us to draw."

"London is your favorite view?"

"London? Is that London?" asked Tommy-Lee.

"Where else could it be? There's the Thames. There's St. Paul's." The rockety thing with the big yellow clock turned out to be the Houses of Parliament. I'd never been to London before. Now Tommy-Lee seemed to have a map of the whole city in his head.

"What I'm wondering is," said Nurse Rock, "where anyone could stand where they'd get that view of London."

I looked at Tommy-Lee. Tommy-Lee looked at me. I thought he was going to say something that would give the game away, but he just shrugged and said he couldn't remember.

"You saw the whole of London and didn't even know it was London?" said Nurse Rock. "What did you think it was? Disneyland?"

"I thought it was . . . ," said Tommy-Lee, ". . . like nothing else on earth."

*W*HAT ADVENTURES DOES THE CITY HOLD FOR OUR HEROES TONIGHT?!

I lay in bed that night—Tommy-Lee still wouldn't turn the light off—just hoping and waiting for him to sleepwalk again. Every now and then I'd ask him a question just to see if he was still awake.

"Where do you think we'll go tonight?"

"We're not going anywhere. I'm not going outside again until we stop being green."

"But Tommy-Lee, we've got superpowers. You can't have superpowers and not use them."

"What superpowers have we got?"

"You can open locked doors in your sleep."

"Opening doors is not a superpower."

"It is if they're locked."

"I always look out for the codes on the doors when they put me in the hospital," he said. "If you watch where their fingers go, you can work it out. I hate being in the hospital, so I always look for the codes. Then at least I know I can escape if it gets too bad."

"Are you in the hospital a lot?"

"I was in for months when I was little. That's how I learned kickboxing."

"They gave you kickboxing lessons in the hospital?"

"No. They gave me blood tests. So I kicked them." Apparently that was when his mum decided he had a talent for violent footwork and that it was only right to nurture it.

He didn't say anything else. I thought he might be asleep. I tried another question.

"Your brain has got bigger—don't you think that's a superpower? Before you could only draw one house. Now you've drawn a whole city."

No answer. I slipped out of the bed to turn the light off.

"I'm watching you," he growled. "I can't get to sleep. Read me a story."

"What story?"

"From a book."

The only book I had was *Don't Be Scared, Be*

Prepared, so I read him bits from that. He particularly liked the bits about jumping out of a moving car or off a moving boat. He made me read those three times. On the third time I put in a bit about the boat rocking like a cradle. His eyes drooped. Then they closed. For a few minutes he looked like a big, sweetly sleeping baby. Then he gave a snore that sounded like a tiger gargling treacle. Then he rolled over. Plonked his feet on the floor. Stood up and started to do the Spooky Playmobil.

I followed him, hoping he was going to go straight to the window cleaners' cradle and out into the night. Or at least go to the staff canteen, where I could get some cheese.

But he didn't. He just wandered up and down the top corridor, going in and out of the side rooms and rest areas, as though he was looking for something. Finally he found a kind of waiting room for kids—with a slide and a drawer full of face paints and some coloring books. All the pictures had been started, but none of them had been finished. There was fake snow on the windows, a big picture of Santa, and a bucket of Legos with tinsel wrapped around it. It was nice doing some Legos with Santa looking down—you could pretend it was Christmas morning. Even though Christmas was weeks off. I ended up building a really tall Big Ben. I only stopped when the sun was coming up and Tommy-Lee was properly asleep in a Wendy house. I managed to get him half awake and make him sleepwalk us back to the Singing Duck door. I'd found an old *Spider-Man Annual* in the waiting room that I'd brought back to the fish tank. Dad had exactly the same annual under his bed back home.

Home. Home was so far away it sounded like the name of a different planet.

It was the same story the next night and the night after and the night after that. We'd get into our beds. I'd ask him questions to see if he was awake. He would answer the first few, such as why he hated leprechauns (long story), how he turned green (same story), what it feels like to have an allergic reaction (you feel like a football and someone is inflating you), and how come he was so good at talking like a supervillain.

"First time I was in the hospital, my mum couldn't come to see me because she was working. There was no telly. All I had was the *Batman Annual* for 1996. I know everything the Joker said by heart. That's how I know you haven't got a superpower."

"How?"

"Because the minute someone gets a superpower, they get big muscles. Even Spider-Man. There's no such thing as a puny superhero. You are puny." I thought about the Spider-Man pajamas I'd had when I was little—the ones with the foam muscles.

I measured my muscles every day after that in case there were signs of improvement.

Some nights Tommy-Lee would ask me questions, such as "Who would win in a fight between a python and a crocodile?" Or—his favorite—who would win in a fight between Rory Rooney and Tommy-Lee Komissky?

"You would win, Tommy-Lee."

"Yeah. So go to sleep before I come and check that fact."

After "Question Time," when it was quiet, he'd float across the fish tank and open the door. The scariest bit was making sure that Nurse Rock didn't notice. But she was almost always staring at her phone and eating chocolate.

She ate a different kind of chocolate every night, by the way. Toblerone one night, Galaxy the next. What kind of person can't settle on a favorite type of chocolate? A 100 percent untrustworthy kind of person, that's what.

I tried everything I could to make Tommy-Lee go back to the roof. I tried to put the idea in his mind by saying the word "roof" over and over when he was drifting off to sleep. I tried walking in front of him to see if he would follow me, but he'd keep veering off into side rooms and cupboards. Like the time he opened one door and thick, wet clouds came pouring out. I thought it must be the door to the outside world and that it was foggy outside. But the clouds were warm and smelled of lavender. Then there was a break in them, and I saw three dark-haired women staring straight at us from behind a row of ironing boards. The minute they saw us, they dropped their irons and made the sign of the cross. The smallest one shouted, *"Aye! Madre de Dios!"* I realized we'd walked into the hospital laundry.

Or the time I looked back and he'd gone into this little round room. It had a circle of chairs arranged around a table, with flowers, a book, and a shoe box on it. The book was the Bible. The room was a chapel. I opened the shoe box. It was stuffed with yellow Post-it notes. Each of them had some sad thing written on it.

- *Help our Sammy get well.*
- *Look after my mum. I need her.*
- *Let Niall come home from the hospital soon.*
- *Please make our baby better.*

There were hundreds and hundreds of them.

There was a poster on the notice board too—showing some little sick kids playing with Mickey Mouse in Disney World. Underneath it said, *The Wish Factory—granting magical wishes to children and young people fighting life-threatening conditions.*

I thought how the whole hospital—the twelve stories, the long, winding corridors, the locked wards—was really one massive shoe box stuffed with sadness. The 200 percent brain could almost hear all the sighs and the worries—the mums and dads sitting in the canteen, waiting for something to happen. Frightened, sleepless children twisting in their beds at night. Patients hooked up to machines that bleeped and buzzed. Relatives watching the machines, wondering what the bleeps and buzzes meant. Nurses and doctors who understood what the machines meant and wished they didn't have to translate. And the injustices too—such as I've Been Brave certificates being given to children who weren't even a tiny bit brave. The children who were made to eat nothing but frog spawn by people who stuffed themselves with different kinds of chocolate night after night. So much sadness. I felt as if I was going to burst.

What was the point in having a 200 percent brain,

or being able to slightly teleport, if you couldn't fight injustice?!

We had to get out of here and do something!

Tommy-Lee must have had the same feelings in his sleep. Because that was the night we finally went outside again.

THE NIGHT CITY . . .

Fragile as a set of fairy lights on a velvet carpet, just hoping that no one will tread on them. Who takes care of the sleeping?

I tried to make Tommy-Lee follow me back to the Moonlight Delight, but just as we were about to cross the road, a big red bus came past, a London bus, open at the back. I'd never seen one up close before. With the yellow bus light behind them, the people on the top deck looked like faces in a stained-glass window. I was so busy looking at them that I didn't notice that Tommy-Lee had stepped onto the platform of the bus and was trundling away from me down the street. I had to run, grab the pole, and swing myself on, like a Routemaster Spider-Man. There was no one else on the lower deck. Tommy-Lee stood there holding the pole, while the bus breathed diesel in our faces as we wandered around the London streets. Finally we drifted into a park. On one side of the road, everything was dark. On the other was a row of big white houses like massive wedding cakes.

While the bus was still moving, Tommy-Lee stepped off and walked into the dark. I'd been pushed off moving buses so often that actually jumping off one was easy. I ran after Tommy-Lee and stuck as close to him as I could, even when he walked right through the middle of a hedge. Branches whipped my face and leaves tangled in my hair. On the other side was a muddy bank. I lost my footing and slithered down it into a stream. My toes curled into the warm mud at the bottom. Tommy-Lee stood still in the middle of the stream, like a moose in pajamas. I thought about saying his name to wake him up, but he eventually slooshed through the water to the other side and grabbed hold of a wire fence to help him out.

The moment he grabbed hold of that fence, his head jerked back like he'd been shot. A couple of seconds later, another jerk, then another. But he didn't let go.

"Tommy-Lee," I hissed. "Tommy-Lee . . ."

He woke up and said, "Ow," and then he said, "Ow" again.

"Tommy-Lee, I think that's an electric fence you're holding."

"Ow!"

"You should probably let go of it, Tommy-Lee."

He took his hand off the fence and stopped being in pain.

"I could feel some force. I thought it was coming out of me, not going into me. Where are we?"

I didn't know the answer, but I knew how to get over an electrified fence. All you have to do is lay something over it that doesn't conduct electricity— like a log or a piece of carpet—and walk across it. There was a big notice saying DANGER: ELECTRICITY on a wooden stand stuck into the bank. Tommy-Lee yanked it out of the ground and plonked it over the fence. We tiptoed over.

In front of us was a wide field with two trees at the far end and a big tire swinging from the lowest branch of one of the trees. Tommy-Lee immediately wanted to use the tire for kicking practice, but as we got nearer, a security light flashed on and the shadows of the branches danced across the grass like claws. We ducked down. In the blaze of the security light we could see there was another, stronger fence, with a gate in it, and beyond that a little house. A man with a bucket slung over his arm came out of the house. He stopped and peered into the bright cone that came from the security light. He didn't see us, though, and after a while he moved off.

Tommy-Lee walked up to the gate in the fence. There was a keypad next to it, just like the ones in the hospital. He punched a few numbers into it, and the gate squeaked open. He didn't even seem to think that was unusual.

The little house had a roof of corrugated iron painted blue. Its door was metal—thick and heavy—and it was bolted on the outside.

"Don't need any superpowers to open this one," said Tommy-Lee.

"If you're on the outside," I said. "But if you were inside, you'd never get out."

We thought for a minute about why you would have a door with a bolt on the outside.

"A prisoner!" I said. "Someone is being held prisoner in here."

I didn't expect Tommy-Lee to be interested in prisoners. I expected him to say, "Okay, let's go and find a bank to rob." But he didn't. He started yanking on the bolt.

"What are you doing?"

"Setting him free, of course. Rescuing him. Come on. Give me a hand. I hate it when people lock other people up."

Tommy-Lee drew back the bolt. We both pulled on the door, and a smell of damp smacked us in the nose. Inside it was surprisingly light, because the front wall was nearly all window. Moonlight was flooding in. The floor was covered with straw, and in the corner there was a huge pile of sliced apples and a bit of banana. I somehow knew that this was what the man had had in his bucket. He'd dumped it here for the poor prisoner.

The straw rustled. Someone was moving underneath it. Some poor soul, trying to get comfortable on the concrete floor. Some of the straw fell aside, and we saw a hairy hand. A very hairy and very massive hand. Long, gray fingers and a wrist as thick as my waist. With my eyes I followed the arm up to the shoulder. There was no neck. Just a huge head with a massive jaw and a frowning forehead.

"We've rescued you," announced Tommy-Lee. "You can come out now."

"Tommy-Lee," I said, "that is not a prisoner. That is a gorilla."

Just like Tommy-Lee, the gorilla woke up when it heard its name. The second it heard the word "gorilla," it propped its head up against the wall and blew down its huge nostrils—bits of straw and mucus whirred into the air.

"Can't be," said Tommy-Lee.

Quick as teleportation the gorilla was up, shoulders like a train, head like a cannonball, leaning toward us on its knuckles.

"What are we going to do?" whispered Tommy-Lee. "Shall I kick it?"

"What? No. Who would kick a gorilla?"

Its lips rolled back like a lion's, showing big yellow teeth.

"Don't look at him," I breathed.

"How can you not look at him? He's amazing." Tommy-Lee was afraid of the dark but apparently not of a cornered gorilla.

He was scared of two cornered gorillas, though. The second one burst out of the straw behind the first one. It pounded the floor with its jackhammer fists and screamed and screamed and screamed.

Tommy-Lee made as if to run, but I pulled him

166

back. "There's no point running," I hissed. "They'll be faster."

"What are we going to do?"

"Look at the floor. Look only at the floor. Crouch down a bit. Try to make yourself smaller. Look like you're not a threat, like you're giving in."

The moment we crouched down, the second one stopped screaming. The first one kept sniffing, though, and coming closer to get a better smell.

Tommy-Lee almost jumped up. I pulled him down again. "If you stand up, that's a threat. Stay down. Do what I do."

"How do you know? Who are you to tell me what to do?"

"I'm someone who has a lot of experience when it comes to being threatened by creatures bigger than himself. Get down, stay down, shuffle backward out the door."

Tommy-Lee followed me. The gorillas didn't. We shut and bolted the door, then sank to our knees and looked up at the big fat moon. We could hear the gorillas scuffling around inside, probably going back to bed.

"What were they?" said Tommy-Lee.

"What do you mean, what were they? They were

gorillas. Wasn't it obvious?"

"Gorillas aren't real."

"What? Of course gorillas are real. You just nearly had a fight with two of them."

"Gorillas are made up. Like dragons and reindeer."

"Gorillas are real, and by the way, so are reindeer."

"What? There are deer that can fly? Deer with light-up noses?"

"Not exactly, but there are reindeer in Lapland and gorillas in Africa."

"We're in Africa?!"

To be honest, I didn't know where we were, but I knew it wouldn't be wise to make Tommy-Lee anxious, so I just shrugged and said, "Teleportation, isn't it?"

The gorilla prison turned out to be in the middle of an island. There were trees full of little monkeys, another fence with a gate in it, then a deep stream. Tommy-Lee opened the gate, and we waded across the stream and came to a pathway on the opposite bank. We found a small wooden hut at a place where the path split into three.

The door of the hut was locked, but there was a kind of hatch at the front which we undid and then climbed through. Whoever lived there had unusual priorities. There was nothing to sit on, but there was a freezer full of ice creams and ice lollies. There was no TV, but there was a shelf of sweets and chocolates. No kitchen, but a big fridge packed with cans of Coke and bottles of lemonade. It was clearly the home of someone who had made some very unhealthy lifestyle choices.

"Flake bars!" said Tommy-Lee, spotting a yellow Cadbury's box on the shelf. "Totally nut free." He grabbed a fistful of the bars and started eating. I wasn't sure we should be eating other people's sweets, but before I could say anything, Tommy-Lee sniffed. A big sniff. Then he rubbed the back of his sleeve over his nose, tucked up his knees, and rested his forehead on them. Tommy-Lee was crying. This was so hard to believe that I asked him, "Tommy-Lee, are you crying?"

"Leave me alone."

"Come on, Tommy-Lee. Superheroes don't cry . . . or supervillains."

"Leave. Me. Alone." He clambered over the hatch and walked off.

I tried to go after him. I tried to call him back, but it was too dark to see which way he'd gone.

In *Don't Be Scared, Be Prepared* it tells you that if you ever get separated from your party, you should stay where you are so that they can come back and find you. If you go after them, you might both end up running around in circles, missing each other until one of you falls into the sinking sands or off the terrible cliffs or whatever. So I shouted, "Tommy-Lee, I'll wait here for you!" then went back into the hut. It probably was wrong to eat so much ice cream without permission, but there really wasn't anything else to do, and I had to stay awake or I might miss him.

Two Magnums and a Mini Milk later, I was getting anxious. I sat out on the steps of the little hut and looked down the footpaths to see if he was coming. I could hear monkey chatter and strange birdcalls. Sometimes something big would flutter past over my head. It felt like Africa. Except that it was shocking cold, plus also when I looked back toward the way we'd come, I could see a dark tower rising high above the trees, which looked like the hospital. So maybe we weren't in Africa, and maybe we hadn't been to China either. Maybe London was a magical city that had everything you could ever want to see in it.

Wonderville.

A shadow strode down the path toward me. For the first time in my life I was pleased to see Tommy-Lee.

"I feel fantastic. Give me a Flake." He crumbled a Flake into his mouth. "You were right," he said.

"Right about what?"

"It's better to be a hero than a villain. I've just been a hero all over this place. All this time I've been thinking I'm only good at being bad. But I can be good when I want to."

"Of course you can."

"I can, can't I?"

"You were never that bad really."

"Wasn't I?"

"Actually, yeah, you were."

"Well, now I've done some good stuff."

I don't know why, but I found the thought of Tommy-Lee trying to be good a bit worrying. I thought he probably didn't have the same idea of "good" as most people. "Tommy-Lee," I said, "what have you done?"

"Them gorillas. Think about them—locked up in that little house. Why would anyone do that to them? Why should they be locked away just because they're big and scary? Big and scary people have hearts too, you know. Big and scary people have feelings!"

"You do know that gorillas aren't people, don't you?"

"That's no reason to lock someone up—just because they're not a person."

A horrible uneasy feeling began to crawl up my

back. "So . . . what was this good thing you did?"

"I let them out."

"The gorillas?"

"Opened their door."

"You opened the gorillas' door?"

"And let them out. Also there was a little bridge over the water with a gate on it. I opened that too. Now they can be free. We should find whoever locked them up and destroy them."

"But . . ."

"I feel great. I wish I'd started doing good when I was younger."

"We need to get out of here."

"In a minute. Just a minute." He leaned back against the wall of the little wooden hut and closed his eyes.

"Tommy-Lee, don't go to sleep. Not here."

"I'm not going to sleep. I'm just resting my eyes."

"No, Tommy-Lee, no. You can't go to sleep. Not if there are gorillas on the loose. . . ."

"Ssssssssssshhhh . . ."

He was asleep. I tried to tug him to his feet, but he just hedgehogged himself into the corner. I couldn't move him. I couldn't leave him. That was probably the worst bit of the whole thing—being alone in the night with an unmovable friend and a gang of gorillas.

WHO WOULD WIN IN A FIGHT BETWEEN A HIPPO AND A FREEZER?

Somewhere in the trees behind me a twig snapped.

Somewhere ahead of me something rustled in the leaves.

Somewhere on the path something was walking toward us with heavy, squelchy steps.

All these sounds seemed really loud.

None of them was loud enough to wake Tommy-Lee.

Then there was another sound.

The big, mucusy snores of Tommy-Lee. Snores that shook the little wooden house and echoed off the trees. Snores you could hear for miles around.

■ ■ ■

I tried to shush him.

I held his nose to try and make him stop.

I was still holding his nostrils together when the snore came again.

It wasn't coming from Tommy-Lee.

It came out of the shadows right in front of me.

It came again.

This time I could see what was making it: something big and pale and fleshy and wet—floating in the air—a watery ghost.

It disappeared. Leaving a horrible compost whiff behind.

It appeared again. Closer. Now I could see what it was.

It wasn't a ghost.

I shook Tommy-Lee. "Tommy-Lee," I said, "did you let any other animals out?" Tommy-Lee grunted. "The reason I ask," I explained, "is that there's a hippopotamus looking right at us."

A hippopotamus can run at forty kilometers per hour.

I know this because that's exactly what it did.

I definitely teleported again, because I was somehow

instantly back inside the little wooden hut with the freezer full of ice creams.

The hut wall splintered. The hippo's head cannon-balled through it. Compost smell bombed the room. I was outside again.

The back end of the hippo was out in the moon-light, steam-shovel feet pushing the gravel. Its front end was jammed into the shattered remains of the hut.

The hippo was fighting the hut.

The hut was fighting the hippo—falling planks smacked its back, the fridge full of drinks crashed across its head.

The hippo whirled around, shoving the freezer, bursting its walls.

Trampled drink cans exploded under its feet. Fanta fountains fizzed in its face.

It must have liked them, because some truly horrible slurping noises were coming from inside the ruins of the hut. At least I now knew who would win in a fight between a hippo and a sweets kiosk.

Tommy-Lee finally stood up. He stood up but he didn't wake up. He Playmobilled off down the footpath. I went after him, and we walked back to the hospital.

The walk home was the most unforgettable journey

of my entire life. First of all, it took ages because we were miles away. Tommy-Lee didn't remember a thing about it. He didn't remember the two gorillas that shambled past us on their mighty knuckles. Didn't recall the little antelopes bouncing by so close their speed breezed our cheeks. He couldn't even remember the leopard that fell into step with us and trotted along next to us, its tongue hanging out, its breath drumming and smoking. He just kept walking.

Maybe it was because he couldn't see them that I survived. If I hadn't been walking next to him, I would've panicked and tried to leg it, and the gorillas and leopards would have hunted me down and beaten me or eaten me.

Instead we got safely back to the hospital, climbed into the window cleaners' cradle, and winched ourselves back to bed.

*W*HO WILL WIN
IN THE FIGHT BETWEEN
GOOD AND EVIL?
(READ ON. . . .)

When Nurse Rock had taken our blood next morning, she said, "Interesting. Tommy-Lee just gave me a blood sample without giving me a hard time. No tantrums. No tears. What's brought about this change of behavior? Maybe you're getting better. Or maybe you've lost the will to live." She sniffed. "By the way, you smell of chocolate. Isn't that interesting—considering you're not supposed to be eating anything except what we give you? And we would never give you chocolate."

She could SMELL chocolate! She really was a bloodhound. It was going to be hard to keep anything secret from her.

I said so to Tommy-Lee. "We're going to need to think up codes or signals or something."

"Wait a minute," he said. "Is this a meeting? Are we having a meeting?"

"Well . . . I was just saying . . ."

"When a team has got things to discuss, it has to convene a meeting. Like in kickboxing. Do it properly. Someone write everything down—that's the secretary. You have to have a treasurer and a special meeting room—like a club room."

"Superheroes don't have club rooms. They have secret headquarters."

"Yeah. We need one of them as well—a secretary, a treasurer, and a secret headquarters."

The minute he said "secret headquarters" we both went quiet and glum. How could we find a secret headquarters if we were locked in a fish tank where everyone could see everything we did, and we couldn't even speak because they could hear us over the intercom? Unless . . .

"Tommy, think about this. We're in a room, high above a big city. No one knows we're here. No one can get in or out without a code. This *is* our secret headquarters. It's so secret that even the people who come in here—the doctors and nurses—even they don't know it's a secret headquarters. Because it's cunningly disguised as an isolation ward in a hospital."

Tommy-Lee looked around the room for a while. There wasn't that much to look at—two beds, two bedside cabinets, a desk, and chair. "It actually looks different once you know it's a secret headquarters," he said.

"Yes," I said. "Especially the map."

"What map?"

"The map you drew."

"It's not a map. It's just a picture."

We were both looking at it. It had everything on it. "That dark bit must be the zoo where we were last night. This is Chinatown. That's the river." I wrote the names on with a Sharpie. It made the room feel like the Center of Operations.

"It is a good map, isn't it?" said Tommy-Lee proudly.

"Maybe cartography is one of your superpowers. You could be the navigator."

"I want to be the treasurer really."

"We don't have any treasure."

"I've got thirty quid that those ladies gave me." He showed me three crumpled ten-pound notes. "Plus a mobile phone that someone gave me to take a picture with just before we ran away. So I've got treasure. That makes me the treasurer. So you're the secretary. You need to write an agenda."

SECRET AGENDA

Item 1: Superhero Names (we need some)

Item 2: Superhero Equipment

Item 3: Superhero Mission

Item 4: Superhero Strengths and Weaknesses

TOP SECRET—EAT AFTER READING

After he'd read it, Tommy-Lee said, "Eat what after reading?"

"The secret agenda."

"What for?"

"To keep it a secret."

"I've only just had breakfast."

"Okay, I'll eat it."

He passed me back the paper, and I chewed it to a pulp. "So item one . . ."

"What was item one?"

"Tommy-Lee, you just read the secret agenda."

"I only read the bit about eating it. It got me so confused I forgot to read the rest."

ITEM 1: Superhero Names.

"We've got to be called 'green something,'" said Tommy-Lee.

"There are too many green things already. Green

180

Hornet, Green Goblin, Green Lantern, Green Knight . . .
We don't have to call ourselves green something just
because we're green. Think of Hulk or She-Hulk."

"Who?"

"She-Hulk. She's a part-time member of the Fantastic Four."

"There were five people in the Fantastic Four?"

"She's like a substitute. Four Fantastics and one on
the bench."

"Who's the Green Knight?"

"Not really a superhero. Just a knight. But if his
head got chopped off, he could pick it up and put it
back on again. So he was sort of invincible. It's in King
Arthur. Let's be logical—Batman is Batman because
he hangs around at night. Spider-Man is Spider-Man
because he was bitten by a radioactive spider—"

"What about Robin?" said Tommy-Lee. "Was he
pecked by a radioactive robin?"

"No."

"Catwoman . . . ?"

"No."

"Frogs are green. We could be called Frogman."

"That's not a superhero. That's a job."

"Tommy-Lee is a good name."

"What superhero uses his first name?! Imagine that.

'Hello, I'm Bruce Batman and this is my friend Peter Spider-Man. Oh, and here comes Dr. Bruce the Hulk.'"

"Frog-Boy?"

"Sounds like a trainee frogman."

"I'm definitely sticking to Tommy-Lee."

"If you use your own name, your enemies might be able to trace your true identity and maybe kidnap your little sister or something."

"I haven't got a little sister. It's just me and Mum."

"Kidnap your mum then."

"Have you met my mum?"

I thought about Tommy-Lee's mum kickboxing. If anyone did kidnap her, they'd soon regret it.

ITEM 2: Superhero Equipment.

"We need capes at least," said Tommy-Lee. "And masks."

"What's the point in wearing masks? The super thing about us is our distinctive green appearance. Why cover that up with a mask? Plus, you can't really pick a costume until you have a name. It just creates confusion. Imagine Spider-Man going around in a bat cape. Or Batman dressed as a spider."

"That is true. But Batman's got a Batcave, a Bat-cycle, a Batmobile, and a butler. What have we got?

Hypoallergenic pajamas. We should have a vehicle at least. Like a Batmobile."

"Or an interplanetary surfboard like Silver Surfer."

A glum look came over Tommy-Lee's face. "That's not going to happen," he said. He lay down on his bed with his back to me, the way he used to when I first arrived. "I can't go running around London in pajamas and bare feet. My feet are important to me. They're my weapon of choice. What's the point in being superheroes if we don't have Superhero Transport Options? Even if we had a Batmobile, we couldn't drive it."

Everything that had happened to us was hard to believe. It was hard to believe we'd turned green. But you could see that was true by looking in the mirror. It was much harder to believe that we'd changed inside too. We both knew we felt different, but if you thought too much about what kind of different, it seemed daft. All we could do was hold on to the feeling and see what happened, and not think too much about it. Like when you're playing Star Wars when you're little. You know that you haven't got a real lightsaber, but as long as you keep making the noises and acting like you've got one, it doesn't matter. So that's why I said to Tommy-Lee, "I can drive."

"No, you can't."

"I can. My cousins live in Ireland. We go every summer. They let me drive a tractor." Tommy-Lee sat up. I said, "A tractor's probably harder to drive than a car because it's high up."

"So if you can drive a tractor, you can probably drive anything."

"Think about it, Tommy-Lee. What's Batman's superpower? He hasn't got one. He's just got loads of gear. Cars and boomerangs and super-lightweight climbing equipment. Which he bought because he's so rich. Batman's superpower is cash."

"That's not really a superpower at all."

"Exactly. We are actually more super than Batman."

ITEM 3: Superhero Mission.

Some people become super by accident—like being bitten by a spider or blown up by a Gamma Bomb. Some people are chosen to be heroes—for instance, Hal Jordan, who became Green Lantern. The Green Lantern was part of the Green Lantern Corps, whose mission was to keep the universe safe from supervillains such as Sinestro.

"Was his name really Sinestro?"

"Yeah."

"So unfair."

"Why?"

"Well, if you're actually called Sinestro, you're hardly going to turn out to be good when you grow up, are you? I hate it when parents give their kids stupid names."

"The point is, the Green Lantern Corps uses the Central Power Battery to fight evil throughout the cosmos. They can turn bombs into water. He was chosen for the job because he was good and fair and could help people. What I'm saying is, we weren't bitten by spiders, or blown up by Gamma Bombs, so maybe we were chosen to be green. For a purpose."

"Yeah, but I'm not good or fair. I've got anger-management issues . . ."

"That's true."

". . . also kickboxing skills."

"Anger-management issues plus kickboxing skills is a terrible combination."

"The worst."

I wrote down, "Purpose of Mission—to be confirmed after further discussion."

ITEM 4: Superhero Strengths and Weaknesses.

All superheroes have strengths and weaknesses. For instance, the Green Lantern has the power to create physical objects out of nothing—that's a strength. On the other hand, he can't stand to look at anything yellow.

Superman's strength is . . . well, strength. He's really strong. Except when there's Kryptonite.

Our strengths were: Tommy-Lee can kickbox and open locks in his sleep, I can slightly teleport and have a 200 percent brain. We have jumped off a high building without getting hurt and survived a close encounter with a silverback gorilla.

"What are our weaknesses?"

Tommy-Lee said he didn't have any. I pointed out he had a severe nut allergy.

"That's true. What about you?"

"I definitely don't have any weaknesses."

"You're weak. That's got to be a weakness."

"That's true."

"I could teach you kickboxing. Then you wouldn't be so weak."

"Thanks."

"And then we can go out and kick bad guys to pieces as a team."

Hurting people takes more skill than you'd think. Even superheroes turn out to be not that good at it. "Look at

Spider-Man in this picture," said Tommy-Lee, opening the old annual I'd taken from the waiting room. "Pulling your hand back like that and taking it all around the houses. He's more likely to break his own wrist than the Green Goblin's jaw. Here. I'll show you."

We put our duvets on the floor to stop us being injured if we fell over. Tommy-Lee asked me what I wanted to do first. "Kicking or boxing? Kicking is best."

"Kicking then."

The first lesson in kickboxing is Tommy-Lee gets hold of your foot and tries to get it to go higher than your head, while you try to stay standing up. But you fall over. The second lesson is pretty much the same. Plus also the third and fourth are completely the same. The fifth is similar but it takes longer to fall over and hurts more.

According to Tommy-Lee, learning to fall over is very important.

"Good job, as I'm getting loads of practice. I could end up World Falling-Over Champion."

When I fell over for the ninth time, he fell on top of me and we were both laughing. Rolling around on the floor laughing with Tommy-Lee is not something I ever expected to do in this life.

■ ■ ■

When I got up off the floor, I noticed something on the glass—a smudge of foundation makeup. It didn't take a 200 percent brain to work out that this meant Dr. Brightside had been watching us.

Somehow this made me feel uneasy.

When she came to call, we tried to act less bouncy so she wouldn't be suspicious. She was unusually bouncy herself. "Guess what—I'm going to give a lecture about you! That's how interesting you are." She took loads of photographs of us for her PowerPoint presentation. "No, no. Don't smile. You're supposed to be sick, remember." We folded our arms and tried not smiling. "Wow," she said. "Fierce!" She showed us the pictures on her camera screen. Neither of us said anything at the time, but we were both thinking the same thing—we looked like Invincible Fighters of Crime and Injustice. After that it was the usual—blow in a tube, blood test, wee in a bottle, stand next to the color chart. "It's a breakthrough, Tommy-Lee," she said. "That's the very first time you haven't asked me if you were getting any less green."

"Oh," said Tommy-Lee. "And are we?"

"Not even a little bit."

"Oh well. Never mind."

"I thought you did mind. A lot."

"I mind less now that Rory's here."

"Still, it must be boring for you both stuck in here. Shall I see if I can get you a PlayStation or something?"

"Weights," said Tommy-Lee. "A bench press would be good. A punching bag. Anything to kick or punch, really."

"There might be health-and-safety issues with some of those things, but I'll see what they can spare down in physio."

In his bed that night, Tommy-Lee flicked through the old *Spider-Man Annual*. "Who would win," he said, "in a fight between the Green Knight and the Green Lantern?"

"The Green Knight only has swords and armor, whereas the Green Lantern could use his ring to create an armor-piercing bazooka if he wanted. On the other hand, if you chop the Green Knight's head off, he can put it on again."

"Yeah, but," said Tommy-Lee, "what if you chopped his arms off first?"

"What?"

"If you met the Green Knight and he was threatening you, all you'd need to do is chop off both his arms quick, *before* you chopped off his head. Then he

189

wouldn't be able to pick up his head to put it back on. See? Strategy."

"That is actually quite good."

"I'm a warrior. We could be called the Green Knights."

"That might be good too."

But Tommy-Lee was asleep.

When I was on my own in the dark, I noticed something glowing on the floor. The phone that Tommy-Lee had stolen. It was warm in my hand, and the first thing I thought was—I could ring my mum. The second thing I thought was—I don't know her mobile number. Or Dad's. I rang the house phone instead. No one answered, but it was good to hear Dad's voice on the answering machine saying there was no one home just now but there probably soon would be. Then I noticed that the battery was only at 39 percent, and as we didn't have a charger, I turned it off and went to sleep.

AND SO OUR ASTOUNDING GREEN HEROES SET OUT ON THEIR MISSION . . .

That night Tommy-Lee went straight to the cradle, as if he knew that something was wrong. We came slowly down the side of the building. London was waiting for us.

A yellow light was flashing across the wheelie bins and bags of litter in our landing area. The cradle shuddered as it hit the ground. Tommy-Lee woke up.

"What's that?"

A loud roboty voice was going, "Reversing . . . beep . . . beep . . . reversing . . . beep . . ." over a grinding engine.

"Look . . ."

The yellow light washed over us, then went away,

then came back. As it swept past us, we saw four men. Big men with thick gloves and woolly hats. They wore white masks over their mouths and noses. They were heading for the bins.

"They haven't seen us," I said, crouching down in the cradle. "I think they must be—"

"Robbers!" said Tommy-Lee.

"I was going to say garbage men."

But Tommy-Lee had already leaped over the side of the cradle. He ran straight toward the men, going "Arrrrgggghhhhhh!!!!" with his hands in the air. The men in the masks screwed up their eyes. They must have been thinking, Is it the light or is that kid green?

Why is he green?

Is he contagious?

Tommy-Lee roared, "COME ON THEN!!! COME ON AND FIGHT!!!!"

So the question of was he contagious didn't matter anymore. The real question was—Is he a completely crazy angry massive mutant bullfrog in pajamas who is suddenly going to flick out a giant sticky tongue and splat one of us?!

It's the kind of question that makes you freeze.

Then Tommy-Lee made the kind of terrifying noise that would make you unfreeze. And run away. Which is what they did. All four big men ran away from that one little boy. Well, one very large little boy.

Tommy-Lee put his hands on his hips, threw back his head, and did the kind of mad, Zorro-ish laugh you normally only get inside a speech bubble. Like, "Mwa ha ha ha ha haaaa! Rory Rooney, hurry up."

"Hurry up where?"

He barged through the wheelie bins, kicked aside bin bags, and planted himself in front of a lorry. Its headlights were so bright and so many and its engines so loud and so smoky, it could have been a neatly parked spaceship. Okay, it had YOUR BINS R OUR BUSINESS written on the side, but I didn't want to bother Tommy-Lee with technical details. The front passenger door even made a kind of starship hiss when Tommy-Lee yanked it open.

"What do you think you're doing?!" shouted the driver. "This is authorized personnel o—"

Before he could finish his sentence, Tommy-Lee roared, "Pow! Kersplat!" and jumped into the passenger seat. The driver took one look at him and shot out of the driver's-side door into the night.

"Rory, get in! We've got our vehicle!"

"What?!"

I clambered on board. It was surprisingly high up.

There were rows of softly lit dials and switches along the dashboard that just seemed to be saying, "Play with me."

"Did you see? They all ran away from me! Like, whoosh. Like I was emitting some kind of force field. In fact, I think I probably was emitting some kind of force field. I think that might be my superpower."

"Your superpower is scaring bin men?"

"Robbers. Didn't you see? They were wearing masks and gloves, and they ran away. From me. And now we've got our vehicle!"

"What vehicle?"

He slapped the driving wheel. The horn blasted the night. "This vehicle," he said. "This is our super vehicle."

"This . . . oh . . . no. No, no, no, no!"

"You said you could drive."

"Yeah, but this is . . . this is a bin lorry. It's huge."

"You said you could drive anything." He looked so sad—like a very large little boy whose football has been confiscated.

"I said I could drive a tractor. Over fields. Not on roads where you have to steer and indicate and stuff."

"You said you could drive anything. That's why I got you this." He waved his hand around the cabin as though he'd made the entire bin lorry in metalwork at school as a special present just for me. He seemed so hurt I thought he might cry. Well, I thought, maybe if you're in a big enough vehicle, indicating and steering aren't that important. You never see the Batmobile indicating, do you?

The engine was already running—so no problem about starting it. The hand brake had HAND BRAKE written on it. The dials were all clearly marked. How hard could it be to drive? I touched the accelerator pedal. The engine raced and so did my 200 percent brain. It filled up with confidence and information like a tank filling up with petrol—I could see in my mind how my dad changed gear, how he checked the mirror; all I had to do was act like him. "Tommy-Lee," I said, "let's do this."

There was a man in a yellow jacket and black beanie jumping up and down in the glare of my headlights. I banged on the horn. It sounded like an army of war elephants. It was so loud it blew him aside like a feather. I slipped the hand brake. Hauled on the wheel. We were off. Wheelie bins scattered around us like bowling pins. I could barely feel the crunch as I drove over them. A fence came down. Some chunks came off a wall, but I was beginning to get the hang of it.

Tommy-Lee whooped with joy! He tried to high-five me, which did lead to a driving-straight-through-a-security-fence situation, but no one got hurt.

On the road it was easy. Turns out I was right about indicating. If you're the size of a spaceship and loaded with rubbish, you can go as slow as you like on whatever side of the road you want. No one seems to mind. I think people make allowances. It's obvious that something that big isn't really going to go around a traffic island. It has to go over it. Also, if you're that big, people can see you coming, so there's no need to stop at traffic lights and stuff. We did crash through a set of Christmas lights that was hanging over the road, but it wasn't our fault that someone hung them so low.

"Tommy-Lee, where d'you want to go?"

"Wherever there is trouble!"

There seemed to be quite a lot of trouble around already. All the cars were flashing their headlights and beeping their horns. I managed to swing around a corner onto a main road. I was quite pleased about that. But Tommy-Lee was going, "Stop! I think you should stop now! Really, you should stop!"

"I'm just getting the hang of this. Why would I stop?"

"Because everyone else has!"

I'd probably been concentrating too hard on the dashboard and stuff and not hard enough on the road. So I hadn't seen the flashing blue light ahead of us and the line of stopped cars until it was too late.

"CRASH!!!" Tommy-Lee actually shouted that. He went, "CRASH!!!" as if the sound of three or four cars turning over and bashing into one another as I sledged into them wasn't loud enough.

Anyway, it wasn't really a crash. Not like in a proper car chase, where the car explodes in a fireball BANG and blows out all the windows of the nearest tower block, BOOM. It was just a few cars that got slightly crunched while I was mastering the brakes.

There were people banging on the doors, yelling at us to get out. We couldn't see them, but they sounded angry.

"What do you want to do?"

Tommy-Lee said he wasn't scared of them. "They shouldn't've got in your way. Let me out. I'll talk to them."

I knew you opened the doors by pressing a switch, but I didn't know which one. The first I tried turned the cabin lights on and then off again. The next one made a rumbling noise start up somewhere behind us.

The third one made the door on my side open, slowly, spookily, with that hissing sound. Even when it was only slightly open, we could hear the angry motorists yelling and telling us to get out. Until one of them shouted, "Oh. MY. DAYS!!!! Look!" and pointed toward the back of the truck. Then they all ran back to their cars.

We climbed down, trying to see why they were so upset. Two big, shining pistons were hoisting the whole back part of the truck upward and tipping it, getting ready to dump all the rubbish inside onto the road. Well, not so much on the road as on the cars that were parked behind us.

No one was interested in us. Everyone was busy trying to get their cars out of the way.

"Police!" yelled Tommy-Lee. "Look!"

Ahead of us, flashing blue lights, shouts, a siren going.

"What are we going to do?!" I was thinking of making a run for it.

"Go and talk to them," said Tommy-Lee.

"What?"

"They're just the people we've been looking for, aren't they? We're crime fighters. They're crime fighters. We should talk."

I wasn't convinced that the police would see the people who crashed a bin lorry into their roadblock as their best friends, but there was no stopping Tommy-Lee. No one even looked at us as we dodged in and out of the trapped cars. They were all too busy shouting at one another, or looking at their twisted bumpers and steaming radiators. There was a line of police cars and beyond that a strip of yellow tape stretched across the road and signs saying, SERIOUS INCIDENT—POLICE ONLY.

There were no police there. They were all sorting out the fighting and mess around the bin lorry. The streets were empty. Strangely empty. Nothing there but puddles and streetlight.

"Tommy-Lee," I said, "what if the serious incident is really . . . serious?"

"'S okay. We are invincible."

I didn't say so, but all of a sudden I didn't feel invincible. In fact I felt definitely 100 percent vincible.

*T*HE STREETS ARE QUIET, TOO QUIET. BUT THE ASTOUNDING GREEN BOYS ARE BRAVE. TOO BRAVE?

*I*t was as though the whole street had been double-glazed. Everything was quiet and still. Nothing was moving. There was another yellow tape across the next corner. Tommy-Lee walked through it like a runner crossing the finishing line.

We were in the square with the stone dragon, the square that had been full of Chinese people and hustle and bustle and stalls full of fruit. Only the stone dragon was still there.

There were no people.

No sound.

Emptiness and silence are actually more frightening than gorillas and hippos. Especially if they go on a long way. Across the square was a narrow alley that led up to the road where the girls in tottery shoes had been queuing to get into the Bank. There were no girls now. The Bank was still there. Its bright neon sign still flashed on and off like a lighthouse beam across an empty sea. No cars. We walked past a massive toy shop. Its windows were full of amazing Christmas stuff—massive pedal cars shaped like old-fashioned Rolls-Royces, a row of dolls with angel wings and tinsel halos, a doll's house that was all lit up from the inside, guns and fighter planes . . . Our reflections walked through them like ghosts that couldn't play.

Something flickered on the window. There was a helicopter, with a searchlight, hovering over the buildings a few streets away. I must have been hearing the engine for ages without noticing it. The searchlight poked and prodded at the rooftops. The helicopter swung closer, balanced on its pyramid of light. It stayed still right over the middle of the road.

Into the spotlight, as though it was a dancer about to start a ballet, trotted a hippopotamus.

It stood still, very still, very big, very confused. It stepped forward. It backed up. Its head went from side to side. It really did look as if it was dancing. It was probably baffled and blinded by the light.

"What's that?!"

"A hippo. I think it's the one that attacked us the other night while you were asleep."

"Maybe that's our nemesis!"

"I think it's just a hippo."

"Actually, it's got a nice face. It looks like it's smiling. It likes us."

He was going to go and pet it. I stopped him. I explained that hippos kill more people every year than lions do. "They look friendly, but they're dangerous and bad-tempered."

"They're probably misunderstood," said Tommy-Lee. "Just because they're big, people probably pick on them and ask them to have fights they don't even want. What's it doing now?"

The hippo's head touched the floor. Its two front legs collapsed beneath it.

"I don't know. Is it taking a bow?"

It rolled over on its side, one leg in the air. A man with a rifle ran into the pool of light. We both realized what had happened—the hippo had been shot. This man had shot it. Now a truck backed into the light, and other men piled off the back of it. They were all in uniform.

"They've killed it!" gasped Tommy-Lee. "Let's get them!"

"I think they're the police." The truth popped into my brain like an urgent message. . . . When Tommy-Lee freed the leopards, the gorillas, the hippos, and the antelope—they must have found their way into this part of town. That's why there was no one here. It had been evacuated. The police truck had a little winch on the back. Men were fastening straps around the hippo and hoisting it on board.

"I don't think it's dead. I think they tranquilized it."

"Even so . . . ," said Tommy-Lee. He was itching to kick someone.

Suddenly the men stopped what they were doing. Radios crackled. There was shouting. The helicopter swept off over the town.

Some of the men carried on winching the hippo, but most of them ran off. A police van squealed into the square, and three or four of the men jumped into it. The man with the rifle jumped in too.

"What could be more interesting than fighting a hippo?"

"Fighting something bigger and scarier than a hippo?" A thought occurred to me. "Tommy-Lee, you didn't let a grizzly bear out, did you? Or a herd of elephants?"

"I don't remember. I opened a lot of doors. I was upset."

We didn't discuss it. We just went straight after the police car. We could see its siren splashing blue light down the street.

It didn't go far. There was a whole pileup of police vans and cars across the road a few blocks away. Beyond that we could see a crowd of people—all shouting and milling around. These must be the people that the police had evacuated from the dragon square and the road where the Bank was. We went nearer. I tried to keep us in the shadows.

No one was looking at us. A line of policemen was trying to get through a crowd of people. The people scrummed together, shouting and pointing. Except for some who were standing farther off, looking worried, talking, pointing. There was something in the scrum. The police were trying to make the people move back so that they could get at whatever it was. Maybe it was the leopard. Maybe it was the gorilla.

We had to intervene. Especially as it was all our fault. I was about to explain this to Tommy-Lee when he took off.

He ran straight at the crowd, roaring and howling, with his arms in the air.

He came at them so fast, people jumped out of his way. I followed him, running in the bubble of his force field, right through the crowd.

A policeman tried to stop him, but he was unstoppable.

"Crash! . . . Pow! . . . Smash!"

It was actually pretty exciting wondering what he was going to do when he came face-to-face with the gorilla—probably pick it up and give it a piggyback.

But there was no gorilla.

No leopard.

No hippo.

There was a scream.

Not a scared scream.

A furious-battle-cry-type scream.

When we shoved our way to the center of the circle of people, we saw what looked like a girl with a paper bag over her head. Some of the police were holding the crowd back. Someone shouted, "Take the bag off, then you'll see!" Then everyone started shouting. Then one of the police pulled the bag off the screaming girl's head.

She screamed again.

Her face was bright green.

WHAT TO DO IF YOU ARE CAUGHT IN A RIOT . . .

Exit the area as quickly as possible. Move with confidence and an air of conviction. Look as if you know what you are doing, and no one will question you.

—*Don't Be Scared, Be Prepared*

The moment he saw her, Tommy-Lee rushed in and grabbed hold of the girl. I ran in and stood next to him.

"Three of them!"

"Grab them!"

The girl and Tommy-Lee were looking at the faces in the crowd, but my 200 percent brain had already noticed the policeman with the tranquilizer gun, standing on the van, possibly taking aim at us. It also noticed the Tasers on the tool belts of the other police.

I put my hand in the air like a traffic policeman.

Everyone went quiet.

Putting my hand in the air made it look like I knew what I was doing. Everyone stared at me as though I was about to explain everything. "Stay calm," I said, "and no one will get hurt."

People started to talk all at once and shuffle around. There were more of them than us. They hadn't really thought about us hurting them until now.

"We're going now," I said. "If you'd all just step aside, please . . ."

And everyone did! They all got out of our way.

Except one big bloke who stood right in front of us.

"Why should we get out of your way?" he snarled.

"To minimize," I said, "the risk of infection." He more or less jumped out of the way at that.

The girl picked up her paper bag and put it back over her head. We strolled across the square. When we'd gone a few yards, I realized that they were all following us—at a distance.

"Don't look now," I said, "but they're all following us—at a distance."

"Shall we run?"

"Not yet. When I say so . . ."

As soon as we got to the edge of the square, I said, "Now!" and we bolted, Tommy-Lee kicking over wheelie bins and empty crates as we went, to make a kind of obstacle course.

We could hear shouting as we dived into the underpass. Tommy-Lee and I both vaulted into the window cleaners' cradle, dragging the girl in after us. I pulled the switch. We were ten meters in the air by the time we heard anyone stumble into the bins area. I stopped the cradle and we crouched down, just in case. We could hear confused and angry voices down below.

"They were definitely here."

"They can't have vanished into thin air."

"Well, they have."

They carried on rooting around among the bin bags for a while. They never looked up.

"If I scream now," said the girl quietly, "you'll be under arrest for kidnap."

"Are you going to scream?"

"Probably not. After the day I've had, being kidnapped is a happy ending."

INTRODUCING . . .
THE INCREDIBLE
KOKO KWOK

Every good superhero team needs a mixture of talents. For instance, the Fantastic Four:

- one genius scientist (Reed Richards, aka Mr. Fantastic)
- one invisible person (Susan Storm, aka Invisible Woman)
- a strong one (Ben Grimm, aka the Thing)
- and a flying one (Johnny Storm, aka the Human Torch)

We had:

- one superstrong kickboxing door opener (Tommy-Lee)

- one who could slightly teleport and had a 200 percent brain (me)
- and now one girl whose super ability was . . . well, we were about to find out.

Her name was Koko Kwok.

When she saw that we were green, she was really pleased. She'd thought she was the only green person on earth—doomed to wander the streets forever with her head in a paper bag. "Thanks for rescuing me from a violent mob," she said. "Also from London, which is overrun with wild animals. There were wolves in the Natural History Museum gift shop."

I was worried that Tommy-Lee might admit that this was slightly our fault. But he was just too excited. "Wow!" he gasped. "Did they do proper howling, like . . ." He put his head right back and howled like a wolf. "Howhooooooowwwww. Howhooooowww!"

Somewhere far away in the streets below, something howled back. "Howhoooowwwwww. How-hooooww!" We all shuddered. There were goose pimples all the way up my arms. Tommy-Lee nearly dropped the blue plastic bin he was carrying.

"Why are you carrying a blue plastic bin?" I asked.

"Just thought it would be nice to have a bin. More homey."

We took Koko up to the fish tank.

"Welcome," we whispered, "to our secret headquarters." We were using the phone we got during our bank raid as a light.

"This," she said, "is a hospital ward. In fact, it's an isolation unit." She was good at spotting detail.

"Our headquarters is disguised as an isolation unit," said Tommy-Lee. We told her all about sneaking out at night and righting wrongs and fighting injustice. We asked her if she'd like to join. We thought she'd be pleased about that.

But she wasn't an easy person to please.

"Why are you in an isolation unit?" she said.

"Because they think we're contagious."

"So"—she folded her arms like an angry math teacher—"even though you're contagious, you sneak out and contage people? So it's all your fault when other people turn green? It's your fault I look like a plate of spinach?"

"Broccoli. The medical term is broccoli."

"First you contage me and then you kidnap me and now you're trying to lock me up in an isolation unit?! I'm calling the police." Before we could stop her, she'd swiped Tommy-Lee's stolen phone off the bedside table.

"No! Wait! We're not contagious. We're not even sick."

"Of course you're sick. You're bright green."

"We're not sick. We're astounding."

"Ever since we turned green, we've been doing astounding things. Maybe you can do astounding things too."

"Okay," said Koko, "astound me."

"We jumped off the roof and didn't get hurt," said Tommy-Lee.

"My brain has had some kind of upgrade. It's sort of a two hundred percent brain. Also, I slightly teleported.

"That's how come we rescued you from a bad crowd and howling wolves," I said. "We're like the Fantastic Four. Except there's only two of us. Three counting you."

"This is a game, right?"

"No. We really, really have become astounding. Honestly."

Before she could reply, the room was filled with a thrashing, scrabbling sound—like someone trying to stab their way out from inside a drum.

Koko dropped the phone. The room went dark. The noise—a wet, slapping noise—got louder. Something sharp poked my leg.

"Wolves," said Koko. "Stand together."

Somehow she found the phone and shone it toward the floor. A tiny wet creature with a sharp yellow dagger where its nose should be was crawling out of the bin.

"An alien?!" I gasped.

"That's not an alien," snapped Koko. "That's a penguin."

"Yeah. Sorry about this," said Tommy-Lee. He tried to scoop the penguin back into the bin, but it slashed at him with its beak and then penguined off toward the toilet.

"Tommy-Lee, why have you brought a penguin in?"

"He was by the bins, all alone. I couldn't leave him there. He looked cold."

"He looked cold?! He's a penguin! He doesn't mind being cold."

"You said we were supposed to be doing good. Well, we did good. We rescued a girl! And a penguin!"

He went after it again, but it slid under the bed.

Koko Kwok got to her feet. "Join hands," she said.

"Why?"

"It's usually best to do as I say first and ask questions later."

We all held hands in a circle. She kicked the bed. The penguin came scuttling out, into the middle of the circle.

"Close up!" said Koko. We all stepped toward one another, and the penguin was trapped—like in a game of Farmer's in His Den. "Okay, shuffle." We shuffled into the bathroom. The penguin had to shuffle with us. Koko turned on the taps in the sink. As soon as it heard the water, the penguin calmed down, put its head under his wing, and went to sleep. It didn't exactly snore, but its lungs made a kind of creaking noise.

"Good night, Peter," whispered Tommy-Lee.

"How do you know it's a boy?" I asked.

"Because his name's Peter, and it's a boy's name."

"But how do you know his name's Peter?"

"He just looks like a Peter."

"So," said Koko, looking us up and down, "you're superheroes? Superheroes who were outmaneuvered by a panicking penguin."

"We've done other stuff," sulked Tommy-Lee.

"Such as?"

"We did a bank robbery."

She looked impressed. "How much did you get?"

"Thirty quid and a phone."

Now she was unimpressed. "What else?"

"We foiled another robbery. Men in masks and everything."

"What were they trying to rob?"

"Bins."

"You saved some bins?"

"Probably there were secret papers or something in the bins."

"So you've got a two hundred percent brain and you can teleport and all you've done is nick one penguin and a mobile phone and just enough cash for one ticket to Alton Towers?"

That's when Tommy-Lee blurted out, "It was us that let the animals out."

She stared at us. "You did what?"

"That was us. Well, it was Tommy-Lee. He let the animals out."

She looked at Tommy-Lee. "You let the wolves out of the zoo?"

"And the gorillas."

"Why would you let gorillas out of a zoo?"

"They looked so sad in those little houses."

"And the hippos?"

"Just because they're big and ugly, is that any reason to lock them up?"

"Lions?"

"Once I figured out how easy the locks were, I got a bit cheerful about it."

"Reindeer?"

"I didn't even know reindeer were real till Rory told me. I just wanted to see them up close. It's rubbish about them flying, by the way. Even when they see lions, they don't fly."

"Fruit bats?"

"Really big? Like big flappy umbrellas?"

"That's them."

"I thought they were vampire bats."

"You thought they were vampires and you still let them out?"

"Everything else was getting out. It didn't seem fair to leave them locked in. They can go fast."

"Most things go fast when there's a lion about."

I pointed out that lions are nowhere near as dangerous as people think. "Statistically lions are a lot less dangerous than wasps."

"You reduced the entire city of London to a state of terror."

"Sorry about that."

"That," said Koko, shining the phone in our faces, "is impressive."

Then she told us the story of how she turned green.

Her school had taken all the clever kids in her year (she was the cleverest) to a special sleepover in the Natural History Museum as a reward for being clever. "We slept in sleeping bags under the dinosaur skeletons. It was educational but also quite cozy. Next morning we were supposed to leave before the museum opened, but no one came to let us out. The teachers were worried that no one would ever let us out. Someone said, "Maybe everyone's dead of Killer Kittens and we're the only survivors, like in that film." I could hear howling coming from the gift shop. I said I thought there were wolves in the gift shop. Everyone said, "You're just trying to scare us." I tried to explain that wolves are not actually that scary if you just stay calm. The teachers went ahead. And what was in the gift shop? Three big, howling timber wolves! So I was right. Even though everyone laughed at me . . ."

Tommy-Lee tutted. "I hate when that happens."

"So everyone was terrified. Even the teachers. Especially the teachers, in fact. So I took charge. Why is it always me who has to take charge? I led the way back to the big gallery—the one with the life-size blue whale hanging from the ceiling—because that's got a door you can lock. The teachers were trying to ring the emergency number, but no one was answering. They were pretty convinced by now that the population of London had been wiped out by the Kittens and the city had been taken over by wild animals.

"I got up to say everyone should stay calm, but everyone started laughing at me."

"Why?" growled Tommy-Lee. "Why do people laugh like that?"

"Because she'd turned green," I said.

"I didn't know I'd turned green. Someone took a photo of me with their phone and showed me. I was so shocked I just ran off. I ran out through the gift shop. I didn't care if I did get eaten by wolves. The wolves were still in the shop, but they seemed to be eating something—maybe the souvenir flapjacks or maybe a shop assistant. I took a very nice paper bag and put it over my head and went outside. I ran as far as I could. I had to lift up the bag to see where I was going. It was fine at first because the streets were deserted. The museum is in one of the exclusion zones—"

"The what?"

"Wherever there's been an outbreak of Killer Kittens, they move everyone out and close the place down. They're trying to stop it spreading—otherwise there won't be any Christmas."

"They're going to cancel Christmas?!" wailed Tommy-Lee.

"They're worried that if too many people catch it, there won't be enough people left to drive the trucks or work in the shops. No shops, no turkey, no crackers, no fun."

"That's terrible," I said. "That means my mum was actually right." All those tins of Spam and piles of toilet rolls. They really were going to be lifesavers.

"Anyway, eventually I got across Green Park and down Pall Mall. I'd just crossed Trafalgar Square when someone spotted I was green. Everyone crowded around me."

"And then we rescued you."

"Yes. Thanks for that. Maybe you are a bit super after all. What're your names again?"

We told her. She noticed that my first name and second name both began with the same letter—just like hers.

"Not to mention Peter the Penguin's," I pointed out.

"And who else has names that sound like that? Other astounding people. Peter Parker (Spider-Man), Bruce Banner (the Hulk), Reed Richards (Mr. Fantastic), and Clark Kent (Superman)."

"And me," said Tommy-Lee.

We both looked at Tommy-Lee. I explained that Tommy-Lee does not start with the same letter as Komissky. "My real first name," he said, "is Karol."

"Karol?!"

"In Poland it's a boys' name. Here it's a girls' name. I had to change it because it was getting me involved in so many fights. I had to use my kickboxing skills because my hands were getting tired from doing so much punching. Karol Komissky—that's my real name."

Karol?! I'd only just got used to calling him Tommy-Lee. "Karol!" I blurted. He stared at me, like he was daring me to say something bad about it. I said, "Karol Komissky sounds really superhero. Three of us with superhero names is too much of a coincidence. We were definitely meant to meet. We are the League of Green Knights. Or the Green Knight League or Corporation or something."

"I am Karol," said Karol. "Just don't call me that."

"Okay."

"Can I just ask . . . how are you going to explain me?"

I looked at Tommy-Lee. He looked at me. We both looked at the penguin.

"If you're not supposed to leave the ward, it's going to be very hard explaining a stray penguin. It's going to be a lot harder explaining a kidnapped girl."

"We didn't kidnap you. We rescued you."

"Besides," I said, "we can explain it easy. We'll say you were admitted during the night."

"Oh, really? Where's my bed then?"

A bed!

"When people are admitted to the hospital, they normally get a bed."

There was one in the next fish tank—the one that Tommy-Lee had disconnected from the wall. We tried wheeling it through, but one of the wheels squeaked so loud we were scared it would squeak Nurse Rock awake.

"Stop," said Koko. She went to the antibacterial-hand-gel dispenser on the wall, squirted a load of gel stuff into her hand, and rubbed it on the axle. "Now try." The bed rolled silently into our fish tank.

Easy.

"Now all I need," said Koko, "is pajamas, a bedside table, a reading lamp, some medical notes . . . oh, and some of those curtains-on-wheels things so I can get some privacy." The list went on. We raided the cupboard for the pajamas. There was a spare bedside unit in the corridor. Couldn't find a bedside lamp, so she took mine.

She pulled the curtains around her bed. "This

superhero thing—I'm beginning to like the idea. I always did feel a bit special."

"Good," I said. "And we like the idea of a girl in the gang. The Fantastic Four had a girl. And there's loads of girls in the X-Men."

"Can I just ask, what have you actually done about this? I mean, do you have costumes? A badge? How do the police contact you?"

"The police?" Tommy-Lee asked.

"If something terrible is happening, how do the police get hold of you? Like Batman has the Batphone."

"Haven't really thought about it," I said.

"Okay. Well, we'll sort all those things out tomorrow. I'm starving. What's the food like in here?"

"Terrible," Tommy-Lee said. "Something called quinoa."

"I'll do something about that too. Karol, turn the light out and let's get some sleep."

I was going to explain that Tommy-Lee wouldn't let us turn the light out. But Tommy-Lee did turn the light off right away. Then he whispered to me, "Tell her not to call me Karol."

"Tell her yourself!"

"She might tell me off."

It seemed that we had a new leader.

*T*HE NEXT MORNING . . .
THE DOCTOR IS ASTONISHED
TO DISCOVER AN EXTRA
GREEN CHILD.

"**T**his is so exciting," said Dr. Brightside, pogoing with excitement, "Look at her! She's soooo green. Why didn't anyone call me?"

Nurse Rock looked uncomfortable. Dr. Brightside was unstoppable. "I'd've been right over. This is our first green female. I had been toying with the idea that girls were immune. But obviously not. You're at least as green as the boys."

"Errmm . . . ," hummed Nurse Rock.

"And what's her name?"

Nurse Rock carried on humming. "Errrrrmmmmm . . ."

"Kwok," said Koko. "Koko Kwok."

"Lovely name. Where are her notes?" There was a

set of notes in a blue folder hanging from a clip on the end of my bed, and one on the end of Tommy-Lee's— nothing on Koko's.

Nurse Rock patted her pockets as if the notes might just be in there.

"Here they are!" Koko whipped a clipboard from under her duvet and passed it to Dr. Brightside. "I hope you don't mind. I was studying them. I'm hoping to be a doctor one day myself."

She'd faked a set of notes for herself!

"Your name . . . Are you Chinese?" asked Dr. Brightside.

"My father is."

"My darling Medical Mysteries, you're all sooooo interesting. You were all different colors and now you're the same color. So, Nurse Rock, does Koko have any food allergies?"

"Errrmmm . . ."

"There's nothing in the notes."

"I do have allergies, though," said Koko. Dr. Brightside took out her iPad to make a note. "Quinoa. I can't eat quinoa. Can't even be in the same room as it."

"Oh." Dr. Brightside looked crushed. "But quinoa is what we've mostly been eating these last few weeks. . . ."

"Makes my hands swell up like boxing gloves," said Koko.

"What a coincidence," snarled Nurse Rock.

"In fact, the only carbohydrate I can eat is"—she looked at Tommy-Lee—"is Snack-a-Jacks."

Tommy-Lee beamed. Which wasn't wise. Nurse Rock definitely saw it. She flicked up her knife-edge eyebrows and sniffed. "Any particular flavor of Snack-a-Jacks?"

"Salt and Vinegar," said Tommy-Lee. Dr. Brightside and Nurse Rock looked at him.

I said, "She was telling us all about her allergies last night. That's how Tommy-Lee remembers that she has to have Salt and Vinegar."

"I see," said Nurse Rock. The way she said it made it clear that she didn't mean, "I understand." She meant, "I see something weird is going on here and I'm going to find out what it is."

Then there was a flippery smack sound from the bathroom. "What was that?" snapped Nurse Rock. As if she couldn't tell it was the sound of a penguin waddling over wet tiles.

"My ringtone!" Koko smiled, holding up Tommy-Lee's phone. "By the way, I meant to tell you—I also eat sardines."

"Sardines?"

"Yeah. Love them. Buckets of them, if you've got them. They're good for the brain, aren't they, doctor? My love of sardines is probably why I'm so clever."

"Sardines it is then! Nurse Rock will sort that out, won't you, nurse?"

"Oh. Of course. Just think of the ward as your favorite restaurant and me as your favorite headwaiter." I could actually hear suspicious thoughts sparking around Nurse Rock's brain. "But first let's do the tests, shall we?"

"Before breakfast?!" said Dr. Brightside, biting her lip. "Oh, go on then. I just can't wait to get a look at your corpuscles, Koko. Send the samples straight to the lab, would you, Nurse Rock?"

"Yes! Great idea!" said Tommy-Lee. "I'll go and do a sample now. In the bathroom."

"I think the doctor meant blood samples, didn't you, doctor?" said Nurse Rock with a smile, whipping out a needle.

"That's right," the doctor agreed, slipping out of the door.

"I'll do a sample anyway," said Tommy-Lee, and fled into the bathroom.

I swear she jabbed us harder and took more blood that morning than she'd ever done before. Also there were no I've Been Brave certificates. There was a rattling sound from somewhere. Her eyes flicked over to the bathroom door. "What are you doing in there, Tommy-Lee?"

"Washing my hands like it says on the notice."

"You're making a lot of noise about it." She had the look of someone who has just figured out where the last person is hiding in a game of high-stakes hide-and-seek. She shooed Tommy-Lee out of the bathroom, went in there herself, and locked the door behind her. No! We waited for the scream. Nothing. She walked out ten seconds later and said she'd be back as soon as she had located some Snack-a-Jacks.

As soon as she'd gone, I dashed into the bathroom.

There was no sign of the penguin.

Maybe she'd eaten it.

It was when I stepped back into the ward that I heard the rattling at the window and saw a yellow beak clamped to the window catch.

"Tommy-Lee, what have you done?"

"I let Peter out so he could fly home."

"Penguins can't fly."

"What? I thought they were birds! He's got wings. Why can't he fly?!"

The penguin was quaking with fear at the twelve-story drop below him, and clutching on to the window catch so tightly with his beak I thought he was going to bite through it. I wedged open the window and dragged him back in.

"Look at him. He's shivering."

"You said penguins didn't mind the cold."

"It's not the cold," I said. "It's the fear. Stuck on a ledge twelve stories up. He's terrified."

Koko wrapped him in her duvet and pulled her curtains closed around him. I said, "This penguin is endangering our whole operation. He has to go."

"What's wrong with endangering things?" said Koko. "Superheroes love danger."

*T*HE MAP OF TREATS

Green Nights

Rongs Righted

Injustisses Fought

Kickboxing lessons availerbul on rikwest

Call—07700 900458

This was the business card Tommy-Lee made for us. Apparently his mum has business cards in case anyone wants to hire her to kick them.

"Kickboxing lessons?" said Koko.

"I'm the treasurer. We need to get money somehow, since Rory won't let us rob banks."

"I'm not sure about the name Green Knights," she said.

"Yeah . . ." Tommy-Lee considered. "You can't be a knight if you're a girl."

Koko's eyes narrowed. "I'll be whatever I want to be. Only I think what's on the card needs to be more obvious. Like if we were selling pizzas, we'd say Dial-a-Pizza."

"Dial-a-Hero?"

"Maybe."

"The pizza place by us," said Tommy-Lee, "is called Chicago Pizza Place."

"That's not really useful. Because we're in London."

"They're amazing pizzas, though. They do one with bacon and egg. The minute I stop having to eat nothing but quinoa, I'm going to go there."

"The best pizza ever is from a guy who sells just slices of pizza on Tottenham Court Road," said Koko. "He also sells little cakes with ice cream inside."

"I feel," I said, "as though we are getting off the subject." I made a few suggestions: Heroes-R-Us, Heroes-4-U, the Hero Helpline, and Heroes-at-Your-Service.

Tommy-Lee said, "Doesn't have to be Chicago. Could be London Heroes."

"Heroes of London," said Koko. "That's it, Karol! Put Heroes of London and make some more. We need to tell the world."

I thought he was going to yell at her for calling him Karol, but no. He said, "You know what we could do? You could come to ours for pizza and then I could come to you for ice-cream cake."

"Yeah, because then you could come to Chinatown for braised lamb with bok choy, which is the best thing ever."

"No," I said. "The best thing ever is the cheese-cake from Dafna's Cheese Cake Factory. It's near my cousin's house. She sends us one in the post on our birthdays."

They drew some more business cards. Koko took over the spelling. "We're a team, Tommy-Lee," she said. "We need to make the most of each other's skills." They carried on talking about food.

I pointed out that there were more important things to talk about, and anyway they weren't even talking right about food, because they had completely forgotten to mention the Ice-Cream Factory—where you can build your own ice-cream fantasy.

"Ice-Cream Factory!" whooped Tommy-Lee— as though he could already taste the chocolate sprinkles—"that's got to go on the list. What we need to do is draw a map—I'm really good at maps—a map of all the best food, and on the day we officially get out of here we can follow the map and eat, like, Chicago pizza in Handsworth as a starter and then down to London for Chinese food and then—oh! me and Mum stopped at Watford services once, and they give you hot chocolate in a tall glass with a flake sticking out of it, so that could go on. And the cheesecake place . . .”

"That's in Liverpool," said Koko. "Near the park."

"So it could be one big meal, but you have to travel around to eat it. A meal with a map instead of a menu. A Map of Treats."

"I," I said, "will keep watch. Someone has to." They didn't even reply. They were 100 percent involved in drawing their Map of Treats and putting it on the wall and admiring it.

Every couple of minutes Nurse Rock came and peered through the window, as if she was trying to catch us out. I could see her and Dr. Brightside having some kind of row, but they had their backs to us so I couldn't lip-read. After a while she pushed in a trolley with a big packet of Snack-a-Jacks on it, and a plate of fish. The moment she brought the fish in . . . we heard CREAK from the bedsprings and SWISH from the curtains, not to mention FLAP, as the penguin lolloped onto the floor. The nurse didn't seem to hear any of this. She just went out and carried on arguing with Dr. Brightside. In the time that it took the door to close itself, the penguin had hopped up on top of the trolley and shoveled all the sardines off the plate into his mouth. When he finished, he jumped off the trolley onto my bed. The door opened again, and Nurse Rock stuck her head around the door. "Urine samples—" she said, but then stopped. She saw the empty plate. "Those fish . . . where have they . . . ?"

"We were really hungry." Koko smiled. "Want to see our pictures?" She was trying to make the nurse look away from my bed, where the penguin was leaning his head right back, stretching his neck, trying to get the fish to go down. Even penguins shouldn't bolt their food.

"Not just now." She went back to her row.

Doctor Brightside had turned around now. She was talking straight into Nurse Rock's face. Now I could read her lips. She was giving Nurse Rock a telling-off. "I have now spoken to everyone who was in A and E last night and everyone in admissions. No trace of her. No trace. How can that happen?"

"Don't know, Doctor." I'd never heard a grown-up being told off before. Even though Nurse Rock was being polite, I could hear that she was angry underneath. If she couldn't be angry back at Dr. Bright-side, she was probably going to be angry at us. She was probably going to be our nemesis.

"You were on duty! What happened? Did she just materialize? Was she beamed down from a spaceship? Do little girls just appear out of nowhere?"

"Not that I know of."

The door banged open. Nurse Rock blew in, grabbed the trolley, and pushed it back out of the door. And when the door shut behind her, the penguin was no longer doing throat-stretching exercises on my bed.

I looked out of the fish-tank window. She'd left the trolley in the corridor. It was rattling and shaking to itself. There was either a very small earthquake, or a penguin had tucked itself underneath the shelf and was squirming around, trying to get comfortable. There was a buzz at the Singing Duck door. Nurse Rock opened it and shoved the trolley out.

"What do you mean, he's gone?" wailed Tommy-Lee. "We can't just let him go. We've got to go and rescue him."

"No, Tommy-Lee, we're not here to rescue wandering penguins. We're here to do what it says on your card—right wrongs and fight injustice."

"It's wrong for a penguin to be wandering. Tell him, Koko," said Tommy-Lee.

"This is a king penguin," said Koko. "They normally live in the very, very south of South America—where there's blizzards and snow. London is summer holidays for him."

"King Penguin? Does that mean we should be calling him King Peter? Maybe he's offended?"

"Stop worrying about the penguin. We've got arch-enemies to fight."

As soon as she said "fight," Tommy-Lee was listening.

"Fight? Fight who?"

"Shhhh, listen . . ." Over the intercom we could hear that Nurse Rock was bickering with someone at the Singing Duck door. The other person was yelling, "It just jumped out and ran off. It was wearing a hat."

"Please step back. This is Isolation. You're not allowed in here."

"What have you got in there? What's going on in there? Little creatures in hats jumping out of the food trolley?! What was it? Is it aliens?!"

"Did you hear that?" I whispered. "What did she see?"

"Aliens," said Tommy-Lee. "She saw aliens."

LONDON IN FEAR-QUAKE! ALIEN PLOT TO CANCEL CHRISTMAS!

"That was no alien," said Koko. "That was our runaway penguin."

"Why," I asked, "would she mistake a penguin for an alien?"

"Because she has poor ornithology skills," said Koko. "And because people have been going on about aliens all week. There are no aliens."

"What do you mean, people have been going on about aliens all week?" I asked.

"Where have you been?!" said Koko. "How can you not know about this?!"

"We've been in isolation."

"Well, weird things have been happening everywhere—viruses that come from nowhere, trains being canceled, shops being closed. Wild animals every-where. People talking about canceling Christmas. But it's just a coincidence. Why would aliens want to cancel Christmas?"

"What do they look like?" asked Tommy-Lee.

"Who?"

"The aliens."

"Don't you ever listen to anything? There ARE no aliens. There's only talk."

"That," I said, "is exactly what they said about the wolves in the gift shop. But were they right?"

She stared at me. "You're right," she said.

"And turning green," said Tommy-Lee. "My mum said no one turns green. But I did turn green."

"Exactly."

"If we're going to fight aliens," said Tommy-Lee, "we'll need rockets and jet packs and lasers."

"We need a mad scientist!" said Koko. "Someone who can invent a special formula for turning aliens into harmless monkeys or whatever." She was very excited about this. She made it sound as if she'd solved all our problems.

"And how exactly do you expect us to find a mad scientist?" said Tommy-Lee. "Are mad scientists even real?"

"When they take samples of our blood and our

wee, where do they send them? To the lab. Where you've got a lab, you've got scientists. Where you've got scientists, you've probably got at least one mad one. All we have to do is find the mad scientist and ask if they'd like to join the team."

"Ever since the day we turned green," I said, "people have been trying to find out how it happened, what's causing it, if it can be stopped, if they can make us un-green. But what I've always wanted to know is why. Why are we green? And now we know why."

"What?" said Tommy-Lee. "I missed a bit. What do we know?"

"Every hero has a nemesis. Batman has the Joker. Spider-Man has the Green Goblin. Superman has Lex Luthor. Why do we need heroes? To fight villains? All this time I've been thinking, What's the point of us being heroes if we have no villains to fight? Now we have a reason. We're heroes because it's Chaos out there. London needs us. England needs us. The world needs us."

"Yeah!" said Tommy-Lee. "We'll go out there and save London from Chaos. . . ." You could tell from the way he said it that he thought Chaos was a person—like Dr. Chaos or Captain Chaos.

"Good thinking," said Koko. "Then everyone will

love us, and we can be in charge."

"Isn't someone already in charge of London?" asked Tommy-Lee.

"Yes, but I'd do a much better job."

Later on, lying in bed, I was thinking, Does Koko sound less like Xavier and more like Magneto?

THREE HEROES STAND ON THE EDGE OF A SKYSCRAPER. WHO KNOWS WHAT DANGERS, WHAT SECRETS, THE SKY ABOVE LONDON IS HIDING?

When Tommy-Lee sleepwalked that night, there were no diversions to the waiting room or the canteen. He walked quickly, as if he had something that he knew he had to do. We followed. Koko was carrying all the business cards and leaflets they had made.

As we were about to go up the steep steps to the roof, Tommy-Lee stopped. He stood completely still, listening for something. There was a sound like a tap dripping but getting louder and louder, as though the tap was coming toward us. Suddenly it was a lot louder. Around the corner came the penguin. He must have been hiding, waiting for us. Tommy-Lee stood still till the penguin flip-flopped past him and self-catapulted up the steps one by one. He was on one step and a second later he was on the next. Like teleporting in installments.

He waddled across the roof, with Tommy-Lee following and us following Tommy-Lee. He waddled straight into the cradle. I pulled the lever and down we went.

The minute we hit the ground, Koko struck a pose and said, "Okay, gang. Green is for Go!"

Peter the Penguin stretched his neck and shook his beak from side to side as if he was joining in. "Look! He knows what I'm saying. He wants to join the gang."

I pointed out that this made no sense. "The whole point of the Green Knights was that we are green. How can someone black and white join the Green Knights? Also, keep your voice down. You're going to wake Tommy-Lee."

She said, "You're supposed to say 'Green is for Go!' too. It's our catchphrase."

"Okay," I whispered. "Green is for Go." But I said it really quietly. "And stay close to him, otherwise he wanders off."

Tommy-Lee had already gone around the corner. He

was following the penguin onto the back of a milk float.

"What's he doing?" said Koko. "We're supposed to be looking for a police station. Or a police roadblock. So we can give the police these leaflets. Or maybe some alien invaders so we can fight them."

The word "fight" was enough to wake Tommy-Lee. His head swiveled around. "Fight! What fight? Has it started? Where are we? What's all this milk?"

Koko said, "The Green Knights/Heroes of London are on a mission! We're going to find the proper authorities and tell them we're here to defend the city."

"On a milk float?"

There was no sign of a milkman. There was no sign of anyone, in fact. So we borrowed the milk float. It was quieter and safer than a bin lorry. Also easier to drive. Basically it's a big, slow dodgem car. There were a couple of crates of bottles on the back. The empty ones tinkled as we floated along, like the bells on Santa's sleigh. There was no one in the streets.

"Where is everyone?" I asked.

"Maybe it's closed," said Tommy-Lee.

"What's closed?"

"London."

"I don't think London closes." But it was closed.

Silence walked the streets like a panther. Koko said, "We're probably in one of the exclusion areas. When there's an outbreak of Killer Kittens, they move everyone out for a while. We shouldn't be here. Oh!"

"What?" I turned.

"Over there, look."

Something was glittering on the side of the road. Little blobs of light floating in pairs. Eyes.

"Wolves," whispered Koko. "Wolves' eyes."

"Wolves," said Tommy-Lee. "Rory, what do we know about wolves?"

"How would he know?"

"He knows about everything scary," said Tommy-Lee.

"Wolves," I said, "are easy. All you have to do is pick out the biggest one, then run at it, shouting. If you can frighten the big one, the Alpha Daddy, the others will run away." That was all in *Don't Be Scared, Be Prepared*, but I tried to make it sound as though I was always fighting off wolf packs, just so Koko would feel a bit safer. Then the floating yellow globules all floated forward at once into a pool of street light. Faces and bodies appeared around them. They weren't wolves. They were cats. A carpet of cats. It turns out that when the Killer Kittens started, people began dumping their cats so they wouldn't catch it from them. The cats had got together and were roaming around the city in big virusy gangs.

"Quick, before they infect us!" said Koko.

I put my foot down harder on the milk float's accelerator, but it didn't make a lot of difference. It certainly didn't go faster than cats.

Suddenly the penguin dived off the van and waddled toward the cats. They yowled and scattered as though they'd been shot at. It seems that cats are penguin-phobic. I don't know how the penguin knew this, but the minute he'd done his job, he jumped back on board.

"Peter, you saved us," said Tommy-Lee. "King Peter is now part of the gang."

"I did suggest that," said Koko, "but Rory said no."

Tommy-Lee gave me his bad look. Exactly the bad look he used to give me in school. I thought he might throw me off the back of the milk float.

"I just said it would be a bit odd, someone who is black and white joining a gang for green people."

"Are you saying he can't join just because of the color of his skin?"

"Nothing to do with his skin. It's his feathers. And the fact that he's a penguin."

"What's wrong with penguins?"

"Think about it, Tommy-Lee—who was Batman's biggest enemy, the most frightening villain in Gotham? . . . The Penguin."

"Are you calling Peter a bad guy?"

"I'm just saying . . ." But Tommy-Lee's attention had wandered. "What," he gasped, "is that?"

We were at a traffic island, but not a traffic island like any I'd seen before. There was a huge white statue of a dumpy woman in the middle, like a wedding cake with a big angry gold angel on top. Behind that was a massive building with hundreds of windows. I seemed to know it from somewhere.

"Is this the police station?" asked Tommy-Lee.

"This," said Koko, "is Buckingham Palace."

I knew I knew it from somewhere.

"We were looking for the proper authorities," said Koko, "and now we've found them. There's no need to mess about talking to the police now. Why bother when we can go right to the top? Let's talk to the monarch."

There are big railings all around Buckingham Palace. Also soldiers in fuzzy hats (we couldn't see them, but we knew they were there from General Knowledge). We trundled the float up and down the railings, but the only way in was a narrow gate, which looked very locked indeed. There was barbed wire on top and about a million cameras perched in the barbed wire, staring down like hungry vultures. There was an intercom.

Koko said, "We could just ask. I'm sure if the queen knew what we were here for, she'd be very grateful. She'd probably give us knighthoods. Then we'd be actual proper green knights. We could sell Green Knight T-shirts and lunch boxes."

I pointed out that it was five o'clock in the morning and that if we woke her now, she wouldn't be pleased.

"She might not be asleep. Look. There's a light on up there."

"Where?"

"Seventy-third window from the left."

There was a light on, but even so . . . Then the gate opened. Slowly, gently, it opened wide, inviting us in.

I looked at Tommy-Lee and said, "Did you do that?"

"Wasn't me."

A voice crackled from the intercom. "Morning, Milky. You're early this morning."

They thought that we were the milkman. After all, we were driving a milk float. We trundled over a field of paving stones. The rows of windows stared down. Surely someone would spot that it was three green children and a penguin on the float and not a milk-man.

A door opened in the wall ahead of us. I stopped the float. "What shall we do?"

"We'd better take the milk in," said Tommy-Lee, picking up a crate. "After all, she is the queen." He carried it in through the door with the penguin following at his heels. We went in after them.

We were in a huge kitchen, full of the smell of bacon cooking. Dozens of rashers were frying on a pan the size of a door. Six people, all in white aprons, stared at us, hardly blinking, frozen by the paralyzing ray of our unbelievable greenness.

I said, "Hi. Don't worry. We are green, but we are also nice. . . ."

Koko shoved me aside, muttering, "Green but also nice? Honestly." She struck a pose and said, "Behold the Green Knights! The mighty Karol, who can do kickboxing . . ." She pointed at Tommy-Lee. He launched into a kickboxing demonstration. His feet flew. His arms whirled. His body swerved and spun. I have to admit it was impressive. The people in the kitchen were so impressed that most of them hid under a table.

Koko pointed at me next, told them my name was Rory and that I could slightly teleport. The frightened heads popped up from behind the table and stared at me expectantly. I put my hand up. "I can't just do it, just like that. It has to be the right time."

"And I," said Koko, "am Koko Kwok. And I"—she thought for a bit—"am In Charge."

My 200 percent brain noticed that the bacon was starting to burn. I said, "Hey, don't burn the queen's bacon." One of the men in white edged toward the pan, never taking his eyes off me. Except for one millisecond when he glanced over my shoulder. My 200 percent brain realized this meant there was someone behind me. I looked round. There was a man with a hefty-looking saucepan raised over his head, as though he was going to hit me with it. He must have been behind the door when we came in. I went to duck, but before I could move, the penguin popped up onto a chair right in front of him. One second he wasn't there. Then he was. He really did seem to teleport. The man was so shocked he dropped the pan. It rang on the stone floor. We all stared at it. Then stared at him.

"Were you going to hit me?" I was quite offended, to be honest.

"Resistance is useless," growled Tommy-Lee. "And especially don't hurt the penguin." The penguin clapped his little flippers at this. "Nice work, Peter," said Tommy-Lee. Then he gave me his Bad Look again. "I bet you feel bad now. You said he couldn't join, and he still saved your life. Say, 'Sorry, Peter.'"

"Not now," I hissed. "I'm trying to explain things to these people."

"Say, 'Sorry, Peter.'"

I said, "Sorry," and patted the penguin on the head.

"We need to talk to the queen," said Koko. That sounded reasonable until she added, "We're going to take over running things here for a while," which sounded Mad. "Is that her breakfast? Give it to us. We'll take it to her. We can explain everything to her over a bacon butty. And some sardines for the penguin."

So they put four bacon butties, a pot of tea, and four cups on a tray. They tried to put some sardines on a plate for Peter, but as soon as they'd opened the tin, he knocked it out of their hands with his beak and gobbled up the contents.

They told us the way to the queen's bedroom. They pointed us up some stairs and told us to follow the long gallery right to the end. "There'll be a man there. He'll help," they said.

The penguin went ahead. We were beginning to get the feeling that he was good at directions. He hopped up the stairs and waddled along the gallery and wasn't distracted by the amazing paintings that lined the walls. They were mostly of animals being shot or chased, so maybe he found them upsetting. We were passing one of a tiger having trouble with some dogs when a bright light flashed on and a big man with a radio clipped to his belt appeared.

"Hold it right there," he said. "Identify yourselves. Be advised that I am armed."

I explained that we were taking the queen her breakfast.

"We're going to have a word with her about running the country," added Koko, which I wish she hadn't. He wasn't listening anyway. His radio crackled into life, and we could hear someone talking to him about intruders in the palace.

"Intruders in the palace?" said Tommy-Lee. "Did you hear that? Where are they? We'll sort them out for you!"

"Get back," said the man, reaching for something on his belt. My 200 percent brain noticed right away that it was a gun. The man's unenhanced brain did not notice the penguin, which seemed to think the gun was an extra sardine. So the moment the man pulled it out of its holster, he playfully leaped up and tried to peck it out of his hands. He really was amazingly quick, that penguin. But not as quick as the bullet that ripped a hole in the painting of the tiger and blew clouds of plaster all over the place.

"You need to be more careful with that," said Tommy-Lee, picking the gun up off the floor, where the penguin had dropped it—disappointed by its lack of fishiness. The man crouched on the ground with his hands over his head. I said we were sorry about the mess and asked him again the way to the queen.

"There, just through there." He pointed at a narrow mahogany door. It did actually have a little brass crown screwed to it, so we were fully expecting it to be the queen's bedroom. We were disappointed when we got inside to find that it was a gents' toilet. There was a row of latrines and some stalls.

"I've never been in a boys' toilet before," giggled Koko.

We tried to go back and explain to the man that he'd made a mistake, but he had locked us in.

"He's locked us in."

"You don't think . . . ," said Tommy-Lee, "that HE was the intruder, do you? Let's get him."

But just then we heard one of the toilets flush. We all went quiet. We were all thinking the same thing.

"But why would the queen use a boys' toilet?" whispered Koko.

"She's the queen. She can wee wherever she likes. Haven't you heard of the Royal Wee?"

The door opened.

It wasn't the queen.

It was a man in pajamas. He was carrying a baby.

He stared at us. He stared at the gun in Tommy-Lee's hand. We stared at him. The baby stared at the penguin. "Tiger!" it whooped, inaccurately.

"Okay," said the man, "what do you want?"

"Are you," asked Tommy-Lee, "a prince?"

"I am. The baby wouldn't sleep. I came for a walk."

"Tiger!"

"Prince!" said Tommy-Lee. The prince put his hand in the air, because Tommy-Lee was suddenly pointing at him with the gun. Only one hand, though, because he was holding the baby with the other. "Let the baby go," he pleaded. "You can do what you like with me. But let the baby go."

"We'd love to," I explained, "but we're locked in. Tommy-Lee, put the gun down. You're frightening the prince."

"There's no need to be frightened," said Koko. "We're here to help. We wanted to speak to your grandma. But you'll do. If we tell you what we think, you can tell her. Okay?"

"Sure. Do you mind me asking . . . ? Are you . . . green? I mean, really green? Like spinach?"

"Broccoli," corrected Tommy-Lee. "Would you like a bacon sandwich?"

While the prince ate the sandwich, Koko explained her ideas about how to deal with aliens. Also some other ideas she had about traffic congestion, extra school holidays, the ridiculous price of Haribo in cinemas, and the way bus drivers are always polite to grown-ups but often rude to children. The prince seemed really interested in this. His baby seemed really interested in the penguin. Things were getting very conversational.

Then from somewhere in my 200 percent brain a memory popped up—a memory of the page in *Don't Be Scared, Be Prepared* about how to deal with kidnappers. It said you should always try to keep your kidnapper talking. The more they get to know you, the harder it will be for them to be nasty to you. The prince was now asking Koko details of which buses she took to school and how much the ticket cost.

He was keeping her talking!

He thought we had taken him prisoner.

I could see things from his point of view now— he was locked in a toilet in his own house with three green children armed with a pistol. I could hear people moving around outside. His bodyguards. Maybe they were getting ready to knock the door down and spray us with sleeping gas or something.

All these thoughts happened at once.

I remembered another page from *Don't Be Scared, Be Prepared*. The page that said if you need to get out of a tall building in a hurry, always use the toilet window as there will be a thick drainpipe just outside, to take all the bad stuff away.

I said, "Let's go." I opened the window. There was the pipe.

"Go where?" said Koko.

"Back to HQ."

"I'm TRYING to talk to the prince," said Koko. "We're TRYING to sort out the nation."

"Koko. Green is for Go!"

In normal life none of us would ever climb down a fifteen-meter drainpipe. But we did it with no trouble that morning. It just seemed like the sensible thing to do. There was a bit of a wobble when Tommy-Lee had to admit that the penguin probably couldn't manage it. But he was fine when I said, "Think about it, Tommy-Lee. He's a king penguin. He's obviously going to be happier in a royal palace."

I was worried about how we were going to get back to HQ, but things turned out okay. When we got into the courtyard, there was a helicopter hovering over a milk float and loads of soldiers pointing guns at a milkman. The milkman was yelling at them, saying, "The intruders were PRETENDING to be a milkman. I'm the ACTUAL milkman. Ask anyone. Ask the queen."

"Step away from the milk float."

He did. The soldiers surrounded him. The helicopter followed them across the courtyard.

We got on his milk float and drove it away.

Tommy-Lee was looking sadly back at the palace, worried about the penguin.

"Oh!" groaned Koko. "I should've given one of our business cards to that prince. What a waste of a networking opportunity."

"Look!" shouted Tommy-Lee. "Peter!" The penguin was waddling toward us with his wings sticking out like training wheels on a bike.

"Peter!" Tommy-Lee yelled. I waited. Peter hopped on board. We floated through the empty streets all the way back to the hospital. The roofs of the houses started to shine as the sun came up.

■ ■ ■

The cradle was dangling above the bins—just out of reach.

"It's okay. We can get up on top of the milk float and jump in," I said. But just as I said it, the cradle motor started whirring and the cradle wobbled down toward us. That's really lucky, I thought.

But I was wrong.

The reason the cradle was moving was that someone was on board.

That someone was Nurse Rock.

She stood, glowering at us. A smile carved itself into her face. Rolled up in her hand was Tommy-Lee's map of London.

"Good morning, children," she cooed. "I've been waiting for you."

AND SO THE HEROES
OF LONDON AWAIT
THEIR FATE . . .

The waiting was the worst bit.

Nurse Rock put us back in the fish tank.

She didn't bring us breakfast.

She didn't stick any needles in us.

She didn't tell us off.

She just left us sitting there.

No one said a thing.

Except Tommy-Lee, who said he was worried about Peter the Penguin. (Nurse Rock had made us leave him by the bins.)

Then he said he was worried that Dr. Brightside would now refuse to make us well because she was so cross with us.

Then he said he was worried that we would all starve to death.

Then he said he was worried that his old badness had come back, because he was feeling very much in the mood to start smashing things up.

Then Nurse Rock came back in. "I've decided not to tell Dr. Brightside what you've been doing," she announced.

We all said thank you, though I'm not sure why.

"I don't know if she could bear to know," she said. "She's spent all this time trying to prevent this terrible contagion from spreading, and now it turns out that you've been wandering all over London, infecting the whole city."

"What will she do?" begged Tommy-Lee, who seemed to be worried that she was going to pickle him or something.

"I just don't know," said Nurse Rock, who was enjoying herself just a bit too much.

"I'll tell you what," said Koko. "If you don't tell her, we won't tell her."

"You won't tell her what?" snapped Nurse Rock.

"That we went out. That the security arrangements were clearly lacking. That we were supposed to be in isolation but somehow we were able to wander in and out all we liked. We just won't mention any of that, if you don't want us to." Koko shrugged.

Nurse Rock bit her lip. I have to say, Koko has great Making-People-Feel-Bad skills. But Nurse Rock is hard to beat. She just shrugged right back at her and said, "Fine. Good idea. You keep that to yourself, and meanwhile I'll reform the security arrangements, as you suggested." She mentioned such things as changing the codes on the hospital doors and making us all sleep in separate fish tanks.

"That's solitary confinement!" I said. "They don't do that even if you murder people!"

"For all I know, you've given a deadly disease to hundreds of people," said Nurse Rock. "You're very lucky to be locked up in here. People out there, they hate anything different. And at a time like this when strange things are happening, if they saw green children, they'd probably . . . well, I don't want to think about it."

I pointed out that people had mostly been quite nice to us so far.

"Really?" Nurse Rock smiled. I knew that smile. It was exactly the smile that Tommy-Lee used to do whenever he saw me taking my lunch box out of my school bag. It was the smile of someone who was going to have a good time by making someone else have a bad time. "Let me point something out," she said.

"No, don't. It's all right."

"How long have you been in this hospital?"

"Errmmmm . . . Honestly, it doesn't matter . . ."

"Your OWN PARENTS have still not been to visit you."

So the waiting wasn't the worst bit after all. That actually was the Worst Bit.

I'd never been in the hospital before.

I didn't know how often your mum and dad were supposed to visit.

But now I came to think of it, why hadn't they come? And why hadn't Tommy-Lee's mum come? Was it really just because we were green?

I could feel all the power and buzz I'd got from being green draining out of me. Nurse Rock must have known that that sentence—"Your own parents have still not been to visit you"—was like Kryptonite, a special formula for neutralizing superpowers.

They moved us into separate fish tanks.

They took all the I've Been Brave certificates and drawings off the wall, and we each took our own with us.

My fish tank was opposite Tommy-Lee's. I couldn't see him, though. I guessed he was just lying on his bed again, wrapped in his duvet like a fat floral caterpillar.

I never in my life thought I'd miss Grim Komissky.

When it was time to do drawings, I drew a square house with a square lawn and a lollipop flower thing at each corner. Just so I could have one on my wall.

I had a blood test and a chromatograph and did my urine sample. When the quinoa came, I ate it. When it was time to put the lights out, I stood at the window.

I could just make out the shadow of Tommy-Lee, pacing round and round inside his own fish tank. Just going from one wall to another, from window to bed, over and over in his sleep, like a big depressed bear in a zoo who can't believe there's no way out of his cage. The more he walked, the more I remembered the other walks we'd done together—walks along secret corridors and over rooftops, walks through the streets and the parks of the nighttime city that we called Wonderville—before we knew it was only London.

Empty London.

It was while I was remembering those walks that it all finally made sense. The empty streets. The police. Of course! The only reason that our parents wouldn't come was if something terrible had happened to them! Maybe the entire population of Birmingham had been destroyed by Killer Kittens! Maybe Captain Chaos himself was holding the whole West Midlands for ransom. Anything could have happened!

We had to escape. Our country needed us!

I'm not saying I planned my daring escape just because I wanted my mum. I'm saying I planned a daring escape so I could rescue my mum. And dad.

A SUPERHERO CAN BE
LOCKED UP, BUT HIS
SPIRIT CAN NEVER BE
IMPRISONED!!!

*D*on't *Be Scared, Be Prepared* has a whole chapter about how to escape when you've been locked away for no reason. It tells you all about the Count of Monte Cristo, who was thrown into a secret cell in a prison on an island in the middle of a sea full of sharks. In the end he escaped, got his revenge, and got really rich. He tapped on the wall of his cell with a spoon so that other prisoners would know he was there. One of them heard him and dug a tunnel right into the count's cell. They became friends. Then this new friend gave the count a secret treasure map just before he died. The prison guards wrapped the dead man up in a sack so they could throw him into the sea,

263

but the count had changed places with the corpse. The guards threw him into the sea, thinking he was dead, but he cut himself out of the sack with a secret knife, swam away, found some treasure, got rich, got married, and got revenge.

He made it sound easy.

Except you really need a dead body to make this work.

Plus, I had a feeling that in this hospital they don't throw you into the sea when you're dead.

I didn't have a dead body.

But I did have a spoon.

I tapped on the radiator.

It rang.

I listened.

No one replied.

I tapped again. This time I seemed to hear the tap of the spoon shiver along all the twists and turns of the pipe leading to the great boiler room, echo in the boiler, swing back out through the heating pipes to all the radiators in the building, ripple through the hot-water pipes into the sinks where the surgeons washed their hands, and the cold-water pipes where people filled the drinking jugs and the vases of flowers, travel under the floorboards, behind the skirting boards, behind the ceilings and in the walls, whispering to doctors, nurses, cleaners, visitors, patients, cooks, porters.

Not one of them answered.

Maybe I just wasn't doing the right kind of tapping on the radiators. Maybe it wasn't enough to make a noise—you had to send a message. In the back of *Don't Be Scared, Be Prepared* there was a section on Morse code. I tried to figure out how to send a cry for help and some information about where I was, but I must have fallen asleep, because the next thing I knew, I was curled up in bed, listening to an inexplicable tapping noise.

Someone had answered me!

I slid out of my bed and crouched down next to the radiator, ready to tap back, when the tapping stopped. It didn't stop. It wasn't coming from the radiator.

Tap.

Tap.

Tap.

Tap.

Maybe from the door?

No.

From the walls?

No.

A tap dripping?

No.

I pressed my face against the glass to see if there was something out in the corridor. Yes. A little dark creature was pecking at the door of Tommy-Lee's room.

*T*HE RETURN OF
PETER THE PENGUIN

The Return of Peter the Penguin was our opportunity.

My enhanced brain was moving so fast that it didn't even tell me what I was doing. It just started moving. I tapped gently on my window. The penguin heard. Turned. Listened. Came over to my door to investigate. When he was right up against the woodwork, I clobbered the door as hard as I could with a chair. Peter was terrified. He flapped. He squelched. He waddled off down the corridor toward the officey bit where Nurse Rock sits. Five seconds later there was a scream, then the sound of a chair falling over, then bins clattering around. The nurse was trying to corner the penguin, but the penguin was too quick. Then came her voice—she was yelling into the phone, calling for help.

I was ready.

The Singing Duck door opened, and two men in overalls dashed in. The door began to close itself, slowly drifting back on its hydraulic hinges.

I was straight out of my fish tank and into Tommy-Lee's. I shook him awake.

"What?"

"Do as I say. We've got thirty seconds till the door closes. Move."

When I opened Koko's door, she was already up and waiting. "What's going on?" she said.

"We've been saved by a penguin. Move quickly while they're busy."

"Green is for Go!" she whooped.

"Shh!" I led the other two out into the corridor.

It was early morning now. The first time we'd been off the ward in the daytime. Light piled in through the big, grimy windows. We looked greener than ever.

"Where are we going?"

"Keep moving. Follow me."

I led them to the waiting room with the Legos and started pulling open drawers. I didn't even know why

I'd done it until I saw them all laid out in front of us.

"Face paints," I said. "Tommy-Lee, you're the best at art—"

"I'm not good at art!"

"What are you talking about? You drew that map. Here's an instruction book." There was a kind of pull-out leaflet in with the colors that told you how to make different designs and how to get the paints to work. "You could try a tiger face—page three. You could make Koko into a butterfly—page forty-seven."

"A butterfly?! Why? Because I'm a girl?! No, thanks. I want to be a gorilla. Here—look."

"What," roared Tommy-Lee, sounding like a gorilla himself, "is going on??!!"

"We're going out to save the world."

"With face paint?"

"Our distinguishing characteristic is our bright green skin. If we want to escape from here, all we have to do is cover up the green with face paint so we look like normal kids. Then we can walk around in broad daylight undetected." I stabbed my finger at the picture on page ten and told him I wanted to be Spider-Man.

I thought of all the times I'd seen kids dressed up as superheroes—at parties, on own-clothes day. One time I'd seen a really big muscley Batman sitting in a KFC eating a bucket of spicy wings on his own. The streets were full of people who looked like superheroes but weren't. I figured making yourself look like a superhero was probably the best way of concealing the fact that you really were one.

"But why do we want to walk around in broad daylight?"

"Think about it, Tommy-Lee. They're never going to let us out of here. Think of all the blood and wee tests you've had. All the quinoa you've eaten. And you haven't got any better. They won't let us out until we're better. But we're not getting better. If we want to get out, we have to break out. If we want to be astounding, we have to do astounding."

Looking around the room, my 200 percent brain could pick up the traces of all the families that had waited in there. Families like mine. There were newspapers. Magazines. Drawing pads. The bin was full of sweets wrappers and broken crayons. There was even a road atlas with loads of pages turned down at the corner, like in my dad's, and a bag with drink cartons, a sandwich box, and a tin of Spam.

"It's the only way," I said, "that we're ever going to see our mums and dads again."

"So," said Tommy-Lee, "we're breaking out of the hospital because you want your mum?"

"No. We're breaking out of the hospital because England needs us. Including my mum."

*I*S IT A BIRD?
IS IT A BOY?

Tommy-Lee turned out to be a face-paint genius. You couldn't see any green on us anywhere. We raided the dressing-up box for hats and capes and masks.

"What do we do now?" asked Tommy-Lee.

"Blend in with the crowd."

"There isn't any crowd."

"Wait and see."

We could hear the hospital beginning to wake up. Doors banged. An electric floor polisher hummed up and down the corridors. The breakfast trolley went past. Then a mum and dad came in with a kid in a stripy top. He played with the Legos while they talked quietly. They were waiting for test results. Then a mum came in with a little girl with curly hair and fairy wings attached to her coat. Another mum with a boy in a Batman suit. There was so much dressing up going on, no one noticed three kids in face paint. We could have left right away, but I think we were all quietly enjoying the sound that families make. Even the grown-ups telling kids off and the kids moaning about being ignored reminded us of home and what life was like before we were locked away for being green. A nurse came in and started taking names. That's when we sneaked off.

Everything was fine until we got up onto the roof. When I opened the door that led to the outside, Tommy-Lee grabbed hold of the handle and wouldn't let go. "I'm not going out there," he said.

"You go out there all the time. You've been out there practically every night since we got here."

"In my sleep. I'm not going out there awake. I'm not stepping off the roof into that cradle thing."

"But you're always awake when we come back here. And you always step out of the cradle onto the roof."

"Yeah. I'll step OUT of it. I'll step out of it because I hate being IN it. I'm not going to climb INTO it awake, am I?"

I tried pleading with him. I asked him to think of

the West Midlands and its people, suffering under a possible alien invasion. Koko didn't say anything. She just grabbed a plastic Iron Man mask and pushed it right down over his head, so he couldn't see.

"What're you doing?! Gerroff!"

"You don't mind doing this when you're asleep. So pretend you're asleep. Or go to sleep. Whichever. We don't mind. Here. Give me your hand."

Tommy-Lee obediently gave her his hand, and she led him across the tarmac roof. The chains that held the window cleaners' cradle jingled in the wind.

"I know we're near the edge," said Tommy-Lee, "because the backs of my legs feel sick. I always get a bad feeling in the backs of my legs when we're up here."

"We're not that near yet," said Koko. Which was a lie because we were right at the very brink of the roof. "Lift your foot up high and then put it down slowly."

"Why?"

"You don't want to trip over when you're twelve stories high, do you?"

"No."

"Then do as you're told."

I said, "We'll get you into the cradle, and then just don't look down and you'll be all right."

Koko guided Tommy-Lee's foot onto the step that led down to the cradle. Then, without warning him, she reached up and pulled his Iron Man mask off and let it drop. It was quite scary how quickly it fell out of sight.

"Arrrgghh. What'd you do that for?"

Tommy-Lee's face was pointing straight down the sheer side of the hospital. Roofs of houses, shops, cars, ambulances were far, far below us. The wind gusted.

"Shut your eyes, Tommy-Lee. Shut them and you'll be okay." That was me, by the way.

"Don't close your eyes," said Koko. "What's the point of being up here if you're not going to look down?!"

Tommy-Lee was already looking down. His neck went stiff like it had been hit by some kind of freeze ray. His eyes bulged. He swayed. I gripped his pajamas a bit tighter. "This," he hissed, slowly spreading his arms out wide, "is"—and his pajamas rippled in the wind like a hypoallergenic kite—"the"—his arms wide now—"best thing EVER!" He whooped. He spun around. I lost my grip, and he did one of his kickboxing moves, right out over the edge of the parapet.

"Tommy-Lee, you'll fall!"

"I feel like I can fly!"

"But you can't, so . . . please don't try."

"Why not?" His bare toes were poking over the edge. He was leaning forward. If he sneezes now, I thought, he'll fall.

"I bet we could if we tried," he said.

"Could what?"

"Fly. Come on, put your arms out."

"We can't fly."

"How do you know if you haven't tried?"

"You don't need to try gravity. Gravity is not in any way unreliable."

"But we're superheroes. That's what you said. Superheroes can fly." He leaned farther out.

"He's got a point," said Koko. She climbed up next to Tommy-Lee, poked her toes over the edge, stretched out her arms, and peered down at London as though it was a pond and she might dive in. I was standing in between the two of them.

Just for a second, it really did feel as though we could fly.

If you stand on top of a high building without feeling scared, you feel like you can do anything. It felt as if my whole body had had an upgrade, not just my brain. I was 200 percent Rory.

Far away a church bell chimed.

"Nearly midmorning," said Koko. "Hey, we'll hear Big Ben striking twelve."

"On the bong of twelve," announced Tommy-Lee, "I'm going to give it a go."

"Give what a go?"

Bong . . .

"Flying. I'm going to try and fly."

Bong . . .

It's great to have superpowers (*bong* . . .), but I strongly believe you should test them (*bong* . . .) in controlled conditions (*bong* . . .) before chucking yourself off a roof.

Bong . . .

Tommy-Lee was up on his toes with his arms stretched wide (*bong* . . .), ready to jump. I could see he wasn't going to listen to health-and-safety warnings.

Bong . . .

"Here I go!" whooped Tommy-Lee.

"No! Tommy-Lee! Don't jump!"

Bong . . .

"Why not?"

"Too conspicuous. Think about it—flying children whizzing around the place." (*bong* . . .) "People notice things like that. They point. They film you with their phones. They tweet the pictures. They put you on the news. We haven't got time for that. We've got work to do. Hero work."

Bong . . .

"He's right," agreed Koko. "We'll take the window cleaners' cradle and save the jump for another time."

Bong.

As we wobbled past the tenth floor, I realized that since we were covered in face paint, we could just have caught the lift and walked out of the front door.

Why didn't I think of that? Why didn't any of us think of that? Because we'd started to think like superheroes.

Superheroes do not use the lift.

It was strange-in-a-good-way to be just walking around the city with normal people as though we were normal too. It felt like being invisible.

We strode along, shoulder to shoulder, buzzing with Superness. "Standing on the edge of the roof," said Tommy-Lee, "has filled my Superness tank to the limit. Let's fight aliens!"

I pointed out that we'd need to find some aliens before fighting them.

"How come London's so full now," asked Tommy-Lee,

"when it was completely empty before?"

"Last time we were out it was five o'clock in the morning," explained Koko. "Also we were in one of the exclusion zones. It looks like everything's just normal here." Extra normal, in fact. Everyone was chatting and texting and going about their business. It was not the way I'd expected things to be during an alien invasion.

"Look!" hissed Tommy-Lee. "Over there!" There were four or five people standing on the corner with blue skin, massive bellies, and antennae sticking out of their heads. "They have got to be aliens."

"Maybe they're just foreign," said Koko. "The whole world comes to London."

"Not with antennae sticking out of their heads." Tommy-Lee barged through the crowd toward the blue people, ready to do battle. We followed him. I noticed that people were stopping to have their photos taken with the aliens and then dropping money into a kind of crash helmet painted with stars which was on the pavement in front of them. "Comic Relief! Give generously," shouted one.

"Do you come in peace?" asked Koko.

"Yes, but we do want all your money."

"Tommy-Lee," I whispered, pulling him back toward me, "I don't think these people are from Mars."

"Mars? No, son. We're from Chelsea. Hence the blue."

"Okay," mumbled the disappointed Tommy-Lee, "we'll let you off. This time."

But by now my 200 percent brain was working. It's amazing how much information leaks out of a crowd of people—the words they say, the clothes they wear, the stuff they carry, it all tells you things. Without even trying, the crowd was telling a story. I could have stayed and listened to it forever. A man with a newspaper, for instance. The front-page headline read ALIEN ATE MY HAMSTER.

Three girls waiting for some more friends to turn up were looking at Facebook on their phones. One of them liked a group called Happy Christmas, Aliens.

There was a big screen on the other side of the road showing mostly adverts. Across the bottom of the screen ran a stream of information about weather, gossip, sports, and what was trending on Twitter. #AliensforChristmas was number one.

Farther down the street, a newspaper seller was using a little black radio to weigh down his pile of papers. I could hear a phone-in playing. A woman had rung in to say aliens had stolen milk from her doorstep. "I seen them do it, Keith," she said, "and with my very own eyes. Two pints of semi-skimmed they had off me. Plus, I wasn't the only one. Mrs. Gable at number eight got a photo of them. There's a big one, a tiny one, and a bossy one."

"You're not the first caller to say this, Eileen. We've had calls from Brent and Brixton, from Southall to Bromley, people saying they've seen aliens. Though you are the first to say that aliens drink milk, Eileen."

There was a girl in a sweatshirt that said LOVING THIS ALIEN.

"Okay," I said, "let's go."

"Go where?"

"There are sightings of aliens all over the city. They're obviously moving quickly. What's the quickest way to move around a massive city?"

"Is it jet packs?" asked Tommy-Lee.

"Think about it. What's got no congestion, no traffic lights, no roundabouts, no flyovers, no parking meters? It's obvious, isn't it? The river."

Keep. away. from. my. penguins.

If you are in a city that is in danger of being destroyed by bombs or missiles or by riots, you should try to travel by water. It's safer, quicker, and helps with orientation.

—Don't Be Scared, Be Prepared

Water buses and pleasure cruisers were jostling in and out of the piers and jetties, heading upriver and downriver. We slid in behind a school group that was boarding a boat heading east. Everyone, including the teachers, was dressed up for charity. I stood next to a fairly short Darth Vader and really tall Yoda, who were having an argument about the future of Arsenal.

We fitted right in. A teacher dressed like Professor Umbridge from Hogwarts counted us on.

Considering we were about to go and save the world, it was all quite relaxing. The wind blew in our hair. There were free packets of Pickled Onion Monster Munch. Tommy-Lee couldn't eat his, but we described the flavor for him. Going under Tower Bridge was probably the best bit. It was funny to think that only a few days ago we didn't even know we were in London.

Then things got slightly complicated. First of all, Tommy-Lee spotted a small black-and-white object in the water speeding toward us. "Peter!" he yelled, and spread his arms out wide—as if the penguin was going to jump in like a puppy.

The penguin jumped into his arms like a puppy.

I can never get over how penguins rocket out of the water.

"How did he get out of secret HQ?" said Koko. "Did he use the lift?" Peter raised his beak as if he was deliberately ignoring the question.

"I've got a feeling he can fly," said Tommy-Lee. "I think he's got penguin superpowers." He put the penguin down on the bench next to him and tried to act like it was normal to bring a penguin on a school trip. Surprisingly this seemed like it was going to work, but then two more penguins shot over the side and stood around Tommy-Lee with their little wings dangling like dripping-wet coat hangers.

"This must be his wife and kid," said Tommy-Lee. "Fancy Peter being a dad."

"You have no reason to suppose that this is a family," said Koko. "For all you know, this is a penguin boy band, or a gang of penguin desperadoes. They might all be girls. It could be a penguin hen night."

But by now the penguins were all clicking beaks and wobbling their heads. Whatever they were, they were pleased to see one another.

And they were attracting attention.

A big lad in a Pirates of the Caribbean costume came over with two even bigger lads dressed as ninjas and said, "What's this?"

"It's not penguins," I said quickly. "It's kids dressed up as penguins." The penguins pulled their necks in and folded their wings into their sides.

"They must be very small kids," said one of the ninjas—obviously the one with the powers of observation.

"They are. Really small."

"You're not from our school," said the pirate. "You don't go to Hackney Free. Who are you?"

284

"You talking to me? Or to the penguins?" Tommy-Lee asked. We laughed.

"You laughing at us?" said the second ninja. "This is our school trip. Who said you could come on our school trip?"

No one is allowed to speak to Tommy-Lee like that unless they actually gave birth to him. That ninja, I thought, will be floating in the Thames any minute, and there's probably nothing I can do about it. By now everyone—Yoda, pirates, stormtroopers—was staring at us. Short Darth Vader turned out to be a teacher. He took his helmet off and peered at the penguins, then at us. He asked who it was hiding under the face paint.

"I don't think we know each other," I admitted, "unless you used to teach in Birmingham?"

"But you're from Hackney Free School, Year Eight, right? From the Thames History Project?"

"Not really."

"But . . . you must be. I mean . . . we counted everyone on. How did you get on here? This is a dreadful mix-up. Mrs. Catermole! We've got a problem."

I have to admit that it was funny watching Darth Vader lose it over three Year Sevens.

"Mrs. Catermole, we appear to have accidentally taken three extra children."

Mrs. Catermole turned out to be the one dressed as Professor Umbridge. "I definitely counted thirteen children," she said.

"But three of those children aren't ours. That must mean . . ."

They stared at each other and both said at once, "We've left three children behind."

Darth Vader sounded out of breath. "The legal implications . . . the health-and-safety issues. Who ARE you, children?" He didn't wait for an answer, just carried on panicking. "We're going to have to turn the boat around and get back to the pier. Your parents or your school must be worried about you."

"Not really."

"Nevertheless, we can't be held responsible for you, can we, Mrs. Catermole?"

Mrs. Catermole agreed that they definitely had to turn the boat around. I tried to explain that this was no good for us. I said, "We're on kind of a mission. We're looking for something and we haven't found it yet. We've got to keep on down the river."

"I'm afraid that won't be possible. We can't be responsible for you. We have to take you back to wherever it is you came from."

Tommy-Lee said that the whole conversation was

stressing him out and went to find the toilet. Professor Umbridge had decided she wanted a proper look at our faces. She pulled a packet of wet wipes out of her handbag and tried to scrub off my face paint.

"I wouldn't do that if I were you," warned Koko.

"How dare you talk to me like that?"

"How dare you talk to *us* like that!" growled Koko. "We don't go to your school. We're outside your jurisdiction."

"Exactly," said Professor Umbridge. "That's why you're going right back where you belong."

"Why are you picking on us anyway?" said Koko. "Why don't you tell THEM to take off their costumes?!" She jabbed a finger at the penguins. Mrs. Catermole looked really confused. "But surely they're real penguins?" she said.

"Oh," said Koko. "So I suppose they're outside your jurisdiction too! I suppose you're going to take them all the way back to the South Pole!"

Before she had time to explain . . .

BANG . . . A door smashed open behind her.

THUMP . . . Something massive stomped onto the deck.

"Oh. My. Days." Teacher Darth Vader looked Tommy-Lee in the face. The face was no longer painted.

The face was Angry. And green.

"Get. Away. From. My. Penguins!" roared Tommy-Lee, rushing toward them.

Pirates of the Caribbean kid more or less jumped over the side of the boat. It was only his lack of jumping skills that saved him from ending up in the river.

"What is it?" yelled Professor Umbridge, dropping her handbag so she could point at Tommy-Lee more angrily. The penguins went for her handbag, which made everything worse.

I did try to calm everyone down. I said that there was nothing to be scared of, but no one seemed to take any notice. Some people screamed about Tommy-Lee's face. Some people screamed about the penguins. Then they all screamed about Koko's face because she had scrubbed the paint off her cheeks with one of Professor Umbridge's wet wipes. It seemed daft for me to carry on being Spider-Man under the circumstances, so I washed off my face paint. Then everyone screamed at my face too.

"Do not be afraid," I said, trying to make them feel better. "We're not sick," I shouted.

But Koko shouted louder. And she shouted something different. "Mrs. Catermole is right. Turn this boat around right now," she shouted, "and no one will get hurt. You heard me. Turn the boat around. I'm counting . . ."

"What are you doing?" I hissed. "You can't hijack a school trip."

"They're scared already," she said with a shrug. "We might as well give them something to be scared about. Trust me. I know where we're going—they'll cheer up once we've saved London."

Batman Drops In!

*E*veryone slid down in their seats as though the boat had made an emergency stop. But it hadn't stopped. It lurched forward, then rocked sideways. All around us the water was churning and boiling as if some massive deep-sea creature was about to surface. The school party—pupils and teachers—screamed in terror. The penguins ran around in circles, bumped into one another, fell over, and rolled around the deck.

"This is it!" whooped Tommy-Lee. "Green. Is. For. Gooooo!"

We gripped the sides of the boat and looked down into the waves. We should have looked up into the sky.

A pair of police helicopters was thundering toward us, flying so low that the wind from their rotor blades whipped the water into foam. So that's why the boat was rocking. And that's why the penguins were scared.

A helicopter dangled over our heads like a massive metal insect. A voice boomed like a bomb, "Cut your engines." The boat's engine coughed and died. The helicopter sounded louder than ever. One of its doors opened, quick as a sting. A bright-yellow cable tumbled out, attached to the helicopter door at the top. The other end clunked onto the deck. A dark figure slid down the cable toward us, wearing a belt that bristled with gadgets.

"Batman!" whooped Tommy-Lee.

"Police!" yelled the figure—who turned out to be the Policewoman with the Loudest Voice in the World—as her massive boots hit the deck. By now other cables had been thrown from the helicopter. Police were dropping onto the deck like water bombs in a water fight.

"Police!" cried Koko, clapping her hands. "Exactly who we wanted to talk to. They'll be really pleased to meet us."

I wasn't sure she was right about that.

"Why not?"

"They've got guns and they're pointing them at us."

Also they had us surrounded.

Tommy-Lee grabbed my elbow and whispered, "Are they going to shoot us?" I tried to put his mind at ease. I reminded him this was England. "The police don't shoot people in England."

"One move," said the Policewoman with the Loudest Voice in the World, "and we'll shoot."

SURROUNDED AND OUTGUNNED, WILL THE LITTLE GREEN MEN SURRENDER?

*A*ll that stood between us and a dozen police pistols was a trio of nervous penguins. Gun barrels were poised like snakes about to strike. It took them forever to take aim. During that forever my 200 percent brain filled up with pictures again. . . .

I saw Teacher Darth Vader and Professor Umbridge sneaking all their pupils around the back of the wheelhouse. We hadn't noticed it at the time because we were all so excited about the police swinging down on their ropes.

The three of us stood alone with the police at the back

of the boat, while they were all herded together out of sight at the front.

I saw the strange, frightening stuff that had been happening—helicopters, guns, police, crowds, and London in a state of panic as wild animals rampaged and Chaos ruled the streets. Pictures of people swearing they'd seen alien creatures . . . Little Green Men . . . just like in a comic.

Other people laughing at these people and saying they must have been drunk.

Drunk people sobering up, looking on their phones, and finding PHOTOGRAPHS of themselves posing with Little Green Men!!!

A news report saying that the Little Green Men have broken into BUCKINGHAM PALACE!!!! And tried to steal the royal baby!!!!

In all these pictures I could clearly see the Little Green Men.

And the Little Green Men were us.

We were little (well, I was little).

We were wearing weird clothes (hypoallergenic pajamas).

And we were green.

■ ■ ■

Suddenly everything made sense. . . .

"Get back!" bawled Loud Policewoman. Koko was coming toward her. "Keep your hands out of your pockets!" Koko was trying to find a Green Knights business card to give to her.

"Okay, okay!" soothed Koko, backing toward me and Tommy-Lee. "What's the matter with them? What are they scared of?"

"Aliens," I whispered. "They're scared of aliens."

"Yeah, but we can help with that."

"They think we ARE the aliens."

"What?! Why?! We're—"

"We're green, we have superpowers, and we have kidnapped the Hackney Free Year Eight Thames History Project."

In every story there are Heroes and Villains. If you don't decide which you are, someone else will decide for you. London had decided that we were the villains. And now London was out to get us.

"Can't we just explain?"

"Explain that we kidnapped a school and set hippos and wolves loose all over London?" My 200 percent brain had already figured out that right now it would be safer to let them carry on thinking we were aliens.

I said, very slowly, "We. Come. In. Peace."

"What?! No, we don't," hissed Tommy-Lee. "We come here for a fight. Don't you remember?"

The Loudest Policewoman in the World pulled back the safety catch on her gun.

"We honestly do come in peace," I said, "but we also have an invisible deadly weapon against which your puny guns are useless. If you fire, we might well annihilate all of London."

"You're lying," said the policewoman.

"Maybe," I admitted, "but then again, maybe not."

A policeman with a mustache the size of a small dog came over and said, "We need a risk assessment."

"What?"

"We can't put London at risk. No matter how remote that risk may seem to be." He looked us in the eye and spoke very slowly, which made his small-dog mustache look like it was barking. "What. Is. It. You. Want. With. Us?"

Before my 200 percent brain could think of exactly the right words, Tommy-Lee said, "Snack-a-Jacks."

"I told you to let me do the talking," I hissed.

But before I could say anything else, Koko said, "Take us to your leader!"

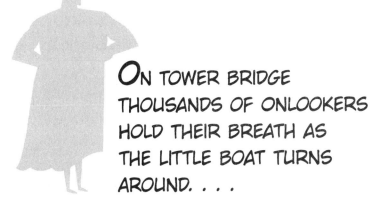

ON TOWER BRIDGE THOUSANDS OF ONLOOKERS HOLD THEIR BREATH AS THE LITTLE BOAT TURNS AROUND. . . .

The police made the captain turn the boat around and head upriver toward a long wooden jetty. We could see the blue, swirling lights of police cars and ambulances. The helicopter was circling overhead.

"Hey," whooped Tommy-Lee, "look! It's snowing!" Flurries of flakes whirled into the choppy brown water. "Is it going to stick?"

"We're not here to talk about the weather," snarled the Loud Policewoman. Even her snarl was louder than the boat's engines.

The boat chugged up alongside the jetty. I was going to climb off, but the loud policewoman yelled, "Freeze!" so loud that I almost fell into the river. "You don't move until we've got these kids off. That goes for you too!" She pointed her pistol at Peter the Penguin, who was waddling toward her.

"He's a penguin," I explained. "He doesn't speak English."

He was standing right up against her now, with his head in the air and his beak wide open.

"Keep him under control or he gets it!"

"He thinks your gun is a fish," explained Tommy-Lee. "He thinks you're offering it to him because you're holding it out. You could try putting it away."

She lowered the gun and started putting it away, but then suddenly jerked it back up again. "Oh no!" she snapped. "You don't fool me that easily!"

The other police were helping the schoolchildren off the front end of the boat. Some of them were crying. Which was a bit much, really. All we'd done was given them an extra-long trip on the river and shown them some penguins. The last one off the boat was a lanky girl in a Disney princess dress. When she got on the jetty she looked back at Tower Bridge, jumped up and down, waved to all the people there, and swished her princess skirts. The sound of applause came at us over the water like a flock of seagulls. Then there was cheering and car horns. People were so happy that these kids had been saved from our clutches. Honestly, you'd think we'd been planning to eat them.

The police kept us at the very end of the jetty while the Hackney Year Eight Thames History Project got on the bus and drove away. "Won't be long now and we'll get this sorted," said Officer Small-Dog Mustache. The mustache was sort of twitching, which I think meant he was smiling underneath it. "Do you need anything in the meantime?"

"Snack-a-Jacks," repeated Tommy-Lee.

"Salt and Vinegar," specified Koko.

"Yes, yes. I've already called Downing Street. The Snack-a-Jacks will be waiting for you. Though I'm not sure I stipulated the flavor." He took out his phone and walked around for a while, trying to find a signal.

The Loud Policewoman took a step closer to us. Koko had found a business card by now and offered her one. "If we can help you anytime," she said, "just give us a call."

"Get back."

"I'll just tuck it in your pocket," said Koko, and did.

"I'll take one," said the man next to her, without lowering his pistol. So she ducked under the barrel of his gun and popped one in his pocket too.

"You know," snarled the Policewoman with the Loudest Voice, "you kids are in a lot of trouble. A. Lot. Of trouble."

Tommy-Lee shuddered and moved closer to me. He hated being in trouble. I sat up straight and puffed out my chest. I tried to make it look like I was taking charge. Just to make Tommy-Lee feel a bit safer. "Trouble," I said, "is our best subject."

"Where did you hear that?" sniffed the Loudest Policewoman. "One of your kids' comics?"

"What makes you think we're kids? We're aliens. Little Green Men."

"Sound like kids to me."

"That could be because we're projecting a reality-distortion force field that makes you think we sound like kids even though we're not," said Koko.

"Could be. But I don't think so. I think the prime minister is going to take one look at you and put you all in jail."

She'd hardly finished speaking when the first splash came.

"What?! What's that?"

She looked up to see the penguins were jumping into the river. First one. Then another. Then the third, and then Tommy-Lee. He stepped backward off the

300

jetty, tucked his knees up to his chest, and bombed into the Thames.

"Tommy-Lee!" I called. And . . .

My teeth rattled in my head.

Incredible pain blazed through my chest.

Everything went black.

BAN WRONG FLAVOR SNACK-A-JACKS!!!

I must have more than slightly teleported, because when I woke up, I was lying on a big black leather couch in a room with dark wood panels and a window looking out into a garden. There was a massive polished table with a bowl of roses in the middle of it. Chairs with gold on. A huge flat-screen TV was fixed to the wall. Apart from the telly, everything was old-fashioned—proper old-fashioned light switches, and instead of a number pad, a proper lock on the door with a key sticking out of it. If they'd locked the isolation ward with one of those, I thought, we'd never have got out.

A man in a suit was sitting at the table, checking

his phone. He was wearing rubber gloves and a white mask over his mouth and nose. He hadn't noticed I was awake. Then someone groaned just beside me, and he looked up. Koko was curled up in a massive armchair. "Where are we?" she groaned again.

"Downing Street," said the man in the face mask. "Number Ten. How are you feeling?"

"Downing Street?" asked Koko. "That's excellent. Are you the prime minister?"

"I'm the personal assistant to his permanent private secretary. I was asked to give you these." He pointed to a silver tureen on the sideboard. Koko took the lid off. "Snack-a-Jacks," she said. "How did we get here? Last thing I remember, we were standing on a jetty in the Thames."

"Did we maybe," I asked, "teleport?"

"I'm afraid," said the personal assistant to the permanent private secretary, "we had to Taser you."

"Oh."

"The electric shock knocked you out and you were brought here. I hope you're feeling slightly better now."

"Yes," said Koko. "Feeling great. I love it here." She got up and sat herself down at the head of the table and stretched her legs. "You can bring the prime minister in now," she said. "I've got loads of ideas for him. These Snack-a-Jacks are caramel, by the way. We asked for Salt and Vinegar. I don't like caramel. Puffed rice is bland. It really needs that vinegar bite. I'm going to tell the prime minister he should ban caramel. Is he coming?"

"Soon. We just have a few formalities to run through first."

There are astonishing scenes here outside Downing Street as reporters and members of the public fight for a glimpse of the so-called aliens. An official government car pulled up to the door of Number 10 just half an hour ago, and the suspected aliens were taken inside. They appeared to be unconscious. Also bright green.

Standing here on this historic pavement, one is bound to wonder if this house—this house that has seen wars begin and end, empires rise and fall—has ever in all its long years witnessed scenes as strange as the scenes it will witness today as the prime minister of the United Kingdom opens talks with what may be two alien life-forms. . . .

*T*OP SECRET MEETING . . .

The "formalities" were X-rays, fingerprints, photographs, and being stared at. A lot. The people doing the x-raying, photographing, and staring were in white overalls, white boots, white rubber gloves, and face masks. You couldn't tell if they were men, women, or ghosts.

"About these Snack-a-Jacks," said Koko to one of them. "They're the wrong flavor."

"We're not waiters," said one of the mask people. "We're top government scientists. We're here to give you blood tests."

Tommy-Lee is not going to like that, I thought. Which was when I remembered that Tommy-Lee had swum away.

"Where's Tommy-Lee? Did you catch him? Be careful with him. He's not as confident as he seems."

"One of your number is still at large. Roll up your sleeve, please. Blood test."

I don't mind blood tests. I've got certificates to prove it. But once these people knew we were just some inexplicably green children, we'd be back eating quinoa in Junior Isolation before you could say "nut allergy."

"We haven't agreed to blood tests," I said.

"You didn't agree to being Tasered. Hackney Free School Year Eight Thames History Project didn't agree to being kidnapped. Some things happen whether you agree to them or not. We need to take blood samples in order to prove to the general public that you're human."

"Why do we have to prove we're human? No one else does."

"No one else is bright green. No one else goes around saying, 'We come in peace' or 'Take me to your leader.'"

By now Koko had figured out what I was trying to do. "What if we're not human?" she said. "What if our blood is full of alien antibodies that could jump out and spread previously unknown and incurable diseases all over the planet, killing everyone on Earth in a single weekend, starting with you?"

The top government scientist seemed flustered. She made a phone call, then said she was going to do a risk assessment.

A few minutes later a man in a dressing gown came in with another silver bowl of Snack-a-Jacks. "Salt and Vinegar," he said, "as requested." He kept sniffing and blowing his nose. "I've got Killer Kittens; you'd better keep back."

"I know you from somewhere," said Koko. "Are you from the telly?"

"I'm the prime minister," said the man. "I'm on the news quite a lot. You're sitting in my chair."

"Oh," said Koko. "Cool." She didn't move. "I'm so excited to meet you. I've got loads of ideas about how to make this into a better country."

"Really?" The prime minister sniffed into his handkerchief.

"Are you sure you're not on some other show as well, by the way? Something funny? Like a funny quiz show?"

"No. I'm not on a funny quiz show. I just run the country."

Koko started to outline her ideas about the price

of sweets in cinemas, also about Peace and Harmony. "See, people," she said, "are all different colors. And this causes friction. Take me and Rory and Tommy-Lee, we were different colors too. Chinese, pinkish white, kind of brown. But then we all went green. I was thinking . . . what if everyone in the world went green like us? Then there'd be no more fighting about who's the best, would there? If everyone was the same color—namely green—there would be Peace and Harmony across the World."

"Excuse me," said the prime minister, putting a hand in the air to tell her stop. He called the government scientist over. "You were worried," he said, "that these creatures might really be aliens?"

"We have to prepare for every possibility, Prime Minister."

"You didn't notice that that that one"—he pointed at Koko—"has a remarkable command of the English language?"

"I can explain that," said Koko. "I've been having lessons."

"And," added the prime minister, "that the other one has a Birmingham accent?"

"How do you know," I said, "that there's no Birmingham on Mars?"

"Is that where you're claiming your home is? Mars?"

"We're not claiming to be from anywhere," I said.

"Where do you think the other one is? Your friend. Might he have gone home?"

Home.

I hadn't been home for so long. It took all 200 percent of my enhanced brain to stop me drifting off into thoughts of Spam, Dad's Rocket Chili Sauce, and Perry Barr Millennium Center. "No," I said, "he can't have gone home. Home is too far away. He doesn't know the way. He's not good with finding his way and things like that."

"Never mind. I'm sure the police will find him."

Of all the strange things that had happened in the last few weeks, the very strangest was realizing that at that moment I was really worried about Tommy-Lee. "He's got a nut allergy," I said. "Tell them if they find him, they mustn't give him anything with nuts. Or even traces of nuts. Not even Wagon Wheels."

The prime minister pulled Koko's chair out so she had to stand up, then sat down in it himself. He pointed to a chair farther down the table where she could sit. He was taking charge. "You two," he said, "have a problem. There are people outside this building who believe that you are aliens. Aliens who threatened the royal baby with a gun."

"We did not!" protested Koko.

"We did slightly point at it with a gun," I admitted, "which may have been misinterpreted as a threat."

The prime minister went on, "Some of the people outside—the nice ones—think that if you really are aliens, I should put you in a zoo. The others—the less nice ones—think I should dissect you in the name of science."

"It's illegal to dissect people without their permission," said Koko. "Even in the name of science."

"It's illegal to dissect people," admitted the prime minister. "But are hostile baby-threatening aliens people? The law is a lot fuzzier about dissecting hostile aliens." He munched a Snack-a-Jack. "The point is, this country—which I'm in charge of—is in a mess. There's this moggy virus. I may have to cancel Christmas. The only inhabitant of this building that the public has any time for is the cat, and I had to have him put down. That's before we even mention global warming and the Middle East. Frankly, I have better things to do with my time than sitting around eating rice cakes with you."

"Snack-a-Jacks," said Koko. "Not rice cakes. No wonder the country's in a mess if the prime minister can't even tell the difference between a Snack-a-Jack and a rice cake."

"But I do know the difference between an alien invader and a funny-colored Brummie," said the prime minister, raising one eyebrow at me. "So let's do some blood tests so that I can reassure the nation."

"Does it have to be a blood test?" asked Koko. "We have had loads of blood tests. I'm surprised we've got any blood left. Could we have X-rays? We like seeing our own skeletons."

"The nation," said the prime minister, "will not be reassured by skeletons."

"We have really green wee," I said. "Is that any use?"

The prime minister didn't seem keen. "The nation," he said, "really wants your blood. Look . . ."

He turned on the TV. Twenty-four-hour news showed crowds of journalists with microphones and cameras swarming around Downing Street. They were talking about all the "inexplicable crimes" we had committed.

"Did you really steal a bin lorry?" asked the prime minister.

"We didn't steal it. We moved it."

"And emptied it over someone's car?"

"That was a misunderstanding. I misunderstood the controls."

"But why were you driving a bin lorry in the first place?"

If you had to explain stealing a bin lorry, where would you begin? I began with me turning up at Handsworth Academy and finding out I was the smallest and that the biggest was also the meanest. "Then when I turned green, I didn't think I was sick. For the first time in my whole life it didn't matter that I was small. I felt huge. I thought I was astounding. My brain was enhanced. I could slightly teleport. Tommy-Lee stopped pushing me around."

"And my brain," said Koko, "filled up with all these great ideas about how to make the country a better place."

"So you thought you'd get revenge on all the people who'd made you feel small? You thought you would bully London?"

"No!!! We thought we were trying to do good things. I thought we were like the Green Hornet or the Hulk or the Green Lantern. We thought we were heroes."

"I thought we could rule the world," said Koko. "I still think I'd be good at it. I've got a great idea for how to stop wars, for instance, and one about—"

"Who's the Green Lantern?"

"He was part of the Green Lantern Corps. Their job was to spread peace through the whole universe. We thought we could do something good. But it turned out wrong."

"I know the feeling." The prime minister sighed. "I became a politician to make the world a better place. Now it looks as if I'm going to be the first British head of government since Oliver Cromwell to pass a law against Christmas." He blew his nose.

"You try to do the right thing, but it comes out wrong. Like when I gave Tommy-Lee a biscuit and he turned out to have a nut allergy. Do we have to go back to the hospital?"

"We're not even sick," said Koko, "so why should we be in bed? You're the one who's ill. Why don't you go to bed and let us run the country for a bit?"

"Is the hospital that bad?" asked the prime minister.

"They make you eat quinoa," I said.

"I actually quite like quinoa. It's better than these rice things. In fact, I might order a bowl of quinoa now." But before he could think any more about catering, the door banged open. A chubby woman came in, plonked an armful of folders on the table, picked up the TV remote, and turned the TV off. Without glancing at us, she said, "Main post office. Central London.

Killer Kittens cluster. Chaps who sort the mail—nearly all got the virus."

"What does that mean?" asked the prime minister.

"It means no Christmas cards. No parcels either. But it also means that nearly everyone who has had mail in the last few days is going to catch it too. The virus has gone viral. Literally. By post. And you know what that means? It means most of London. In bed. With twelve shopping days to the big day. Are they," she said, pointing at us, "the aliens?"

"Rory Rooney," said the prime minister, "and Koko Kwok, meet the home secretary."

Koko explained that the home secretary isn't really a secretary at all and has nothing to do with homes.

"What an unusually politically aware little girl," said the home secretary. "Politically aware. And bright green."

"You're really in charge," said Koko, "of locking people up. I'd be so good at that. I can think of loads of people that should be locked up. But you probably want to lock us up."

"I should think so," said the home secretary. "Emptying the zoo, kidnapping half a school . . . Why aren't you languishing in chains as we speak?"

Some more important people came in. One of them was the lord chancellor—a fat bloke with very red hair. I forget who the others were. Only that they were very serious, except the lord chancellor, who winked at us. The prime minister said this was a Top Secret meeting—strictly off the record. No one should take any notes. There was a pad and a pen in front of each minister, but when he said this, they all pushed them into the middle of the table.

"What about a few selfies, though?" asked Koko. "This is my first cabinet meeting. I'm really excited."

"No," said the PM. "In fact, could you all please leave your mobile phones on the desk outside."

They all sat at the far end of the table in case we were contagious. Every now and then, one of them would give us a dark look, just like Ms. Stressley had. Except for the chancellor of the exchequer, who fell asleep.

The prime minister asked for any suggestions.

Koko's hand shot up.

"Not you," said the prime minister. "You're the problem we're trying to solve."

"The problem is often the solution seen from a different point of view," said Koko.

"That doesn't make any sense," said the PM.

At the time I agreed with him, but in the end she turned out to be right.

"The whole nation is in a state of panic," said the defense secretary. "We should go out and show them that it's all a fuss over nothing. Just some naughty little children. It would be in the National Interest if we just took them outside and fed them to the press."

"Just to be clear," said the prime minister, "that they're not naughty. It was all a bit of a misunderstanding." It was kind of him to stick up for us like that. He probably did it because he knew what it was like to be misunderstood.

The most serious-looking of the serious-looking people coughed. "Has the prime minister," he asked, "considered the implications of this for the reputation of our security services?"

"Not really," admitted the prime minister, grabbing another Snack-a-Jack. "I've been ill, you know."

"Panic has swept London. The Royal Family has been threatened. There has been traffic chaos. . . . Are we happy to admit that two little kids could do that to our capital city?"

"There were three, in fact," mumbled the prime minister through his cracker, "and there's no need to keep stressing how little they are. There's nothing wrong with being little. Einstein was little."

"Even taking into account their height, it will be a grave embarrassment for the government, and the police will be a laughingstock."

"It is actually pretty funny when you think about it," chuckled the prime minister. The chancellor of the exchequer actually snorted—possibly a laugh, possibly a snore.

"What about," said the home secretary, "if we say they ARE aliens and then we send them into space? Wave them off. Have a good-bye party. I think people would like that. You'd like it, wouldn't you, Rory?" I got the feeling that the home secretary was not very concerned about my safety.

Luckily, the education secretary was. "When people find out what these children did," she said, "they will most likely want to see them suffer."

"So we have to tell the public it was just a childish prank," said the prime minister, "but we have to avoid saying which children, in case people want to kill them."

"What about," whooped Koko, "instead of saying we are children, why don't you say we are terrorists disguised as children? And now you've caught us and there's nothing to worry about. Then you look good and we can just sneak off."

"That just might work!" said the culture secretary.

"What are you talking about!?" said the prime minister. "How can anyone disguise themselves as a child?! You can't make yourself smaller, can you?"

"Small terrorists, dressed up as children? Trained-monkey terrorists?" suggested the culture secretary. Everyone shook their heads. "Well, have you got a better idea?" he snapped.

"Anyone fancy a bowl of quinoa?" asked the prime minister. Why would anyone fancy a bowl of quinoa? "I think I have to go out and admit that three children fooled the nation. Then say that we can't reveal who those children are. Because they're so small. Rory is very young. I'll say that the amount of ridicule and anger that people will show those children would be too much to bear, so they'll be under police protection. All you two have to do is keep quiet and keep out of sight until this is all over. As long as no one discovers your true identity, then we can keep you safe."

All this talk about secret identities was bringing back my own feelings of Superness.

A man, young and breathless and wearing a suit, came in, looked at the prime minister, said, "Sorry, sorry," then looked at the telly and said, "Who's got the control?"

"Of the nation?" asked the prime minister. "I have,

of course. I resent the implication that—"

"For the television. The remote thingy."

"Television! Not now, Tristram. We're having a meeting!"

"You have to see this."

Koko found the remote control behind one of the cushions of the big couch. "I've got it, everyone," she said. "Panic over." She made it sound like she had saved Christmas.

Tristram flicked through the channels. "There," he said, stopping on a picture of London's tallest building. The Shard. Three hundred meters high. Seventy-two stories. A giant splinter stuck in the sky.

"Why are we looking at the Shard?" asked the prime minister.

"Listen," said Tristram. "And watch."

He turned up the volume. A reporter was talking about how people all over London had seen the aliens. Tweets scrolled across the bottom of the screen. . . .

Big, angry, dripping wet, accompanied by penguins #scaryaliens

Penguins on the South Bank—lovely. Big wet smelly green creature with them—not so much #scaryaliens

In our car when Bang . . . the alien walked over our car roof like Godzilla. Tried to run it down but foiled by penguins #scaryaliens

They were talking about Tommy-Lee. "They're talking about Tommy-Lee," I whispered to Koko.

"I know."

"Sightings," said the reporter, "are coming in from all over London." He played a conversation from a radio phone-in. . . .

"I got a photo of him, Chris, on my phone. I nearly lost my life. Opened the back door and there he was on my front step, drinking the milk straight from the bottle. He looked right at me. Like he wanted to speak. He's green all over, and I think he's got three eyes. One in the middle of his forehead."

"Did you speak to him?"

"I did not, Chris. I slammed the door right shut. I took a peep at him through the little peephole in my front door. He didn't try to break the door down, I'll give him that. I was terrified, though. I thought the smell of fish off him might be some kind of nerve gas that would make you do his will or whatever."

"All afternoon," went on the reporter, "the police have pursued the creature across London. Their efforts have been frustrated by the many false alarms. There's no way it could have been in central London one moment, then ten miles away in Brixton the next. Unless, of course, it can teleport. But now the chase is over. Now we have this. . . ." The reporter pointed to the Shard. The camera zoomed up to the roof. It was so high above the Thames, there was a little scarf of cloud around the top. Sticking up out of the cloud—like the legs of a great magical bird—was a bright-yellow crane. You could see the cabin where the driver sat, and you could see its great steel arm reaching out across the river. You could also see, working their way along it, the big, bulky shape of Tommy-Lee Komissky and three wobbly black dots that must be his penguins.

Shift to a clip on YouTube—showing two green children upending a dumper truck full of rubbish onto a parked car. Someone had filmed this with their phone. It already had ten million hits.

"Nine million of those hits," said the reporter, "came in the last hour. The world is watching London. Government sources refuse to confirm or deny the existence of Little Green Men, insisting that the creatures who have been spreading fear across the city are just three children with an unusual skin complaint. It's difficult to see, however, why or how a child with a skin complaint could climb London's tallest building and stand up there like King Kong. What does he want? Is it a prank? Or a serious threat to national security? How did he get up there? Surely he must have some kind of ability—a superpower, if you will—that no earthly child would have."

The prime minister looked at us. Everyone stared at us. Like they were trying to figure out if we really did have superpowers. "Couldn't the crane driver just go up ·there and make the crane swing around?" asked the culture secretary.

"What for?"

"Well, if it was pointing over the river instead of the road, at least he'd fall in the river instead of on the road."

The chancellor snorted a laugh. "That YouTube clip actually is very funny, you know. The face on the driver! Have you seen the one with the baby and the subtitles?"

"Would the chancellor please engage with the very serious predicament before us?" said the home secretary.

Exactly! I wanted to shout. How can you just sit there making jokes about Tommy-Lee?! He may be big, but he's still just a kid. What kind of government sits back and makes jokes while kids, or aliens for that matter, are dangling off the ends of cranes?

But before I could open my mouth, the 200 percent brain had already clicked into action. It had noted all the useful things about the room—the long table, the key in the door, the mobile phones on the desk in the hall. I sneaked one of the notepads from the middle of the table, scribbled on it, and passed the note to Koko.

We have to rescue Tommy-Lee.

Underneath she wrote, *You're kidding!! I'm not leaving these people to run the country by themselves. They need help. You go. I'm staying.*

If you get bullied at school, you learn to be inconspicuous. The best form of defense is not being noticed. Sometimes walking down the corridor with my big folder clutched to my chest, staying close to the wall, I was practically invisible.

I used those skills now.

Bit by bit I slid down in my chair until I was actually under the table.

I crawled along the floor, avoiding the feet of the

cabinet ministers, under the chair of the foreign secretary and out of the room. Once outside in the hall, I
reached around and took out the key, eased the door
shut, and locked them in.

The collected mobile phones of the cabinet ministers were all clunked together on a desk. It was easy
to spot the prime minister's. His screen saver was a
picture of him with one of his children. I went through
his address book until I found someone called Sam
with "Driver" after his name. I texted him: *Sam, come
around to the front. Do whatever Rory asks. PM.* I put
his phone in my pocket and headed for the front door
of Number 10.

*I*NVISIBLE BOY ADDRESSES THE NATION

There were hundreds of news cameras waiting out there. I knew that. The prime minister wanted to hide us away from them. I quite liked the idea of getting a permanent secret identity from the government, but the truth was I didn't want to hide from Trouble anymore. If I'd learned one thing, it was this—there's no point in hiding from Trouble. Trouble comes looking for you. Wherever you hide, Trouble will find you.

The prime minister had said he was worried that I would get ridiculed and laughed at. So? I've been laughed at most of my life. My whole class saw me turn green. My whole class saw me fall off the bus every night. I'm used to being laughed at. Laughed at doesn't worry me. I might be the smallest in my year, but I was big enough for this.

I opened the door. There was a lightning storm of flash light. I blinked. Hundreds of journalists held their microphones out over the crash barriers. I walked up to them. I sort of knew what I was going to say.

I was going to say something like "Sorry. It was all my fault. We're not aliens. We're just three kids. Now my friend's in trouble. Let me go and help him."

That's really, honestly what I was planning to say.

But when I got out there and saw all those microphones, all those cameras, my mind just changed. They all looked at me and then past me, at the open door of Number 10. They were waiting for the prime minister to come out. I went back and closed the door.

There wasn't going to be a prime minister.

There was just me.

Everyone went quiet.

Everyone was just a little bit nervous.

Everyone was just a little bit confused.

Everyone was thinking, If a person is standing on the doorstep of Number 10 Downing Street, that normally means that person is in charge of the nation.

"Who are you?" shouted the journalist with the biggest microphone. "What have you done with the prime minister?"

I could have answered, "I'm the smallest in my year. I've locked the prime minister in the cabinet room. Why not push me off a bus?"

I raised my hand. I appeared confident—just like it says in *Don't Be Scared, Be Prepared.* I said, "Don't be scared."

They all looked at one another. Nothing makes people more scared than being told not to be scared. Especially if the person telling them not to be scared is a possibly little green alien.

Some of them shouted out questions, but I raised my hand again. There was silence.

I said, "No one will get hurt."

Now they were really worried.

I looked up into the sky, as if I was expecting a delivery of secret super-weapons.

Someone shouted, "Are you from space?"

Someone else shouted, "No. He's from Birmingham."

"Where's the prime minister? Who's in charge?"

"Your prime minister," I said, "is quite safe." Then I added, "But . . ." just to see. They all went quiet. I couldn't actually think of a "but," though. In my pocket, the prime minister's phone buzzed. Out of the corner of my eye, I could see a glossy blue car sliding toward me in front of the crash barriers. Everyone was staring at me expectantly. It seemed rude not to say something, so I said, "People of Earth—stop pushing people off buses just because they're small. And just because a person is big, that doesn't mean they're not frightened sometimes." I didn't know I thought that until I said it. "And what does it matter if a person is green? We . . . I mean, you . . . are all human beings. Every one of you—tall or short, green or whatever—is useful. Be nice to each other. And"—the car was pulling up in front of me now—"don't try to follow me." I jumped in.

"Where to?" said Sam the Driver.

"Shard. As quick as you can."

Sam slipped the car into gear. Camera flashes glittered all around as we moved forward. Then the back door opened, and someone climbed in next to me.

How are you supposed to apologize to a prime minister who's caught you in the act of trying to steal his car after you've locked him in a room in his own house? The prime minister didn't even give me a chance to try. He just said, "To the Shard, Sam. And make it snappy."

Journalists were yelling and engines were roaring as we sped out of Downing Street. He didn't look at me, but he snarled out of the corner of his mouth, "I'm the prime-bloody-minister—did you really think I don't have my own key to my own cabinet room?" I couldn't think of anything to say. Police sirens swirled around us. I thought they were coming to arrest me. "Relax," said the prime minister. "I asked for a police escort. To speed things up. No one's going to put you in jail. Yet. Now, can I have my phone back, please?"

I finally thought of something to say. "You look smart." He was wearing a suit now. He'd still been in his dressing gown a few minutes ago.

"I put the suit on over my pajamas," he said. "It feels a bit lumpy, to be honest." There was a TV in the back of the front seat. He turned it on. I kind of screamed when I saw who was on there.

"Someone you know?" asked the prime minister.

"My geography teacher." Yes. It really was Ms. Stressley.

"This was when you were at school on Mars, I suppose?"

"No. Birmingham."

The television news people had already worked out who we were and where we came from. They were interviewing people who knew us, asking them what we were really like. Ms. Stressley said I was a problem child who was always seeking negative attention. "I'll give you one example. On a class trip, we went on a nature walk. Everyone else stuck to the path. Rory, on the other hand, threw himself in the river. This business of turning green is completely typical of him, I'm afraid." After her it was Kian and Jordan saying, "He was always a bit evil. He tried to kill our friend with a biscuit." Bonnie Crewe came on and said I was a loner who never spoke to anyone! As if anyone ever spoke to me! She also said I was a bit weird. "When he turned green—which was actually quite funny—he made us all think he was incurably ill and probably going to die. You know, to get sympathy."

I probably was sitting there with my mouth open in shock, because the prime minister said, "Don't worry about it. People say nasty things about me too." Then he said, "So why is your mate on top of the Shard? And how are we going to get him down?"

I looked out of the window, pretending that I was thinking of a great plan. I pressed a button that I thought would open the window, but instead it made the backseat massage our bottoms.

"I get the feeling," sighed the PM, reaching over to turn it off, "that we are going to be winging it. Again."

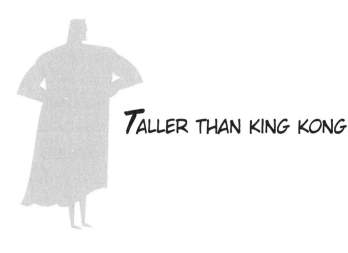

Taller than King Kong

The observation deck of the Shard is on the seventy-second floor. Until I saw the view from there, I thought twelve floors was high. Compared to seventy-two stories, twelve is a mushroom. Even without going near the windows, you know you're high up. The floor was moving around as though it couldn't get comfortable.

"Wow!" said the prime minister to the loads of police officers who were waiting for us. He didn't go over to them. He waited for them to come to him.

The police all stared at me.

"He's possibly contagious," said the prime minister, "so keep your distance. So am I, by the way. Killer Kittens." He sneezed.

The policeman in the fanciest uniform said, "If you could step over to the window, Prime Minister, I'll be able to show you the suspect."

"Do I have to go nearer to the window, Commissioner?" asked the prime minister. "I'm usually okay with heights, but this is . . . it gives me a bad feeling in the back of my knees."

"Me too, if I'm honest," said the commissioner. "Julie, binoculars, please."

Julie turned out to be the Policewoman with the Loudest Voice in the World. Only she didn't have a loud voice when she was talking to the prime minister. She was all, "There you go, Prime Minister, this is how you focus them. Great to meet you, by the way." She didn't say anything to me, not even, "Sorry about Tasering you."

At first when we all looked up, there was nothing to see but a thick gray cloud. "Looks like we're going to have more snow," said the prime minister.

"There!" shouted the commissioner. "See the crane. Look right at the end."

The prime minister swung the binoculars around to a hole in the cloud, then said, "Actually, I can't. Back of the knees again." Without looking at me, he handed me the binoculars and asked the commissioner what the plan was.

"We've been in touch with the crane driver—"

"Why *is* there a crane on top of the Shard? They're surely not trying to make it taller?"

"Installing a new aerial on the top, Prime Minister. Mobile phones."

"How do they get the crane up there?"

"I can find that out for you in due course, Prime Minister, but in regard to the possible alien at the end of the crane . . ."

I could see him now. Right at the far, thin end of the crane's arm stood Tommy-Lee, hands on hips, penguins at his side, their stabilizer-wings outstretched, all enjoying the view. For birds that can't fly, they certainly seemed happy being high up.

"We've sent for the crane driver," said the commissioner. "We were hoping that the crane arm was retractable—that we'd be able to wheel him in. But no. He can, however, swing the crane through forty-five degrees to the north."

"What for?"

"Then the end would be over the river. So when he falls, he'll fall into the water."

"You're the second person that's said that today. Why do we want him to fall down? Can't we get him off there?"

"Health and safety, sir. If he does fall, we don't want

him to fall on people. Just on fish."

Another man in uniform said, "Speaking of fish, the penguins—"

"Penguins aren't fish," said the prime minister, sounding confident for the first time.

"No, but fish made me think of penguins. And with regard to the penguins—"

"The penguins are not a priority."

"I think you'll find that the British public thinks they are," said the man in the uniform.

"This is Roger," said the commissioner. "He's from the RSPCA."

"Oh," said the prime minister, "great. But can we talk about the suspected alien? He has a name. It's . . ."

"Tommy-Lee," I said.

"Can we talk about Tommy-Lee? How are we going to get him down?"

"With respect, Prime Minister, suspected alien Tommy-Lee got himself out there, so presumably he can bring himself back in."

"The penguins, on the other hand," said Loud Julie, "were probably tricked into going up there."

"Very true," said RSPCA Roger.

"Just because Tommy-Lee can get INTO trouble," I said, "that doesn't mean he can get out of it again."

"We could shoot him down," suggested Julie. "Once he's over the river."

"Why would you want to do that?" asked the prime minister.

"Just an idea."

"It's not a good idea," said RSPCA Roger. "The penguins could be hurt by a stray bullet. Also be stressed. They're probably quite stressed as it is. . . ."

"I imagine Tommy-Lee is pretty stressed too," said the prime minister. "Can we get a helicopter close enough to rescue him?"

"The wind from the blades would blow him off the edge. Are we sure he wants to be rescued? He must have gone up there for a reason. I hesitate to put my men at risk for someone who doesn't want to be rescued."

"I'm pretty sure that if someone's clinging to a crane three-hundred-plus meters above London, they don't want to stay there forever. Have you tried talking to him? To find out what he wants."

"Too windy," said the commissioner. "We thought of a megaphone, but . . ."

"That would stress the penguins too."

". . . we could make ourselves heard, but we couldn't hear him. I've sent for a kind of directional microphone, but it'll take time. I can't think what else to do. Pigeon post?"

Then I remembered something. "He's got a phone," I said.

"A phone?!" said the prime minister. "Do you know his number?"

"Not by heart, but it's on his business cards."

"He has business cards?"

"Yes. And Koko gave one to that lady." I pointed at Loud Julie. Loud Julie went bright red. "I'm afraid I didn't keep that," she said. But as she said it I saw one of the other armed police pat his pockets. Of course. Koko had given business cards to everyone she could reach. The policeman pulled out the card. I took it. I said it was probably best if I called him. He'd feel happier talking to me. The prime minister rolled his eyes and handed me back his phone. So I rang Tommy-Lee from the prime minister's phone.

It was ringing. Roger from the RSPCA was watching Tommy-Lee through the binoculars. "He's moving. He's going to answer. The penguins are moving too."

"Hello?"

"Tommy-Lee? It's me, Rory."

"Rory—you've got to help me." His voice was

shivery. He sounded tired. Or maybe it was just a bad signal. Maybe that's why they were putting a new mast up there. I moved away a bit to see if it was any better.

"They want to help you. There's police and animal rescue and the prime minister even." I didn't mention that none of them had any idea how to help him.

"You come and help me now, or I'll come down and get you."

"That might be easier."

The line went quiet. The silence was terrible. I thought he'd fallen. I ran back onto the observation deck. The prime minister, the police, and the man from the RSPCA were still looking up at the crane. The prime minister was saying, "Are jet packs real? Could we send someone up on a jet pack to bring him down?" I knew then that they were never going to get Tommy-Lee down. I had to do it myself.

I slid out of the room, dialed the number again, and asked for directions. I didn't really need directions. If someone is fifteen stories higher up than you are, then the directions are obvious—just keep going up—using stairs, elevators, service ladders, whatever . . . but it was good to keep Tommy-Lee talking, and when I got to a metal door marked AUTHORIZED PERSONNEL ONLY. HARD HAT AREA. HARNESSES MUST BE WORN. TOKEN MUST BE LODGED

WITH FOREMAN, he remembered the code for the keypad. I typed it in. The door opened. Cold air punched me in the face. A white ladder went straight up in front of me into the clouds. I was at the foot of the crane. Top floor of the Shard. Ground floor of the Sky.

*W*HO CAN SAVE THEM NOW?!

*S*omething that looked like a dead bat was dangling right in front of my face. A safety harness. Attached to a long orange cable that I hoped was attached to something else at the far end. I couldn't be sure, though, because of the cloud. I strapped myself into the harness and started to climb. The metal rungs were freezing cold to touch. I almost slipped off on the first step. When I fell back, though, the orange cord tightened and yanked me up a little—as though someone was pulling me up from the other end. I kept climbing. As I climbed, the cord kept slackening and tightening. Sometimes I floated past two or three steps at a time. Sometimes I had to climb. After a while everything turned dull and the air was damp. I realized I was inside the cloud. I kept climbing and bouncing, floating and clambering.

Everything turned bright again. I looked up. It was like something from that story about the magic beans. At the top of the ladder there was a house, with a door like the giant's castle in the story. Of course. The crane driver's cab! This was the ladder that the crane driver used every day to get to work. Just thinking about him made me feel safer. Climbing up here wasn't an adventure for him. It was his walk to work. He probably had his sandwiches in his pocket. Maybe he had his headphones in. He probably had to do it in the rain, and the wind. Maybe it was still dark when he went up in the mornings. Maybe it was already dark when he came down at night. As I got higher, a great bird flew a lazy circle around the ladder, its wings barely moving. As it passed in front of me, I saw its wide, dark eye and its bright, curved beak. It looked like an eagle or something. Maybe the crane driver threw it one of his sandwiches every morning on his way to work. Maybe the crane driver was friends with the eagle.

Inside the cabin was everything a sky-high crane driver might need to make himself cozy. Newspaper.

Kettle. A pair of binoculars and a chart about birds of prey. A pair of gloves. A bottle with a wide neck and a rubber stopper—just like the ones we had to wee in in the hospital. So that's how crane drivers go to the toilet. There were baby wipes and one of those very excellent plastic things that warm your hands when you squeeze it. I settled down in the chair, took out the phone, and called Tommy-Lee.

"Tommy-Lee, I'm here. I'm in the cabin. Can you see me? I'm waving." I was probably a bit too relaxed. "Come over. There's biscuits."

"I can't."

"Why?"

"Something terrible is happening to me. You've got to come and get me."

"But . . ."

The tower crane is like a giant seesaw. Tommy-Lee was out at the far end. Behind me there was a kind of bridge to balance it all out. The cabin is right in the middle. But it's lower than the arm. To get out along the arm you have to climb onto the roof of the cabin. I kept the harness on. The harness was attached to the cabin. If I fell, I would just kind of bungee jump into the ladder or something. It wouldn't be the best way to spend the afternoon, but it might stop me being pavement jam.

The arm of the crane stretched out in front of me like a railway track. The buzzard (I knew now it was a buzzard because it was on the driver's chart) swept past me like it was getting a good look at its dinner. Tommy-Lee was crouching at the far end. Far away. Too far away. I tried shouting to him, but the words blew back in my face.

Just thinking about putting my foot on the arm of the crane made my brain light up like a Christmas tree. The first thing I saw in my mind was the road atlas and the sandwich box that we'd seen in the waiting room. They reminded me of my mum and dad.

Of course!

They *were* my mum and dad's. Mum and Dad had been there the whole time. They just weren't allowed to come and see us for medical reasons. Nurse Rock had lied to us. But then, what do you expect from a nemesis?!

The medical reason being that we were sick.

That was the second thing I saw. Really clearly.

I was not astounding.

Never had been.

Falling off a twelve-story building does not make

you astounding. Opening doors in your sleep—so what? Turning green like the Hulk—it's a virus.

All along, we had been sick—not super.

I'm not astounding.

I'm the youngest and smallest in my year.

There's nothing special about me.

And if there's nothing special about me, then what's the point of going to try and rescue Tommy-Lee? What can I do? Why should I do anything? What had Tommy-Lee ever done for me apart from push me off the bus and leave me lunchless?

I could hear him now, yelling at me. "Come on! COME HERE! COME HERE RIGHT NOW! OR YOU'LL BE SORRY!"

He was shouting at me just like he did at school. Only when he did it at school I used to be terrified. Today when he did it, I could hear that he was the one who was terrified.

I knew I couldn't leave him.

Why?

Why couldn't I leave him?

Because he was my friend.

When did that happen? How did it happen? How did I end up friends with Tommy-Lee?

Never mind. We were friends—that was the point.

Maybe if we weren't, I could have just climbed back down to the cabin and sat back and enjoyed the view. But he was my friend, so I put one foot on the girder.

Fear surged through my body like electricity. My fingers tingled.

My heart banged.

My brain went faster. Had there been anything in *Don't Be Scared, Be Prepared* about walking out on a high-rise crane? Nope. If anyone was going to write that paragraph, it would have to be me.

Fear felt exactly like a superpower.

Maybe fear is a superpower.

I put one foot on the metal strut. It felt so horrible that I put my other foot up there too. To keep it company. That felt worse, so I took a step. And another. And another. Stopping felt more frightening than moving. I was scared to look back. Scared to look down. So I just kept looking forward. And moving forward. My brain was whispering to me, saying stuff like "These metal struts are about the same width as our staircase back home. You can walk upstairs, so you can walk along this. What difference does height make?"

Just the difference between life and death.

Apart from that?

Maybe I wasn't astounding.

But I was doing an astounding thing.

Tommy-Lee was crouched down in a little ball, his hands clutching the girder under his feet. But as I got closer, I could see him uncurling. He let go of the girder. He started to stand up.

The penguins were watching me too. As I got nearer, they put their heads in the air, made a weird croaky sound, then came waddling straight for me. Maybe they thought I was going to attack Tommy-Lee. Maybe they were going to defend him by pushing me off. I couldn't make myself smaller so I'd be less threatening, or bigger to look more threatening. I know you're not supposed to look at a dog when it's angry with you. So I looked away from the penguins.

And where I looked was . . .

. . . down.

I thought that Time had stopped.

Up ahead of me was the hoist—the thing for lifting things. Under my feet a big grubby rug of cloud with a hole in the middle. Through the hole I could see the river. London. All of it, like when you look down from a plane. And all of it was still. When you looked down from the hospital roof you could see things moving—cars, buses, trains, boats, people. But below me nothing was moving.

I know now that I was just too high to see things moving. But just then I thought that Time had stopped. Completely.

Even the buzzard seemed to be stuck in the air. Its shadow spread on the top of the cloud like a stain.

I couldn't move.

Then Tommy-Lee called my name. I looked up. He was standing up, his hands straight down by his side like when he sleepwalked.

"Come on, Tommy-Lee. Take a step toward me. I'm wearing a safety harness. See? If we're together . . ."

"I can't."

"Why?"

"Look at my hands." He held his hands up. They were pinky-white. All except the fingertips. It was as though some invisible soap was washing the green off his hands. And his arms. And his face. My brain could nearly hear the thoughts chugging around in his brain. Well, one thought anyway. The thought was . . .

If I've stopped being green, then I've stopped being astounding.

■ ■ ■

"Tommy-Lee," I said, "don't worry about it. It's probably just the cold." It was really cold up there. "Everyone's hands turn a different color in the cold."

"Is my face still . . ."

His ears and nose were still green. But his forehead wasn't, or his cheeks or his chin. They were all back to the way they'd been when we were in school. I tried to say he was still a bit green, but he could see from my expression that it wasn't true. He quickly grabbed the crane.

"Now what am I going to do? When I came up here, I thought I could do anything. Now I can't do anything. I was green and now I'm ordinary. I'm going to die. And the penguins—they really trusted me, and now they're going to die too."

I thought about saying to him, "We never were astounding. It was all a mistake." But it didn't seem like the right moment. Instead I said, "Tommy-Lee, I'm still green, aren't I?"

"Yes."

"Really green?"

"Really green."

"So I'm still super, okay? I'm also wearing a safety harness. See? So if I do fall, we'll be okay twice over.

All you've got to do is take a few steps toward me."

"I can't."

"One step then. One step for now."

"Can't."

"Tommy-Lee, you've got to. The harness is at full stretch. I'd have to undo it if I was going to come closer."

"Okay. Just two steps."

"Take one for now. And another one in a minute." Tommy-Lee was holding on to the struts with his hands behind his back. Now he let go and took one step forward. "No hurry, Tommy-Lee."

"What do I do now?"

I didn't have a plan. I thought we might have to stay like this forever. But I had to say something. "I'm going to hold my hand out. All you have to do is reach it. Not from there, though. Take another step nearer first."

"You're not going to push me off?"

"What? Why would I do that?"

"I used to push you off the bus."

"This is not quite the same thing."

"I'm sorry I pushed you off the bus."

"I'll push you off the bus when we're back home."

"Okay. That's fair."

"Keep coming. You're nearly there."

He took a step. Reached his hand toward me. I grabbed it.

"Thanks, Rory." He squeezed my hand. "Thanks, and I'm sorry." He squeezed my hand a bit harder. Like he really, really meant it.

"I really, really mean it," he said. "Thanks, and sorry."

"Yeah, but don't squeeze my hand so hard. It hurts."

"Sorry." He let go.

He let go too quickly.

His hand swung back behind him.

He lost his balance.

He fell.

That's when I discovered that I really could teleport.

My eyes were scrunched up like a pair of old paper bags. When I opened them, Tommy-Lee's face was in my face. I had my arms around him. I was in midair. But I wasn't falling.

I'd teleported. I'd grabbed him.

We were dangling from the crane. I could hardly breathe. Something was tightening around my chest, squeezing the breath out of me. It was the harness. It was twisted around one of the metal struts. It was trying to reel me back in.

I turned my head to catch my breath. I saw what was underneath us.

"Tommy-Lee," I whispered, "I'm going to let go of you."

"Nooooo!!!! Don't!"

"It's okay. You have to trust me."

"But I don't trust you."

We were dangling right above the crane's huge hoist. The bit where they put the stuff they wanted to lift. It was big—like a piece of floor in the sky. It was just a meter or so below us.

"I'm going to let you go. You're going to be all right," I said.

I let go.

But Tommy-Lee didn't let go. He slipped a bit; then he grabbed me round the waist and squeezed so tight I could hardly breathe.

"Tommy-Lee, let go. Please. Reach down with your toes. Feel." He let go. But grabbed again.

My knees this time.

Then he let go again and dropped onto the hoist. He landed standing up and really steady. Like a cat. Kickboxing really teaches you to fall properly.

"Hey, this is great!" shouted Tommy-Lee.

I wasn't listening.

The minute he had let go, the cable pulled me up again. I didn't want to go up. I wanted to go down. Before, I'd been just above the hoist. The hoist was all I could see. Now I was dangling three or four meters above it, and I could see tiny London. I didn't want to see tiny London.

The 200 percent brain had already made its decision.

My hands were doing something I didn't want to think about.

They were snapping me out of my safety harness.

I stared at the hoist. I tried not to think. I tried to leave it all to my hands.

I dropped.

I landed on top of Tommy-Lee. He fell, but neatly. We lay there on our backs, looking up at the struts and oily chains of the crane. Penguins plopped around us like ripe black fruit. I held my hand up in the air. It was still bright, broccoli green against the blue, blue sky. Tommy-Lee was still laughing his head off. "Thanks, mate," he said, and shoved me in the shoulder.

"Anytime," I said, and pushed him back. "If they can't rescue you when you're dangling from a crane three hundred meters above London, well, what are friends for?"

"Ahhh." He shoved me again.

Something was sticking in my bum. The prime minister's phone was in my back pocket. "I could call," I said, browsing through his contacts, "the president of the U.S.A. and ask him to get them to lower it down."

"I'm not in any hurry," said Tommy-Lee, stretching out with his arms behind his head. "Are you?"

"Not really."

The phone quacked like a duck being trodden on. I thought this was a pretty immature ringtone for a prime minister. The penguins croaked in reply.

"It's the mayor of London." I declined the call. As soon as I did, the home secretary rang. Declined that. Then the prime minister's mum. Declined that. I turned the phone off after that.

I was worried the ringtone was stressing the penguins.

The hoist jolted. One link of its chain clicked through the pulley. Then another and another. Down on the observation deck, they must have been watching our every move through their binoculars. Now they were lowering us down. It takes a long time to lower a hoist eighty-odd stories. We watched the links of the chain pass through the pulleys one by one like the words in a story. High above us, a pair of helicopters was buzzing around like fat summer bees.

"I'm not going to move," said Tommy-Lee, "until we're on the ground."

"Me neither. I'm not even going to think about the police or the prime minister or the hospital or all the millions of people who probably want to put us in jail. I'm going to just lie here and forget about them all. This is probably what Spider-Man does when he wants a break. He probably swings up to somewhere no one can get him and enjoys the view." The view! What were we doing just looking up at the sky?! Sky looks the same wherever you are. But the city looks different from very high up. "Tommy-Lee," I said, "remember what Koko said. What's the point of going all the way up if you don't look down?" I rolled onto my belly. Then I carefully shuffled to the edge and looked over. We were in the cloud. I couldn't see a single thing. Then we came through the cloud, like coming through a curtain. Tiny London was completely still and silent.

"What's that shiny thing?" asked Tommy-Lee, shuffling over to join me.

"That's the Thames, that you jumped into."

"It looks cleaner from up here." It looked like a glitter-pen scribble. "I can't even swim."

"What? You jumped in a river when you knew you couldn't swim?"

"I just wanted to get away from the police. Whenever I'm in trouble with the police, it gives my mum anger-management issues."

"What? You mean she hits you?"

"No. Course not. She hits the police. I thought if I jumped in the river, I'd probably be suddenly able to swim, in a superheroey kind of way."

"And could you?"

"No. I sank, but I grabbed a penguin. I hid under that jetty for ages. Then I got out of the water, and I was just completely lost. I thought I'd know where to go and what to do, but I was completely lost and wet and smelly with mud and everyone was laughing at me. And I didn't feel a bit super or astounding. I felt like an idiot. Then I saw this building and thought, I'll get up on top of there and then everyone will see. That'll show them not to laugh at me. You had to put thirty pounds in a ticket machine to get inside, and I had exactly thirty pounds from when we robbed the bank. Somehow that made up my mind. But once I got up there, I realized it was so high up that no one would even see me. Not even birds, really."

"They saw," I said. We were passing the observation

deck. The prime minister, Loud Julie, the RSPCA Roger, they were all still standing there, watching us go by. They were so near that we could see the worried expressions on their faces. We waved to let them know we were all right.

"We weren't really superheroes at all, were we?" said Tommy-Lee, looking at his white arms and hands.

"What are you talking about!? I just did a daring rescue of you. And look where we are. I don't remember Spider-Man ever getting this high up." I tried to get up to do a superhero pose, but it was like standing up in a rowing boat. The hoist tilted and the penguins scuttled around in fright. So I lay down again and we both looked over the edge.

I could just feel the slightest bit of warmth from the winter sun on the back of my neck.

"Hey," I said, "we're green. Maybe we can photosynthesize?"

"What?"

"It's the green in their leaves that lets plants feed on sunlight. The sun comes in through the leaf and it hits this stuff called chlorophyll, which makes it into oxygen. They eat sunlight. Maybe we can eat sunlight."

So we gave it a go. We lay there waiting for the sun to fill us up, and I thought about the sun shining on the ocean and filling all the plankton and on the forests and the grasslands.

"Is this working for you?" asked Tommy-Lee. "Is the sun feeding you?"

I was thinking how all the grasslands and the forests and the plankton were filling the air with oxygen. And everyone breathing the oxygen and going about their business and how all of that could only happen because some things were green. So I said, "Yes. Yes, it is."

"Well, it's not feeding me," said Tommy-Lee. "I'm starving."

Then there came a moment when suddenly you could see things moving. Cars, a train, boats on the river. As though the city had been stopped by some kind of freeze ray and now had come back to life and was running to catch up with itself. And my 200 percent brain saw how much of that running was done by heroes—by firefighters putting out fires, ambulances chasing through traffic, doctors and nurses saving lives, bin men emptying smelly bins, mums and dads looking after their kids, young people looking after old people, old people helping young people. Heroes were everywhere. When you thought about it, a city was nothing but heroes. Heroism is everywhere. It's the petrol that makes a city go. A few minutes later we could hear noises—ships' horns, traffic, and last of all, cheers. It turned out that our dramatic descent was being streamed live on the internet. People had been tweeting and texting about us, and now there were hundreds of people jammed onto the pavement waiting to see us land. When they could see our faces, they cheered. Tommy-Lee leaned right out so he could see better. "Tommy-Lee, don't!"

"We're almost on the ground," he said.

"We're still five floors up. It doesn't look much to us. But it'd be enough to smash us to pieces."

But he jumped up and struck his superhero pose— arms on his hips and his face in the air. I got up and did the same. My stance wasn't as good because I'd only had that one lesson, but the two of us standing together looked pretty strong, I think. Down below there were a lot of police. We weren't sure if they were there to protect us from our admirers or to throw us in jail. But just then we didn't care.

We too busy being Astounding.

If this really was a comic, that would be the last picture— me and Tommy-Lee dangling over London. And everyone talking and tweeting and texting about us. They never really stopped talking about us, by the way. There's a clip on YouTube of us coming down on that hoist, and it's got a gazillion million hits or something. The whole bin-lorry incident has had loads of hits too. Also clips of us dancing with the chickens in the Bank. There's also a crazy film claiming that we really were aliens and proving it by showing photos of the prime minister pushing through the crowd of VIPs to make sure he was the first to talk to us. The crazy film says he was telling us not to tell anyone we were aliens in case it created fear and a possible breakdown of Law and Order. In fact, he really did push through the crowd to be first to speak to us, but what he said was "Can I have my phone back now? You know, just in case the nation's at war or something. Thank you."

I said, "Sure. You've got a load of missed calls, by the way, from your mum."

Meanwhile in a zoo on the far side of town . . .

So loads of people have seen our faces. In fact, probably nearly everyone in the world saw us that day. But even though this was all just a few months ago, no one recognizes us anymore. Because we've both changed so much already. I've had a growth spurt, probably thanks to the fact that Tommy-Lee no longer steals my sandwiches so I'm finally getting some nutrition. He sometimes even lets me share his—actually he doesn't, but he sometimes makes Kian and Jordan give me some of theirs. I'm still the smallest in the class, but I'm not THAT small. Tommy-Lee's got even bigger, but mostly around the shoulders. He's also got stubbly, and his voice now sounds like someone raking cement.

Also I'm not green. Not anymore.

Ciara was with me when my color started to fade. She was disappointed. "I was hoping you were going to grow gills and maybe webbed feet."

I was sort of disappointed too. I liked being the only green boy on Earth. Now I'm just the same as I was before. On the outside. On the inside everything is different.

Even when we went back to London Zoo to meet up with Koko and visit Tommy-Lee's penguins, no one recognized us. That was the first time we'd seen Koko since 10 Downing Street. The sweets kiosk that lost the fight with the hippo had been rebuilt, and we had ice cream sitting at a table next to it. We gave Koko the prime minister's mobile phone number—which was still on Tommy-Lee's mobile—so that she could ring him whenever she thought of an idea for a new law. We thought he'd like that. It's always good to hear new ideas. There were people at the penguin pool who recognized the penguins. "That's the penguin who was on top of the Shard!" But no one said, "That's the boys who were on top of the Shard" or "They're the kids who plunged London into a state of panic," either.

■ ■ ■

Before we left London, Dad gave Koko a lift back to Chinatown. We all had braised lamb and bok choy for tea, followed by ice-cream cakes on Tottenham Court Road.

But this isn't a comic book. It's our life, and that doesn't end with us dangling over London. Because the most astounding thing we ever did came after that. We got sent back to Woolpit Royal Teaching Hospital in a special car. Dr. Brightside hurried me off to the lab and took about a million more blood samples. She kept muttering, "Stay green, stay very green, stay my broccoli boy."

OFFICIAL STATEMENT FROM THE PRIME MINISTER'S OFFICE . . .

"**W**e are happy to announce that our concerns about the so-called Killer Kittens virus can now be forgotten. . . ." The prime minister was speaking to a crowd of journalists from the steps of Downing Street. We were all watching it—Mum, Dad, Ciara, and me—sitting on the couch in front of the telly the day we finally all went home. We were eating Pringles from a bowl. It was just like things used to be before I turned green. The moment the prime minister said that, the journalists all started shouting. Mum pointed at the screen. "There's that nice Dr. Brightside, look. Standing with the prime minister. And there's that nurse . . . hang on . . . is she . . . ?"

We all peered closer at the screen. Nurse Rock was standing just behind the prime minister. She looked slightly uncomfortable and . . .

"She's turned green!" said Mum.

She was definitely a light broccoli color.

"I will now hand you over," said the prime minister, "to Dr. Bernadette Brightside of Woolpit Royal Teaching Hospital."

Dr. Brightside stepped up to the microphone. "I have been working," she said, "with three brave young people who have recently had the traumatic experience of inexplicably turning green. As has my equally brave assistant, Nurse Rock."

"I told you," said Mum.

"She's talking about you!" said Dad.

The journalists were all yelling again, but Dr. Brightside calmed them down.

"My tests have shown that their green discoloration was in fact an allergic reaction. An extreme allergic reaction, yes, but one that had a good side. Killer Kittens turned them green, but it didn't make them ill. In fact, the very opposite. It made them immune. In the fight against Killer Kittens, they were bulletproof. The children selflessly submitted themselves to a series of rigorous blood and urine tests.

(Their urine was incredibly green, by the way—I've never seen anything like it.) I have in this way been able to isolate the enzyme that caused this reaction and incorporate it into a live vaccine. The Killer Kitten vaccine can be delivered to the vulnerable and to key workers so that even if the infection reaches epidemic proportions, we will be able to keep going as a nation. Britain, possibly the world, owes these children an apology. And a debt. They were branded a problem when in fact they were the solution. These children—Rory Rooney, Tommy-Lee Komissky, and Koko Kwok—are heroes."

Tommy-Lee got quite excited when he heard this. He thought Dr. Brightside's serum was going to turn everyone green. I explained she was just sharing the bit of us that had been fighting the virus with everyone else. Then he got even more excited.

"Most people spread germs," he said. "We sneeze superhero power."

So Mum was right. When there's a chance, however small, something can happen. But this was something even my mum couldn't prepare for. There was a billion-to-one chance that I would have the antidote to the

Killer Kittens virus in me. That I would go green. And I was that billion-to-one kid.

I slightly missed being part of a gang and having a secret headquarters. Sometimes me and Tommy-Lee met up in the geography storage cupboard and sat by the model of the West Midlands in the Ice Age. We acted like we had got serious stuff to plan, but mostly we just talked about food. We did show Dad the Map of Treats, and he wrote the names of the roads on it for us with a Sharpie, so now we know that after we've eaten the Handsworth Chicago pizza on the A34, we need to take the M6 to the M1 to get to the Watford Hot Chocolate. Then back up the M1 and across on the M6 and M62 to Dafna's famous Cheese Cake Factory (nut-free recipe).

The Birmingham Christmas lights usually go on in November, but this year was different. Due to a shortage of manpower caused by Killer Kittens and to fears about the possible cancellation of Christmas, the lights had gone up but stayed dark. Now the crisis was over, the council decided to save the lights until Christmas Eve itself. Dad took us all into town for the Big Switch-On. There were fireworks and people selling chestnuts (which obviously Tommy-Lee couldn't eat) and even some real reindeer. ("I still don't see how they can fly," said Tommy-Lee.) We were in the middle of a massive Christmas crowd, but we were sort of invisible. People were wearing Santa hats and tinsel, but no one who looked at us had any idea that we were the Kids Who Saved Christmas. We knew then how it felt to be Peter Parker, walking around New York, with no one knowing he was Spider-Man. It was a good feeling, a superhero feeling. Everyone is good for something. We turned out to be good at saving Christmas.

When the lights went on, everyone went, "Oooooohhhhh!" And all of their upturned faces went orange, then blue, or red—because of the changing colors of the lights. And I thought, The best thing about people is how different they are. When we went green, people wanted us to stop being green, to be the same as everyone else again. But it was only because we were different that we could be Astounding. The thing that makes you different is the thing that makes you Astounding. The thing that makes you different from everyone else—that's your superpower. Like they say in the comic books . . . The End.

AFTERWORD

There really were green children in England once. A monk called Ralph of Coggeshall told how two green children had turned up in the village of Woolpit during the reign of King Stephen, in the twelfth century. They were found hiding in a pit during harvesttime. They were frightened. They couldn't speak English and wouldn't eat any food. The lord of the manor took them in, and after a week or so they agreed to eat raw beans. Eventually they learned to speak English. They said they had come from a place called St. Martin's Land, where it was always twilight. They had been looking after their father's cattle when they heard bells ringing. They had never heard bells before. They followed the sound into a cave and came out in England. The little boy died quite soon, but the girl grew up and married a man from King's Lynn.

I've always been haunted by this strange, sad little tale. I'm not the only one. Herbert Read told their story in a novel. Kevin Crossley-Holland and Alan Marks made a picture book about them. Some people said the children came from underground. The philosopher Robert Burton in his *Anatomy of Melancholy* said they probably fell from the heavens.

But the reason I was fascinated wasn't because they might be fairies or goblins or something from Lord of the Rings, but because I change color too. I have a strange blood condition that means when I am under stress—for instance, late delivering a book—I go bright yellow. Like a walking, talking daffodil. I don't feel any different when this happens, so the first I tend to know about it is when people stare at me in shops as if I've just stepped down from Mars or up out of the grave. When I was a teenager, maybe it should have made me feel like hiding, but I always remembered the story of the green children and it made me feel as though changing color was all right, really. Weird and maybe embarrassing, but also mysterious and interesting. Maybe it meant I fell out of the sky.

The other thing from my life that is in this book is

teleportation. I definitely did it once. When our eldest son was little, we were still quite young and silly ourselves. We went on holiday to a farmhouse in France without really checking if it was safe or not. It turned out we would be sleeping in a loft that was reached by a very steep staircase. The gaps between the railings on the banister were very wide—easily wide enough for a toddler to slip through and fall onto the stone floor below. We thought it was romantic and beautiful. It was also extremely dangerous—a sheer drop to a stone floor. One afternoon I was playing with my son up there and got so absorbed in the game that I forgot to keep watch on him. When I looked up, he had toddled over to the top of the stairs and—I still can't even type this without feeling sick—he was just stepping through the railings into the empty air. The next thing I knew I was holding him by the arm and he was dangling in midair over the fatal drop. I have no memory of how I crossed that room. I was in one place. Then I was in another. It's impossible to cross a room quicker than someone can fall, but I did it. I really did slightly teleport.

One last thing that is real in this story is Dafna's Cheese Cake Factory. It's owned and run by a tiny woman called Mrs. Lev. Her superpower is making astounding cakes, but she also once saw off an armed robber just by giving him a very dark look. All of us are superheroes when we really need to be.

Last of all, this is where I get to thank my inspirational editor Sarah Dudman, who doesn't rest until I've done my best. Venetia Gosling, who protected us. Talya Baker, who wouldn't let us get away with anything. I also have to thank Dr. Mary Bunn, who talked to me about viruses. Above all Heloise and Xavier, who read every draft, and my wife, Denise, who sticks by me through pink and through yellow, through two-thousand-word days and days with no words at all.

FRANK COTTRELL BOYCE

is the author of *Cosmic*, *Framed*, and *Millions*, the last of which was a *New York Times* bestseller and was made into a movie by Oscar-winning director Danny Boyle. His books have won or been nominated for numerous awards, including the Carnegie Medal, the *Guardian* Children's Fiction Prize, and the Whitbread Children's Book Award. Frank is also a screenwriter, having penned the scripts for a number of feature films as well as the opening ceremony of the 2012 London Olympics. He lives in Liverpool with his family. You can visit him online at www.frankcottrellboyce.com.